DEVIL'S GUARD
VIETNAM

ERIC MEYER

DEVIL'S GUARD VIETNAM

ERIC MEYER

FOREWORD

Vietnam – a name that conjures up so many things to so many people. To the Americans, it was a horrific war that saw a great many of their people dead and wounded, brave soldiers whose lives sometimes seemed to be callously thrown away for little or no gain, their incredible courage sacrificed in the name of political expediency. To the world at large it was perhaps the first war of truly modern technology, from the weapons used to fight it, the complex fighter and bomber aircraft used to wage war on the communists to the broadcast media that brought it to our television screens as it happened. And to the Vietnamese people, a war of liberation or a war of enslavement, depending on your fate after the last bullet had been fired in 1975.

Yet this is not a story of nations, it is a story about one man, a personal story of a man who hacked his way through the slaughter of the Eastern Front during World War II, through the jungles of Indochina during the first French Indochina war, only to be sucked into the killing machine again when he thought his fighting days were over. As in my previous book Devil's Guard – The Real Story, some might ask the question 'did this really happen?' The answer would have to be yes and no, unfortunately. The main characters certainly existed, although some of the names have been changed to protect their identities. I have told Hoffman's story as it was given to me, with certain alterations and a few literary enhancements to make it read more fluently.

Yet essentially most of the events in the story did happen, as they are described. After the end of the French Indochina war many civilians and combatants stayed on in the Republic of South Vietnam. Some did get caught up in the American war, having so much local knowledge to offer of both North and South Vietnam. And the American approach to war is just as depicted, the bravery of the soldiers on the ground often merely a tool to be used in the name of Realpolitik and government expediency, whether for the benefit of the US, the Republic of South Vietnam, The People's Republic of North Vietnam, the Soviet Union or China.

That the French government welcomed former SS veterans of the Eastern Front to the ranks of the Foreign Legion is a matter of public record, at least until 1947. So is the nickname 'Devil's Guard', as it was applied to the Foreign Legion Units that some of these men fought in, although contrary to popular belief, there never were Foreign Legion units comprised only of former SS and German soldiers. All foreign legion units were a mix of nationalities, without exception, led by French officers. The records of French nationals who stayed on in Vietnam are fragmented at best. Hoffman was one of those who did stay behind and make his home there and common sense dictates that anyone who had fought and survived the bitter savagery of the Eastern Front and the endless jungle warfare in Indochina would quickly find their fighting knowledge of the communist enemy becoming highly valued by the new arrivals, the Americans.

How much of this story is true and how much exaggerated will never be known. What is known is that it all happened, almost every bomb, every bullet, every death, and every deceit. What is also known is the indisputable bravery of those soldiers of all sides who fought in the Vietnam War. The world will never be the same again after their sacrifice.

Eric Meyer

DEVIL'S GUARD VIETNAM

INTRODUCTION

It was a long journey from the hell of the Russian Front during World War II, through the jungles of Indochina fighting for the Foreign Legion to the modern reality of the Vietnam War. Yet it was a journey that Jurgen Hoffman had survived. With his beautiful wife Helene and his partner, former SS-Totenkopf Sturmbannfuhrer Paul Schuster, they set up a ramshackle civilian airline to serve the fledgling Republic of South Vietnam.

The arrival of the Americans and the inevitable escalation of the war as the communists infiltrated more and more fighters into the South meant that they would not be left in peace. The services of the two men, experienced, skilful and brutal fighters in every theatre of warfare are increasingly called upon by the American military. Once more their SS training and toughness is needed to survive the risky charter contracts they are forced to accept by the American military and their shadowy counterparts, the CIA.

An innocent charter to carry two Americans to Hue develops into a full blown clandestine rescue mission into the North. A combination of bureaucratic stupidity and CIA treachery results in a debacle that can only be unravelled by once more unleashing the vicious, cold killing skills of the SS. Even in peace, the Devil's Guard are once more at war. This is their story.

CHAPTER ONE

'The confidence of the Kennedy team prevailed through the early months of 1963, even after South Vietnamese Army units, supported by US helicopters, had failed to destroy a far smaller Viet Cong force in the ARVN's first pitched battle, at Ap Bac.'
CIA and the Vietnam Policymakers

We were in serious trouble even before our wheels left the runway. Heavily loaded with a mixed cargo of military equipment and various boxes and crates we were transporting for a civilian contractor, we had only just begun our take-off roll when the starboard engine started to misfire. Normally I would just abort the take-off and taxi back to the terminal so that we could take the time to remedy the problem. Paul had already reached forward to cut power, anticipating my command, when the first mortar shell hit the tarmac yards away, showering us with debris and shell fragments. We both looked out of the windows but there was nothing else to see, no sign of any attacking force.

"Do we abort or go?" Paul asked.

Calm as ever, it was as if he was asking me the time of day. Schuster was a veteran of the French Indochina War and before that the Eastern Front during World War Two, an officer in the Waffen-SS. A survivor.

It was my decision as pilot in charge, and a tricky one at that. We could abort and become sitting targets for another mortar strike, or we could continue and find ourselves having to crash land the aircraft with a faulty engine. We were approaching take off speed and I had only seconds to decide. In the event, the decision was taken from us, two more mortar shells hit the runway one hundred yards ahead of us and we had to swerve away to avoid our wheels falling into the shell holes or the tyres being shredded by debris.

"Reduce power to both engines," I ordered as I wrestled to hold the aircraft straight, bumping as we hit the first of the debris from the two explosions. "We'll go around again, I want to get out of here, this could be the start of a major attack."

I threaded the C-47 carefully around the fragments and shell holes and cut across the grass to the taxiway, heading back for our take off point. Another explosion hit the runway and then two more shells fell directly on a fuel dump, causing a vast pillar of smoke and flame to jet up into the sky. Behind the roiling black smoke I could see armed men rushing through a gap in the perimeter wire, Viet Cong, brightly illuminated by the burning fuel. We both worked calmly to keep the aircraft headed towards the end of the runway, we'd both been under fire enough times to ignore any threat that wasn't immediate and concentrate on getting out of trouble. We were taxiing at high speed, a hazardous activity on the bumpy taxiway, but the alternative was even more hazardous. Eventually we arrived back at our start point and I put on the brakes. Paul got out his binoculars and scanned the runway ahead of us.

"There's debris scattered halfway along the tarmac, it covers the whole width of the runway, we can't avoid it. We'll shred our tyres if we try and go over it."

"Could you clear it by hand?" I asked him.

As I said it, another mortar shell struck the grass strip, hurling up earth mixed in with a hail of metal fragments.

He looked thoughtful. "It'll only take a few minutes, but I'll be out there without any cover."

"It's the only way, Paul. I'll taxi up there and try to take the Viets' minds off you while you're doing it."

He nodded and I opened the throttles, released the brakes and began taxiing towards the debris. Then I swung the aircraft off the tarmac onto the grass strip, if any mortar shells landed the soft earth would absorb the worst of the blast and resultant shrapnel. I slowed to let him jump down to the tarmac, and then I opened the throttles and headed towards the Viet Cong, who by now were moving steadily across the airfield, putting the aircraft between them and Paul.

They'd lost interest in us for a few moments but when they heard and then saw the aircraft taxiing towards them at speed they transferred their fire towards us. I felt the impact of bullets striking the fuselage, ducked as a round went straight through the windscreen leaving it shattered, a gaping hole in the front of the cockpit. Then I swung the aircraft right around and began heading back, there was no percentage in being killed by charging them head on with an unarmed plane. Paul had finished clearing the debris and I slowed to let him jump aboard, then throttled up to once again head back to our start position at the end of the tarmac. He came into the cockpit and sat down.

"Verdammt, Jurgen, I thought you were doing the Charge of the Light Brigade there," he laughed.

"That's a thought," I grunted as I swung off the grass and onto the runway, then turned a full circle to get ready to take off. We looked at each other. Paul grinned. "Let's go for it, Jurgen. We need to get out of here fast."

I throttled up both engines to full, let off the brakes and we surged forward. A volley of machine gun fire ripped over the roof of the cabin, I stared ahead and could make out the shape of a medium machine gun manned by two men, set up on the side of the runway. Their intention was obvious, to destroy our aircraft. I turned to Schuster. "The M2s in the locker on the bulkhead, they're loaded and ready to fire. They've thoughtfully provided us with a firing port, perhaps now would be a good time to use one of them."

"Good idea, at least I can try to spoil their aim."

I hoped he'd do more than that. Paul Schuster was a veteran of the Russian Front and the French Indochina War here in Vietnam. Even now he was as muscular, tough and hard as I could ever remember him, almost six feet tall with cropped blonde hair and piercing clear blue eyes that were as sharp as the day his unit crossed the border into Poland.

He'd survived innumerable firefights and one of the skills

that had helped him survive was the ability to shoot accurately, especially when under enemy fire. He got up, took down the rifle and expertly checked the clip. He quickly grabbed three spare clips that were in a bag hanging next to the gun, and then pushed it through the cockpit window. We were getting near the Viet machine gun position and a burst of fire hit us, this time going low, I guessed they were aiming for the tyres but instead they hit the belly of the aircraft. God only knew what damage they were doing but if we survived this there'd be plenty of time to repair it.

We were still seconds away from reaching take off speed, Paul still hadn't fired and I could clearly see the faces of the machine gunners. Again the starboard engine faltered, I leaned forward to work the throttle to try and encourage the engine to run smoothly again and steered to port to correct the swing as the port engine tried to push us off the tarmac, at the same time another burst of fire hit the aircraft. This time their aim was slightly better, a burst hit the cockpit, putting holes in the metal skin and punching through into the cabin behind. Their aim was getting better as we got nearer, I didn't think we'd survive another one. Then the starboard engine picked up and I corrected our course once again. Paul still hadn't fired and I called out to him, "What's going on out there?"

"Two seconds, Jurgen, I'm almost on them."

I held us on course and kept my eye on our speed, and then three things happened at once. His M2 fired, a long burst that emptied the clip, the two machine gunners were flung to the ground as the hail of fire smashed into them and I reached take-off speed, hauled on the column and we were airborne.

We were heavily loaded and I retracted the wheels immediately and kept the aircraft in a long, slow ascent, refusing to sacrifice speed for height. We barely cleared the trees as we flew over the jungle a half mile from the airport, but it was the only way. Too steep a take-off meant we would have been a high, slow moving target, a sitting duck for any enemy guns that decided to take an interest in us. But no more enemy fire hit us and we were airborne.

Paul removed his assault rifle from the window and went aft to find something to block the shattered window. Once we reached cruising altitude it would be a problem with the icy slipstream blasting into the cockpit. He came back with an old army blanket and stuffed it in the hole, the airflow hitting us from the outside stopped and he sat down in the co-pilot's seat.

"Good shooting," I smiled at him.

"Good enough," he grunted. "I thought I'd really have time for just one clip so I had to be sure. There wouldn't have been enough time reload, it all happened so fast. If I'd needed to change clips it may have been a different story."

He looked across at the top of my seat and his eyes widened. "Jurgen, that last burst, did you lean forward as they fired?"

I said I had.

"Behind your head there's a bullet hole right through the seat, exactly where your head is."

"I had to adjust the starboard engine, it was faltering again."

"It's just as well."

I felt an icy sensation in my stomach. How many times

in my turbulent life across the world's battlefields had I come that close to death? More than a few.

"Paul, when we get back to Tan Son Nhat don't tell my wife it was that hairy, will you."

He grinned. "You're more afraid of her than the Viet Cong."

"Too right."

We flew steadily south, the starboard engine didn't give any more trouble, I tuned the radio into AFN, the American Forces Network station playing The Locomotion, sung by an American known as Little Eva. Not quite the cultured classical pieces I remembered from the many fine orchestras of my homeland, at least when I was last there more than twenty years ago. But this music was modern, young and alive, a world away from the doom laden arias of Hitler's favourite, Richard Wagner. It was the music of optimism, besides, Adolf was dead, Wagner was dead and Little Eva was alive and singing her songs. Several hours later we were approaching our home airport. When I called for landing clearance the familiar voice of Nguyen Cam Le, the air traffic controller at Tan Son Nhat sounded in my headphones.

"SGN-SS1 this is Tan Son Nhat, you're cleared for immediate landing, winds south easterly, speed ten knots and the sun is shining as usual on our beautiful city."

I smiled at his cheery voice. "Thank you Le, I'll buy you a beer when I see you."

"You always say that, Herr Hoffman, I calculate you owe me at least twenty by now."

"I'll pay you when the war's over, Le."

"You mean after we're all dead?" he chuckled. "Tan Son Nhat out."

It was good to hear the familiar joking voice of the friendly Vietnamese in the control tower. We went straight down onto the tarmac and taxied over to our hangar where we supervised the unloading of our cargo. I left Paul to talk to our ground engineer Johann Drexler, another Waffen-SS and French Foreign Legion veteran, about repairing the damage to the C-47. Feeling battered and exhausted, as if I'd used up one of the few remaining lives left to me, I went home.

My bungalow lay just outside the perimeter of Tan Son Nhat Airfield, its surface pockmarked with the patches that covered the shell holes from the mortar rounds that struck regularly. I often wondered if we should move further away from the danger zone, but our home was convenient to our hangar. Besides, was anywhere really safe here in Vietnam? I smiled as the tempting fragrances of Helene's French cooking came out to meet me. In this ramshackle, broken, crazy dumpster of a country of Vietnam that we called home, I sometimes thought that without her none of it would be worth it. She rushed out to hug me, as passionate now as the day when we first decided that we were made for each other, flung together in a dank, jungle clearing whilst fleeing an avenging horde of Viet Minh savages. She was just as beautiful as she was then, more than ten years had passed but not one day slipped by without me counting my blessings for having met this girl. I hugged her to me and felt myself becoming erect, she could drive a man wild almost with a look, even now when she was in her mid-thirties. She felt me against her body and smiled.

"No, Jurgen, down boy, you're a typical soldier, back from a mission there's always one thing on your mind. Dinner first, my love, get yourself washed."

Despite Helene's charms, I felt distracted, we'd been having a few problems with the starboard engine on our C-47, the aircraft that was our main source of revenue. If the engine had failed completely on the last run we could have lost the aircraft to enemy action.

The Douglas C-47 Skytrain, also known as the Dakota, was built as a military transport aircraft developed from the DC-3 airliner. It had a reinforced fuselage floor and the addition of a large cargo door to allow for the loading and transport of quantities of military supplies. Used extensively by the Allies during World War II it had remained in front line operations through the 1950s. The Skytrain was at one time the standard transport aircraft of the US Army. Since they began to replace them with other, larger transport aircraft, many of them appeared on the surplus market, where we had picked up our own aircraft at a knock-down price.

The phone rang and I held Helene to me while I answered it. It was Drexler, he'd already taken a preliminary look at the starboard Wright Cyclone GR-1820 engine and suspected a faulty centrifugal supercharger. Paul Schuster was on his way into Saigon to buy a replacement unit that Johann understood from his contacts could be found in an engineer's shop in the city. Probably stolen from the US military, I reflected, but that wasn't my problem. I turned my attention back to Helene, kissed her again and detached myself to take a shower. Newly changed into clean cotton trousers and bush shirt, I went to check out my dinner, but in the lounge two guys were sitting waiting, sipping cold drinks, I hadn't heard them come in.

"Jurgen, these two gentlemen have called to see you, I'll leave you to it."

I nodded my thanks, she was a soldier's woman, and knew when my clients would require privacy. I looked at them, they were as different from each other as chalk from cheese, a soldier with the insignia of a lieutenant colonel and a civilian. The civilian's clothes gave away his occupation as much as the soldier's uniform gave away his own. The colonel was sitting almost to attention, alert and as ramrod straight as it was possible to be on our old couch. His name badge said Goldberg and I guessed his age at about forty. He could only be Special Forces, the unique units that the Americans had formed to come and train their South Vietnamese allies, and a glance at the green beret he was holding under his arm confirmed it.

Disliked by the army brass, the green beret had been adopted from the style worn by the British Special Forces group, the Royal Marine Commandos. The military hierarchy had initially banned its use, but on visiting Fort Bragg, President Kennedy asked General Yarborough to encourage all of the Special Forces to wear their green berets to attend the event. Kennedy delivered a speech whereby he made the green beret "a mark of distinction in the trying times ahead".

I had no doubt that Goldberg had earned his own 'mark of distinction'. He looked fit and tough, about medium height, his jungle green uniform razor sharp, clean and neatly pressed, his hair cut so short as to make him almost bald. He carried a side arm in a holster on his belt, Vietnam was a war zone, of course. But I doubted the weapon was for show, he had a hard look in his eyes, the cold, calculating stare of someone who has seen much action and spilled a goodly amount of blood. A look I had seen often during my own career.

The civilian was wearing clothing so unsuitable for the climate, for the humidity and filth of Vietnam, that I briefly wondered why they had become almost a mandatory uniform for intelligence operatives. Beige chino trousers, pale blue button-down long sleeved cotton shirt and mid-brown Docksiders on his feet, the kind with a little tassel on the toe. He'd obviously left his bow tie and pipe at home, together with his tweed jacket. I could almost sense his discomfort at travelling without the outward trappings of his American WASP upbringing that would have taken him directly from Harvard or Princeton to a career in the corridors of Langley, Virginia. He may as well have been wearing a badge similar to his companion's, but his would have said CIA.

"Gentlemen, what can I do for you? I see my wife has brought you cold drinks."

The soldier looked straight at me and we shook hands. He came straight to the point. "Mr. Hoffman, it's quite simple, we have a charter for you if you have an aircraft to spare."

"That's how I make my living, Colonel. If it's just the two of you, I can have the Cessna 170B fuelled up and ready to go in the morning, where do you want to go?"

Our four-seat Cessna 170 was a light, single-engine, aircraft produced by the Cessna Aircraft Company in 1954. It had a metal fuselage and tail and fabric covered wings, and was fitted with a powerful 145 hp Continental engine and large fuel tanks. For simple jobs ferrying passengers or small loads around Vietnam it was the perfect workhorse, able to operate out of the smallest and roughest of the airstrips and it made the jungles of this hostile country a little more accessible.

"To Hue," he replied, "Tay Loc. Is that a problem? Just the two of us, myself and Mr. Anderson here, not really much in the way of luggage."

"That's fine. Journey time is about three hours in the Cessna, she's a four-seater so we won't be fully loaded. When do you want to leave?"

"Is ten in the morning ok with you?"

"Fine, that'll give me time to get back here the same day. I'll see you at the airfield just before ten, the flight plan will be filed ready and the aircraft good to go."

We discussed the price, when carrying military men I had a rule of thumb, think of a price and double it, but they just shrugged when I told them how much and Goldberg said it would be fine. Anderson suddenly took an interest in the conversation, he looked up and spoke to me.

"Do you ever miss Germany, Mr. Hoffman?"

The room suddenly felt as chill as his gaze. I could tell that Helene had been listening in the kitchen, she had stopped what she was doing when she heard his words.

"Why do you ask, Mr. Anderson?"

"You've got an interesting past, lots of rumours about you. You were in Russia during the war, I gather?"

It wasn't really a question. What did he want?

"I was here in Vietnam too," I replied. "I was a soldier in the French Foreign Legion. I am also a citizen of France, but I do not miss France any more than I miss Germany. Surely you'd know that, your people, wouldn't you, Mr. Anderson?"

He shrugged. "I've seen your file, Hoffman."

"So why do you ask?" I pressed him. "Do you have a problem with Germans?"

He smiled a superior, knowing smile. "No, of course not. Not all Germans were members of the, you know..."

"The SS, Mr. Anderson?"

"Something like that. Amazing, eh? One minute you're all fanatical Nazis, the next minute half the country is commie. Which side were you on, Mr. Hoffman?"

"I can assure you I was not on the side that your agency is fighting a cold war against, Mr Anderson. The side that is supplying arms to their communist allies here in Vietnam. The side that I was fighting while you were still in kindergarten, my friend."

His expression darkened and Goldberg jumped in before the conversation deteriorated further.

"Miles, we're all allies now, you know that, Mr. Hoffman is a French citizen, so leave it alone. We'll be at the airfield in the morning, Sir, see you then. Would you say goodbye to your charming wife for us? And wish her Happy New Year."

"Yeah, do that, Herr Hoffman," Anderson added, putting the accent on the 'Herr'.

I smiled at them, "Of course, gentlemen, see you in the morning. Happy New Year to you."

It was January the first, 1963.

So what the hell was wrong with Miles Anderson, CIA agent? The Second World War had ended eighteen years ago, yet some people seemed able to harbour a grudge for life. But he'd need watching, he was one of those people that naturally had to knock people down, perhaps to make himself look good. There was something else, too, something about Miles Anderson that was dark and hidden.

I told Helene I'd be going to Hue in the morning and then I telephoned Drexler and made sure he'd have the Cessna fuelled and ready to go. As I went to sleep that night, I thought more about the two men. One thing I'd learned about Vietnam, everyone had their own agenda and most were on the make too. And one other thing, of course, life was cheap here. Very cheap.

In the morning I said goodbye to Helene and walked out to the Hotchkiss jeep, Schuster had called in early to pick me up. The former Waffen-SS officer had stayed on in Vietnam when his enlistment in the Foreign Legion ended. We had both spent our termination pay on acquiring pilots' licenses in the US, where it was cheap. Commercial and type approval licenses were not difficult to obtain in Vietnam, like most things here it was simply a matter of money changing hands. We drove the short distance to our hangar at Tan Son Nhat in our Hotchkiss, the French copy of the Willys jeep, open to allow the breeze to cool some of the sticky humidity, our clothes were already sticky with sweat.

The Willys MB US Army Jeep was initially built from 1941 to 1945. In the SS we had the radically different and inferior Volkswagen Kübelwagen. Based on a small automobile, the

VW Beetle, it used an air-cooled engine and lacked four wheel drive. Before the Americans arrived in Vietnam the French Army produced the Willys derivative, the Hotchkiss M 201, in considerable quantities. When they left Indochina, a large number were put up for sale and our workhorse was one of these French built vehicles.

I noted with approval that Drexler had the Cessna ready to go, the engine already ticking over to warm it up. My preflight checks were almost completed when Goldberg and Anderson arrived. Goldberg had changed into Tiger stripe camouflage, almost a copy of the old SS pattern. He still carried his sidearm, but in addition he was carrying an AR-15 assault rifle with pouches of spare clips hung on his belt. Built of black plastic and aluminium, the Colt AR-15 was probably the most lethal assault rifle ever produced. It was light in weight, easy to shoot, and extremely accurate, so that it was fast becoming the standard infantryman's weapon of the US and ARVN forces.

Anderson was dressed identically to the previous evening, I suspected it was the only type of clothing he possessed or would ever deign to wear. The only difference was that he was wearing a shoulder holster with a huge Colt automatic pistol in it, the standard sidearm of the US military. And of the CIA. He saw me looking at it.

"Yeah, don't worry Hoffman, if we come down in Gook country, I know how to use this thing."

I nodded at him. "That's very reassuring, Mr. Anderson."

Goldberg smiled. "Are we ready to go, I'd like to keep to schedule?"

"Yes, if you would like to climb into the aircraft and strap in we can take off straight away."

They climbed into the Cessna, Anderson in the back and Goldberg next to me. I called the control tower and got immediate clearance from Nguyen Cam Le.

"You're ok to go straight out, Jurgen. If you're headed anywhere nice you can bring me back a nice present. Something small, like a Rolex watch," he broke off, laughing to himself.

"Yeah, we'll see, thanks Le."

I taxied down the runway and took off, heading north towards Hue.

"That guy fancies himself as a bit of a joker," Goldberg said.

"Le? Yeah, he's always cheerful, but don't let the jokes fool you, he's a good man, very professional, runs a tight ship. Hates the commies, too," I replied.

"Why is that?" Goldberg continued.

"Le's family were murdered while he was in the US doing his air traffic control training. Apparently the communists accused them of supporting the Americans by allowing their son to train in the US. When he came back he tried to enlist in the ARVN, wanted to shoot every commie in sight, but he was too valuable in air traffic control so they ordered him to stay there."

Goldberg grunted an acknowledgment as I concentrated on climbing to our operating altitude.

We reached five thousand feet as quickly as possible. I burned up more fuel that I would have liked but ground fire was becoming increasingly common and I preferred not to offer the Viet Cong a tempting target. We reached operating height and I set the throttle to cruise. Goldberg leaned nearer to speak to me, out of the corner of my eye I could see that Anderson had moved closer to listen.

"Do you know the area around Ap Bac, Mr. Hoffman," the soldier asked me.

I thought for a moment, Ap Bac was a village about forty miles to the south west. I nodded.

"We'd like you to detour and fly over it if possible, we want to take a look."

A strange request, I wondered what was behind it.

"It's in the opposite direction, Colonel. It'll add almost an hour to our journey time and put us on the limits of the fuel reserves."

"I'll add a fifty percent bonus if you'll do it," he replied.

It was a very good deal, I nodded, they both seemed to relax as I banked the Cessna around through one hundred and eighty degrees and set course for Ap Bac.

We flew on in silence, just the drone of the engine for company and the unending sight of the jungle below, hiding everything that was both good and bad about this benighted country. I heard the action of a pistol being worked and looked around. Miles Anderson was checking his Colt automatic, as I watched he removed the clip, checked the load and slid it back into the pistol. He saw me looking.

"You ever fired one of these or seen any real action, Hoffman, or were you just a desk jockey in those old wars?"

"I've fired a few guns, yes," I replied.

Colonel Goldberg sighed with irritation.

"Christ, Miles, I thought you'd read Mr. Hoffman's file."

"Well yeah, I did glance at it, he was in the Nazi SS and the French Foreign Legion, I read some of it. That doesn't mean a thing, he could have spent the whole time behind a desk."

"Did you read the bit about him being an SS-Sturmbannführer, a major, a highly decorated combat veteran of the Eastern Front? Or his Foreign Legion record, a shitload of medals including their Legion D'Honneur, like our Congressional Medal of Honor, for leading countless engagements against the Viet Minh?"

Anderson looked at me, then at Goldberg. "I just glanced at it, Aaron. So he got lucky, did he?"

Goldberg and I looked at each other, we both smiled briefly, then he looked out of the window at the jungle below, I busied myself with the chart I had unfolded on my knee.

Four minutes later we were approaching the area of Ap Bac, I was about to call out to the passengers that we were almost there when there was a bang on the starboard wing. I looked across and there was a ragged hole about an inch in diameter punched right through it. While I looked, another bullet struck further out on the wing. I flung the Cessna in a tight bank to port, set the throttle to maximum and pulled back on the column to start gaining height.

"We're taking ground fire, I'm going to get more height," I explained to them.

I looked around, neither of the Americans seemed surprised, although Anderson had gone deathly pale. Just then a voice came over the radio.

"Unidentified Cessna over Ap Bac, you are entering a battle zone, turn back immediately. Acknowledge."

I looked around, there was another Cessna, an army O-1 Bird Dog liaison and observation aircraft about half a mile away and closing on us.

The O-1 was the first all metal fixed wing aircraft flown by the United States Army since the U.S. Army Air Forces separated from the Army in 1947, becoming its own branch of service, the U.S. Air Force. The Bird Dog had seen a lengthy career in the U.S. military as well as in other countries, they were a common sight in the sky over Vietnam where they were used for artillery spotting, directing battle and a range of less glamorous but equally valuable tasks.

So there was some kind of a battle going on here, that's why they were so interested.

"Mr. Hoffman, would you circle the area for a few minutes," Goldberg said to me. "Could you let me have a communications headset, I'll talk to the army spotter."

I passed him a spare headset. "Colonel, I don't know what's going on here, but I'll give you five minutes over Ap Bac, no more. I have no intention of being shot down in an unarmed aircraft."

"Five minutes will be fine, Mr. Hoffman."

He put on the headset and clicked the send button.

"This is Lieutenant Colonel Aaron Goldberg, Fifth Special Forces Group, flying in civilian Cessna over Ap Bac, who am I talking to?"

I listened in my own headset, the radio was silent for a few seconds, and then it crackled to life.

"John Paul Vann, United States Army assigned to Col. Huynh Van Cao, commander of the ARVN IV Corps as advisor to the Seventh Division. Colonel, I'm observing and directing a battle right at this moment, I don't have time to make conversation."

"I read you, Vann, we'll just watch for a few minutes and then head out of here. How is it going? Those ARVN boys shaping up well?"

Vann replied immediately. "It's a miserable damn performance so far, Goldberg. These fucking VCs are outnumbered five to one but they're still giving the ARVN a hammering. There's gonna be some heads rolling after this little lot, I can tell you. Colonel, we've got a battle on our hands here, I'll catch up with you some time, I suggest you clear the area immediately."

"Understood. Good luck, Goldberg out."

He took off the headset and turned to speak to Anderson, who had not heard both sides of the conversation. I looked down, two CH-21 Shawnee helicopters were visible sitting drunkenly on the ground, clearly casualties of the battle. I wondered if the troops they carried had got out safely. While I watched, a flight of five Huey UH-1 helicopters flew in and discharged a platoon of ARVN troops on the ground. There was an explosion in the middle of them, mortar fire, I noted, and the survivors scattered to take cover. It didn't look very good. Five to one, Colonel Vann had said, that was by how many the Viet Cong were outnumbered, yet they were hammering the ARVN soldiers who didn't seem to understand what was required of them. Several ran back to the Hueys, if they hadn't lifted off the troops would have jumped back in them. Perched on a hilltop not more than two hundred yards away I could see the distinctive sight of a Type-24 7.92mm Chinese made heavy machine gun, a copy of our German First World War Maxim gun, belt fed, it would be deadly if it opened fire on the exposed ARVN. I shouted at Goldberg, "Colonel, the VCs are setting up a Maxim down there, a heavy machine gun, it'll destroy those ARVNs that have just deployed."

He looked down where I was pointing. "Yeah, I see it, Colonel Vann is bound to have seen it too, we have to leave it to him."

Anderson leaned over and put his face close to me so that I would hear him. "It's not your war, Hoffman, so I suggest you stay out of it and leave it to the experts."

I smiled at him. "With pleasure, Mr. Anderson."

I threw the Cessna in a tight bank and put her on a course for north east, to Hue. Anderson looked furious, but Goldberg only smiled at him. "Miles, you did tell him to stay out of it. Anyway, we've seen enough. You're going to need those Montagnards, I don't think the ARVNs can do it all on their own."

The French term Montagnard, meaning people from the mountains, referred to an indigenous people from the Central Highlands of Vietnam. In 1950, the French government established the Central Highlands as the Pays Montagnard du Sud under the authority of Vietnamese Emperor Bao Dai. When the French withdrew from Vietnam and recognised a Vietnamese government, Montagnard political independence was drastically diminished. The U.S. Special Forces were beginning to develop base camps in the area and recruit the Montagnards to fight alongside ARVN and American soldiers, and were intending that they would become a major part of the U.S. military effort in the Central Highlands.

I flew the Cessna steadily on towards the ancient imperial city of Hue, home of the Emperor of Vietnam, or more correctly, South Vietnam. I was concerned about the fuel, it was cutting it fine after the diversion to Ap Bac, but I throttled back to the most economical speed and at nearly seven thousand feet we should get there with a little fuel to spare. I didn't think it likely that we had taken any hits to the fuel tanks, there were three of them on board the aircraft. If we were losing fuel, the gauge would have shown it.

Anderson and Goldberg were arguing about the Montagnards. It was no secret that the CIA regarded Vietnam as their own little war, a chance for them to cover themselves in glory. Nor was it a secret that the U.S. forces saw Vietnam as a chance to muscle in with their own advisors and weapons inventories, perhaps like our German forces did during the Spanish Civil War when the Luftwaffe tested their air war theories prior to declaring war on the whole of Europe. I was faintly amused, these Viets had shown extraordinary tenacity in defeating France, the final battle of Dien Bien Phu demonstrating that Ho Chi Minh's troops were the equal of any in the world, and often better led and better motivated. It was well known that the French had treated their colonials as little more than slaves. What better motivation was there to fight hard than to gain your freedom from a colonial oppressor? A lesson we Germans had learned the hard way from the Russians during the war on the Eastern Front.

"We were talking about the Montagnards, Hoffman, what's your take on these people?" Anderson asked me.

I had met a few of them during my time in Indochina, most I had found to be decent folk, if a little primitive in their strange costumes.

"They're no friends of the communists, if that's what you mean."

"Exactly what I mean.   We're meeting some of their leaders in Hue, setting up a programme to help their people."

I smiled at him. "By giving them guns to fight the Viet Cong, I suppose?"

He bristled at that. "Maybe we will, sure, why not? The VCs have given them a hard time, they sure want to fight back. Nothing wrong in that."

"No, of course not. The French armed the Montagnards during their war with the communists. Giap sent his men into the Montagnard villages and wiped them out in droves, especially after partition when much of the Montagnard region lay in North Vietnam."

"The difference is this time we're gonna win, we'll beat those commie fuckers once and for all."

"Like you were doing at Ap Bac, Mr. Anderson?" I asked him.

Even as I said it, I knew I shouldn't have opened my mouth, the CIA paid well and seemed to have an endless pot of money from which to pay for their schemes. But I had seen those ARVN troopers thrown into the mincing machine, facing down a heavy machine gun like the badly led soldiers of the First World War. This American prick wanted to send more men into the lion's mouth to enable him to play his stupid war games, as if they were pieces on a chess board. I'd seen too many sacrifices of good men not to be angry. Goldberg put his hand on Anderson's arm and gripped him tightly.

"Leave it, Miles, it's just a difference of opinion, not worth you getting riled about."

Anderson gave him a murderous look, threw off his hand and sat back in the rear seat, a petulant look on his face. He didn't speak for the rest of the journey.

The beautiful city of Hue came into view, the emperor's palace clearly visible. I got clearance from Hue tower, asked my passengers to fasten their seat belts and dropped in to land. I helped them out of the aircraft, passed them their bags and shook hands with both of them, it seemed that even Anderson had decided to let bygones be bygones.

"I hope you have a good stay here in Hue, gentlemen. Can I offer to arrange your return journey?"

Anderson sniggered. "No thanks, buddy, we're not coming back this way, the agency has got it all taken care of."

Goldberg frowned, but Anderson rambled on. "Once we get these mountain men organised, we'll go out and kick some ass."

I smiled. "I certainly hope you do, gentlemen. No one has so far succeeded in kicking the ass of the Viet Cong, no doubt you'll be the first."

"You bet," he replied, totally missing the irony of my words.

Goldberg gave me a cold smile. "Take care on…"

Several shots echoed across the field, I counted a total of four. We dived to the ground as a Vietnamese of about twenty years of age dressed in black trousers and white shirt and carrying an automatic pistol came running from behind one of the hangars. He sprinted towards us, saw us on the ground near the Cessna and took a snap shot that went wide. He was screaming something in Vietnamese. I'd heard it before during my service in the Legion, shouted by Viet Minh as they charged at our legionnaires, intent on killing us at all costs. Then another man came around the corner dressed the same as the first one, this guy carrying an AK-47.

Goldberg was fast and accurate. He brought up his AR-15, clicked off the safety, aimed and fired all in one smooth motion. The first man screamed and fell heavily to the ground. The second guy was still running, Anderson whipped the pistol out of his shoulder holster and aimed. At the last second, I knocked his arm up, ruining his aim, the pistol fired harmlessly into the sky.

"What the fuck are you doing, Hoffman? Colonel, shoot that Gook fucker while I deal with this German."

"Leave it, Miles, for fuck's sake shut up and stop making yourself look like an ass," Goldberg shouted back. The CIA man's eyes widened and he tried to bring the pistol down to point at me, but in combat terms he was nothing more than a child, I simply took the gun out of his hand, removed the clip and handed it back to him. His mouth opened making him look like a goldfish, but he was unable to get any words out. We watched the second guy walk up to the first, put down his AK-47, kick the fallen man's pistol away and start to examine the body.

"Miles, the guy is airport security," Goldberg said, "He's on our side."

The CIA man looked at me silently, his eyes filled with impotent rage. He then stomped off to the terminal building, a single storey structure that served as an airline office, departure lounge and customs shed. Goldberg looked at me sympathetically.

"I'm sorry about Anderson, he's just not very experienced in this country. He'll learn, sooner or later."

"Either that or he'll be dead, Colonel."

"Yeah, I expect. Hey, I like your tail number."

I looked at the tailfin of the Cessna, SGN-SS1. SGN was the international prefix for Saigon, SS1 was someone's idea of a joke. We smiled at each other.

The Colonel went after Anderson and I walked over to the terminal and arranged for the Cessna to be refuelled for the journey back to Saigon. As usual it meant parting with more cash for bribes, in Vietnam, no one did anything, their paid job included, unless they were bribed. I wondered if Miles Anderson realised that, then it occurred to me that his ancestors had probably invented the system. I genuinely like Americans and got on really well with them, they were some of the best people I had come across, friendly and generous to a fault. But there were bad ones too, as with every nation on earth and when they were bad they were, well, like Miles Anderson. I sat down in the coffee bar and downed a cup of coffee, the radio was playing and I listened to the news. Already, the battle of Ap Bac was making news with reports of a casualty list of one hundred and eighty men, of which eighty were dead, and the loss of five helicopters. There was no mention of Colonel Vann, but I pitied him, once the final tally was added up the commanders would look for scapegoats and I guessed that he would fit the bill exactly.

I walked into the office and filed my return flight plan for Saigon, then went out on the tarmac. Fuelling had finished on the Cessna and I could leave as soon as I was ready. I started the pre-flight walk around, almost immediately I spotted Cessna Bird Dog, painted all black, positioned at the far end of the field. Even from three hundred yard away I could recognise the figures of Lieutenant Colonel Goldberg and Miles Anderson standing next to the black Cessna, talking to a couple of soldiers. It all added up to a Special Forces night insertion. No doubt the two Americans would be dropped into the Central Highlands to conduct negotiations with the Montagnards. Did these people never learn? If it was obvious to me what they were up to it was obvious to every Viet Cong sympathiser and spy on the airfield and there would certainly be no shortage of those. Wherever the two men were headed, the North Vietnamese would know about it even before they took off. I wanted to walk over and warn them, but I knew that they would take no notice of an ageing civilian. They would just have to learn the hard way.

I checked the two bullet holes in the starboard wing, they were not really serious and we'd repaired plenty of those in the past. I made a note to remind Johann Drexler to patch them when I got back, holes in the wing made the passengers nervous. Then I climbed into the cabin, started the engine and got clearance from the tower.

The journey back to Saigon was uneventful, nobody took shots at me from the ground and there was no spoilt American secret agent to spar with. I landed at Tan Son Nhat after receiving Le's customary greeting and clearance from air traffic control and Johann came out to help me tie down the aircraft.

"Did Paul have any luck finding a supercharger?" I asked him.

"No, nothing yet. I've done a temporary repair on it, Jurgen, it's just as well. We've got a full load to pick up from Da Nang first thing in the morning, a delivery to Vung Tau. Paul is preparing the C-47 right now."

"Ok, thanks, Johann. I need to get home for a shower, I'll take the Hotchkiss and call back later."

I drove back to my bungalow and Helene was waiting for me, as beautiful, graceful and warm as ever. Thank God for the French. She kissed me and led me to the shower, helped me undress and then undressed herself.

"You must be stiff after all that flying, Cherie," she grinned and felt my cock. "Ah yes, I thought so. Do you want me to wash it for you or did you have something else in mind?"

"Maybe you could soap my back?"

She smiled. We made love while the tepid water cascaded down over us, revelling in the passion of our lovemaking, and exploring each other's body. She squealed with joy as she came and I followed shortly after, both of us for a short time at least able to forget the humidity and hatred that were so much embroidered into the fabric of our adopted country.

Afterwards we got dressed, Helene made up food for all of us and we drove back to the airfield. We sat eating happily in the passenger cabin of the C-47, Helene and me, Paul and Johann. Afterwards, Paul dropped us home and went off with Drexler to a nearby bar. At dawn he was back to collect me and we took off in the C-47 for Da Nang. There would be no need to refuel, the Douglas C-47 had a range of sixteen hundred miles, enough for the entire round trip and back to Tan Son Nhat, another routine flight that was the bread and butter of our little business. When all of the crates were loaded we got clearance and headed back for Vung Tau, a resort town near the Mekong Delta and a frequent jumping off point for Special Forces operations.

"Any idea what's in the crates?" Paul said as we neared Vung Tau."

I had wondered too what was inside them, but in Vietnam is was not always wise to know everything. Some things were best kept hidden.

"None of our business, my friend, and I want it to stay that way."

He nodded his agreement. We landed at Vung Tau in the early evening, as we were taxiing towards the freight hangar Paul said, "I could murder a cold beer before we take off again."

It was an attractive idea, it was getting dark and we would be staying overnight before unloading the crates in the morning and returning to Saigon.

"Me too, I'm sure the airport bar will accommodate us."

Then a mortar round hit the tarmac immediately in front of the aircraft and the port wheel dropped into the crater, we heard the snap as the leg collapsed and I quickly shut down the engines as the aircraft slewed violently to the left.

We shuddered to a stop as another mortar round exploded nearby. There was no need to say anything to each other, we both ran for the locker at the rear of the cockpit and took out weapons, the M2s, the fully automatic variant of the famous M1 carbine together with our two Tokarev pistols. We had tried carrying AK-47s, but their distinctive shape had once brought friendly fire down on us while we were on the ground in the Mekong Delta, guarding a shipment of vehicle parts, or so the crates said. After that, we bought the more expensive M2 which hopefully would not be the cause of any mistaken identity.

Paul pushed open the fuselage door and we jumped down, the first thing we saw was the port leg, smashed beyond use. The second was the flashes of gunfire and exploding mortar rounds. A harassed looking ARVN lieutenant came running over to us.

"It's a VC attack, you need to find somewhere to get under cover."

"How many of them are there?" I asked him.

"How many?" He looked surprised that I had even bothered to ask the question. "I don't know, maybe ten or twelve."

"Are you engaging them, Lieutenant?" Paul asked him.

"Well, we've got a Marine company here, I expect they're forming up now to counter-attack."

"In that case," I said reasonably, "we should be safe, a company will surely take care of them. We'll stay with the aircraft, just in case any of them slip past you."

He shrugged. "As you wish," he said, angry that we weren't taking his advice, "but keep your heads down, this isn't a game you know."

He said it so gravely that Paul and I had to look away to stop ourselves from laughing and embarrassing him further, which would not have earned us any favours.

"Thank you, Lieutenant, we'll bear it in mind," I replied courteously.

He ran off to find his unit. We took cover in the crater, crouched next to the port wheel of our Douglas.

"It seems you were wrong, my friend," Paul said to me.

"Wrong?" I looked at him, puzzled. He pointed across the field, four shadowy shapes were running towards us, their intention was obvious.

"About it not being our business. It seems that these gentlemen have made it out business."

We clicked the selectors of our rifles to full auto and waited.

* * *

The message on Vietnam is the same: vigorous American action is needed to buy time for Vietnam to mobilize and organize its real assets; but the time for such a turnaround has nearly run out. And if Vietnam goes, it will be exceedingly difficult if not impossible to hold Southeast Asia.'

General Maxwell Taylor

The President was looking at a cable in his hand. He was sat awkwardly on the couch in the Oval Office, one of his bad days for the injury he still suffered from twenty years after his patrol boat was shot out from under him in the China seas. He looked up.

"Robert, you've seen this?"

Robert McNamara, Secretary of Defense, nodded. "Yes, Mr President, I have. I contacted General Harkins at MACV in Saigon and asked him for his opinion too."

Kennedy looked around the room. Who could he trust to give him an honest opinion about the war in Vietnam? The only one here he could really trust had no real influence with the military, his brother, Robert F. Kennedy, Attorney General. The two brothers exchanged glances. Kennedy looked back at McNamara. "Go on, what does he say?"

"He concurs, Sir. Our troops, our advisors, are making a difference, but there just aren't enough of them. With a few thousand more troops, the communists can be beaten and the South Vietnamese government will be able to hold their own."

"Yeah, so you keep telling me." He sighed and looked around the room.

"Look, all this advice I'm getting, then word comes in from this," he paused and shuffled through papers on the low table in front of him. "Lieutenant Colonel Vann. These South Vietnamese troops together with units of our own people outnumbered the Viet Cong five or maybe even ten to one!"

He raised his voice and the advisors looked at each other uncomfortably. Upsetting the leader of the free world was not a good way to handle your career.

"Ten to fucking one, anyone got any ideas, people? These communists field a hundred thousand men, you want me to send a million Americans to fight them and even then we might not win? Because that's what these figures tell me. Bobby, what's your take on this?"

The others barely concealed their sneers. A staunch supporter of civil rights, Bobby Kennedy was no friend of the more militaristic members of Kennedy's cabinet. They joked about his lack of experience, even his own brother President Kennedy had laughed at the criticisms of Bobby and said, 'I can't see that it's wrong to give him a little legal experience before he goes out to practice law.' But what he lacked in experience he made up for with a razor sharp mind. Architect of his brother's successful presidential campaign, he had no direct influence on this meeting. But the President wanted someone he could trust to help him steer his way through the minefield of personal political agendas and prejudices that were part of every president's cabinet.

"Has anyone read the history of these Vietnamese people?" Bobby asked unexpectedly. "For the past thousand years, these people have been fighting one foreign invader after another. China, Laos, Cambodia, you name it, they've scrapped with them. And when they're not fighting someone else, they're fighting each other. These aren't a bunch of slant eyed rice farmers with the thoughts of Ho Chi Minh in one hand and an AK47 in the other. They're hard and they're tough. Sure, this current bunch are communists, but if they weren't commies they'd be called by some other name. Fact is, they're no pushover, anyone that says different hasn't done their homework. Sure, our boys are tough too, but the South Vietnamese? Fact is, Diem doesn't want them to fight the commies too hard, as long as they keep him in power."

McGeorge 'Mac' Bundy, the National Security Advisor, spoke up. "These people threaten the stability of the whole of South East Asia, Bobby. No matter how tough they are, they're a direct threat to U.S. foreign policy and trade in the region, they need to be beaten."

Kennedy looked at them tiredly. "Ok, so we know what we need, we know the problem, so what do we do? Send more troops?"

Robert McNamara muttered under his breath.

"What? What was that Robert?"

"I said Diem needs to go," the Secretary of Defense said.

Bobby jerked upright. "Jesus Christ, Robert, he's the head of state."

"He's a number one pain in the ass," McNamara said. "He singlehandedly invented the word corruption, his brother's an opium addict and he terrorizes any of the population that aren't Catholic, and that's the vast majority, they're Buddhists and they hate him. Get rid of Diem and the war is winnable, otherwise..." He let his words hang.

"Ok, ok, let's tie this up. Bottom line, do we send more advisors or not?" He looked around and received affirmative nods.

"Very well, Robert, get me some figures and I'll take a look at them. Stay behind, would you. That's it, thanks."

They drifted out, the great and the good who steered the

fate of the free world. When they were alone, Kennedy turned to his Secretary of Defense. "About Diem, Robert, I want a report, I especially want to know who would replace him if the worse came to the worse. Thank you."

"Thank you, Mr President."

CHAPTER TWO

'Secretary McNamara summed up such concerns in 1962 when he told Congress that US strategy was to assist indigenous forces in Third World crises rather than commit US forces to combat there. Avoiding direct participation in the Vietnam war, he said, would not only release US forces for use elsewhere, but would be the most effective way to combat Communist subversion and covert aggression in Vietnam: To introduce white forces, US forces, in large numbers there today, while it might have an initial favorable military impact would almost certainly lead to adverse political and in the long run adverse military consequences.'

US Library of Congress

It seemed obvious that our aircraft was the intended target of the four infiltrators. The normal VC tactic was to strip the contents from the aircraft, especially if they thought it contained arms or military equipment, and then destroy the plane. In this case with the whole airfield a battlefield it seemed unlikely they would take the time to pillage so they were probably planning to just destroy our C-47.   We waited until they got within fifty yards, sure enough we could see that they were already removing the pins from their grenades. We opened fire in the same instant, after so many battles and so many wars, we were both able to finely judge the moment. They didn't stand a chance, we dropped all four between our first two bursts. They tumbled to the ground, some screaming in agony, then the grenades went off and we ducked lower as shrapnel flew through the air. The screams stopped and we looked around again.   There was a firefight in progress at the terminal building, difficult to make out in the dark, but we could distinguish the sounds of the AK-47s carried by the communists and the sharper crack of the M16s, the new infantry rifle developed from the Armalite AR-15, increasingly being adopted by the ARVN.   The sounds of the AK-47s were gradually petering out as the shooters were either killed or crept away in the darkness.

Eventually it all went quiet, the lights blazed again in the terminal building and a siren sounded the all clear. We climbed out of our hole to check the VCs we had shot, but they were all dead, either from our bullets or shredded from their own grenades that exploded after they were hit. We returned the rifles to the aircraft, it wouldn't do for unidentified civilians to be walking around carrying rifles. The sentries would be nervous enough for the rest of the night in case a second wave of attackers came, but we still had our automatics tucked into our waistbands. Finally we walked cautiously to the terminal building and went in.   There was no damage, the attack hadn't got that far, they'd even restarted the sound system, Ray Charles was singing, 'I Can't Stop Loving You' softly in the background. We found a telephone and I called Johann Drexler. As expected he was in our office inside the hangar at Tan Son Nhat, we liked to keep someone there to stop the locals from pilfering our supplies and shipments. I told him about the damage.

"I've got a spare leg here, Jurgen, I can bring it to you in the jeep and do the repair," he said. "What about the wheel and the tyre, is that damaged?"

I thought for a moment, then told him to bring a spare wheel and tyre as well, it was unlikely that they were completely undamaged. He promised to go and speak to Helene and leave for Vung Tau in the morning, about a two hour drive cross country. Then we went to the terminal office where I filed a report of the damage and amended our flight plan to leave later the next day.

We eventually got our cold beer at the bar, which had already re-opened. There was a big crowd of ARVN troopers already drinking, I briefly wondered why they were not out mopping up after the attack, chasing down the VCs who had got away. But only it was only a brief thought. It was an open secret that President Diem feared and despised his majority Buddhist population as much as he did the Viet Cong. He deliberately spared the ARVN troops from engagements that might risk them taking heavy casualties. That way he hoped to keep them as a loyal reserve in case his own people tried to depose him by force, as well as not incur the army's wrath by forcing them to undertake dangerous assignments. To say that Diem's rule was authoritarian was to understate the case. His most trusted official was his brother, Ngo Dinh Nhu, leader of the primary pro-Diem Can Lao political party. He was an opium addict and fervent admirer of another corrupt, authoritarian dictator, Adolf Hitler, the architect of Germany's misfortune. Both Paul and I still bore many scars from Hitler's disastrous attempt to rule Europe.

Indeed, Diem modelled the Can Lao secret police's marching and torture styles on Nazi designs. Ngo Dinh Can, his younger brother, was put in charge of the former Imperial City of Hue. Although Can did not hold any official role in the government, he ruled his regions of South Vietnam with an iron fist, commanding private armies and secret police.

Another brother, Ngo Dinh Luyen, was appointed Ambassador to the United Kingdom. Diem's elder brother Ngo Dinh Thuc was the archbishop of Hue. Despite this, Thuc lived in the Presidential Palace, along with Nhu, Nhu's wife and Diem. Diem was nationalistic, devoutly Catholic, anti-Communist, and preferred the philosophies of Confucianism. The result was that in a situation such as this one, the troops were drinking in the bar instead of chasing down and destroying a defeated enemy force. Sadly, we'd seen it all before.

"So Colonel Goldberg and Miles Anderson think that a few thousand Montagnards will make all the difference?" Paul said, shaking his head in disgust. "Even the SS would have had a hard task defeating the Viet Cong, this place is going to become another Eastern Front if this is all they have to fight with."

He was right, of course. The communists had defeated

the French, it seemed that the Republic of South Vietnam was militarily very weak even with American support, it could only be a matter of time.

"What if the Americans lend even more support?" I asked him. "Do you not think it would make a difference?"

He laughed. "Sure, of course it would make a difference, but they can't be here forever. Ho Chi Minh is in it for the long haul. Do you remember the communists handing out free land to the peasants? What is this government doing to help these poor bastards? I tell you, Jurgen, if I was a peasant here I think I'd fight for the Viet Cong myself, and I hate the communists."

It was true, Diem initially limited individual land holdings and reimbursed the landlords for the excess which he sold off to peasants. This being Vietnam, many landlords evaded the redistribution by transferring their property to the name of family members. In addition, the three hundred and seventy thousand acres of Catholic Church land were exempted. As a result, only thirteen percent of South Vietnam's land was redistributed, it was estimated that only ten per cent of the tenants had received any land at all, resulting in a lasting legacy of bitterness and hate towards the government.

We drank several more beers and then went back to watch over the aircraft and its cargo. The ARVNs were still in the bar drinking, I had no doubt they'd be there all night. The airfield had gone quiet and we took turns to stay on watch, but there were no more attacks. We waited as the humidity rose, at just after ten o'clock a lorry and two jeeps arrived to unload the cargo. A short, scrawny looking young Viet was in charge, accompanied by two tough looking Americans with aviator dark glasses and shoulder holsters, probably Special Forces or CIA. So the crates were filled with weapons, I wondered if that was the reason for last night's attack, and how the VCs had found out. Their intelligence was amazingly good, they seemed to be able to communicate better than the army with their sophisticated radio equipment. Six Viet civilians jumped down from the lorry and began to transfer the cargo. The Viet in charge, Le Van Dao came and paid me for the freight and they drove away. It wasn't long before the welcome sight of our Hotchkiss jeep came towards us, the back laden with the spare wheel leg, the wheel and tyre and a selection of tools and jacks lashed around it. Johann climbed out and we shook hands, then he went to look at the damage.

"Yeah, we can fix that, no problem. First thing is to jack her out of there, I'll put some support under the wheel and we can replace the whole unit."

It was good news, we worked through the sweltering heat of the day, drenched in sweat, jacking up the port wing, removing the broken leg and replacing it with the spare. While Johann finished adjusting and testing the hydraulics, Paul and I loaded the broken parts into the empty hold of the C-47, they would be repaired and re-used when we got back to Saigon. I started the engines and slowly taxied the aircraft away from the pothole. When he was satisfied, Johann jumped in and came through to the cockpit.

"I want you to slowly taxi a couple of hundred yards and I'll walk along to give a final visual check on that leg."

I nodded to him and he went out and jumped back down to the ground. I started to taxi again, after two hundred yards

I stopped and Johann jumped back into the aircraft and came into the cockpit.

"It all looks fine. I'll drive back to Saigon now, I'll see you there."

"Thanks, Johann, I'll have a couple of cold beers ready for you when you get back," Paul laughed.

"You'd better." He jumped down to the ground and was halfway across to the Hotchkiss when there was a massive explosion and the jeep disintegrated in smoke and flames. Mortar! The shock wave of the explosion had blown Johann to the ground.

"Paul," I shouted, "go and get Johann, we need to get going."

He was already running out of the cockpit, through the window I saw him run up to Johann and help him to his feet. Thank God, he didn't seem to be badly injured. There was another explosion near the terminal, and then the answering sound of heavy machine gun fire as the ARVN detachment guarding the field opened up in the general direction of the mortar. Paul got to the door and I ran back to help him in with Johann. We helped the mechanic climb on board and brought him forward to the cockpit where he sat down on the navigator's jump seat.

"You ok, Johann?" I asked him.

He smiled. "I will be when we get out of here."

"Yeah, we're leaving now, don't worry." I sat down in the pilot's seat, the engines were still ticking over.

"What about clearance?" Paul called to me.

I laughed. "I don't think they'll be worrying too much

about procedures just at the moment. We'll get in the air and call them afterwards."

I throttled forward all the way and the aircraft began to gather speed. Another mortar hit the airfield, this time on the runway about three hundred yards ahead of us. I made a slight correction to avoid the pothole, then we were past and I rotated the plane off the tarmac, we were airborne. Yet another mortar shell hit just where we had taken off, it had been a near thing. I could see the ARVNs crouched behind their M60 machine gun as it blazed away, shredding the distant jungle foliage where they thought the mortar was sited. Scattered groups of them were lying on the ground blazing away with their M16s, but so far none were advancing to tackle the enemy. I wanted to get down there and shout at them to get out and start doing what they were paid for, to kill the enemy. But I was a civilian now, not a soldier, and I had to suffer the consequences of their failures like every other civilian in this country. We gained height rapidly and I set course for Tan Son Nhat and now that we were safely away Paul went back to check on Johann. My headset crackled.

"C-47 SGN-SS1, you departed Vung Tau without proper clearance, please clarify."

I deliberately didn't answer for a few moments, sometimes these people went just too far, did they want us to wait to be hit with a mortar shell?

"Vung Tau Control, it was a medical emergency, we're taking a badly injured man back to Saigon."

"Understood, SS1."

It was near enough the truth.

We landed safely at Tan Son Nhat. The loss of the Hotchkiss was a blow, not least to Paul Schuster who regarded it as his personal toy. Helene was waiting for us, she checked Johann over thoroughly and pronounced him fine, except for minor shock and concussion that he would recover from in a day or two. She came and held me tightly.

"Jurgen, things are getting worse here, I was very worried about you."

"It's just a blip, I'm sure the government will have it under control soon," I replied. I was a rotten liar, she pushed me away and looked me in the eyes.

"That's rubbish and you know it. The only good thing for you is that the more they make trouble, the more you make money transporting people and equipment around this rotten country. This has been going on for nearly twenty years, they beat the French, they're beating Diem's people, what next?"

"The Americans, my dear, they're arriving in force. Every day, more and more of them are coming into the country to fight the Viet Cong."

"Do you think the Americans will succeed where everyone else had failed?"

I had been thinking about the increased American efforts for some time. We Germans had swept into Russia and were eventually defeated simply by the fact that we alienated most of the population and they fought back willingly, even fanatically. Shoot ten Russians and fifty would step forward to take their place, blinded by their hatred of the Nazis and the golden promises of their commissars. Diem's troops were becoming no less hated than we were, and the Viet Cong commissars were promising the people everything that the government refused them. Could the Americans reverse things? They would need to change the whole system of government, effectively overthrow the Diem regime and rebuild from top to bottom. But that never worked, only the population could achieve proper change and they were cowed by the brutality and corruption of the Diem regime and enticed by the false future offered by Hanoi.

I looked back into her beautiful eyes. "No, Helene, ultimately they will not. They'll make a difference, but not enough, I think. I hope I am wrong. If other countries get involved, perhaps it will help."

Already Australia, a near neighbour, had sent troops to Vietnam to shore up the anti-communist government. But they were few and the VCs were growing rapidly.

"We should leave, Jurgen, get out of here while we still can." She didn't say before one or both of us were killed, but I understood.

"You know that we have debts to pay off on the loans that we took out to buy the aircraft. Perhaps when everything is clear we could consider moving then."

"Let's hope we're both still alive to make the move," she said bitterly as she stalked off.

I went home to a chilly reception and a silent dinner. In bed when I tried to talk she just rolled away from me, what the hell was wrong with her? She had a fiercely independent streak but she wasn't usually this moody about the future. I satisfied myself that it was Vietnam, this damned country got to all of us in the end.

The next morning she was still ignoring me so I made an early start. I got to the hangar to find Johann already at work hammering away at the bent and broken leg.

"You should be resting, Johann, not at work, you were hurt quite badly. Helene said to take today off."

"And if you break another wheel leg on the next job, where do we get a spare?" he asked.

I didn't reply, he was right, of course. Without a spare leg, we'd still be on the field at Vung Tau, a target for every VC mortar crew that happened along.

Paul came into the office, we had a new charter, a cargo to take up to Lang Vei, a small base just south of the DMZ, the local agent had just phoned through, it was already on the way here and would arrive within the hour.

"What are we carrying?" I asked him. "Freight or people?"

If it was people we had snap down seats in the fuselage of the aircraft, but on this occasion it was freight. A civilian lorry turned up driven by a Vietnamese, it was loaded with more of the inevitable anonymous wooden crates, they may as well have stencilled them 'military equipment', everyone knew what they were. Two Americans jumped out of the passenger side, another four men, Vietnamese, got out of the back and began transferring the crates to the C-47. The two Americans approached us.

"Change of plan Mr Hoffman, we're going to accompany the load to Lang Vei. Any problems?"

I looked at them warily, jeans, t-shirts, shoulder holsters with Colt automatics, each carried an AR-15. Short crew cuts, jungle boots and canvas packs on their backs, they could only have been Special Forces. It was fine with me, if we had to make an emergency landing they would come in handy if we hit any trouble.

"No problem at all," I smiled and shook hands with them. "What's up at Lang Vei, why are you taking so much equipment up there?"

They both looked at me suspiciously. Then one of them said in a friendly way, "I guess if you're flying us up there you'll know soon enough anyway. It's a CIDG camp we're setting up near a village called Khe Sanh."

I'd never heard of Khe Sanh, but we had all heard about the Civilian Irregular Defense Group programme. It was a programme developed by the United States to develop South Vietnamese irregular military units from the minority populations. It had been devised by the CIA in early 1961 to counter expanding Viet Cong influence in South Vietnam's Central Highlands. Beginning in the village of Buon Enao, small Special Forces A teams moved into villages and set up Area Development Centres. Focusing on local defence and civic action, the Special Forces teams did the majority of the training. Villagers were trained and armed for village defence for two weeks, while localised Strike Forces would receive better training and weapons and served as a quick reaction force to react to Viet Cong attacks. The vast majority of the CIDG camps were initially manned by inhabitants of ethnic minority regions in the country especially Montagnards, who disliked both the North and South Vietnamese and therefore quickly took to the American advisors.

I nodded and went to supervise the loading. Paul was already at work lashing down the crates, I told him about the CIDG camp we were headed for.

"Let's hope it works, this CIDG programme, he said gloomily. "From what I've seen the locals will just sell their arms and equipment to the VCs."

I laughed, it wasn't entirely fair, from what I'd heard and encountered the CIDG programme was proving to be quite successful, even though it was unlikely that there would ever be enough recruits to fully counter the Viet Cong who had limitless numbers of ethnic Viet peasants from which to recruit. Unlike the fortified hamlets scheme which appeared to have exactly the opposite effect and did little or nothing to deter the communists. While the loading was going on, Johann finished fuelling the aircraft. When he was finished he came with me for the pre-flight inspection.

"Will you be back tonight?" he asked me.

I shook my head. "It's not likely, Lang Vei is fairly new, there won't be any lights for us to attempt a night take off, so we'll leave at first light, we'll be back late morning. Johann, things are not getting any better here, would you mind if I sent Helene to sleep here in the hangar with you?"

He looked surprised. "In the same bed?"

I felt my anger rising, then saw the grin on his face. I gave him a friendly punch. "Schweinhund! But it's much easier to defend here than our bungalow."

"Of course, send her over, I'll look after her."

When I went back to the bungalow, Helene almost spat fire at me for suggesting that it would not be safe for her to spend the night in her own home, but in the end I pressured her and she gave in.

"At least I'll be safe with Johann," she grinned.

"What do you mean?"

"I mean that he's not overly fond of women, Jurgen, hadn't you noticed?"

"So, you're saying that…"

"He's queer, Jurgen, haven't you seen him in town with one of the local pretty boys on his arm?"

I was astonished, so Johann was a homosexual. Well, that was his business, I'd encountered plenty of men that were that way inclined, it made no difference to me as long as they did their job. My face must have looked shocked, because she said to me, "You don't need to worry about him either, Jurgen."

"Why's that?"

"Because you're too damned old and ugly, not his type at all," she laughed

"That's alright then. But please will you stay in the hangar tonight, I'm thinking about strengthening security around the bungalow, but until then you need to be more careful."

"I will, yes, I promise," she said.

She came and kissed me, I felt the love and the warmth flowing out of her. If anything happened to this woman I knew I would have little or nothing left to live for. I picked up the pack she had prepared with food and drinks for the flight, then walked across to the airfield, we had yet to replace the Hotchkiss.

The cargo was already loaded, the two Special Forces soldiers were laying in the grass sipping cold cans of beer, without doubt Paul's gesture to keep the paying customers happy.

"I'll radio the tower for advance clearance, as soon as we're ready I'll give you a call and we can take off."

They both waved an acknowledgment and I got into the cockpit and contacted the tower. Paul had lodged our flight plan and they were expecting me, quite apart from the small envelope of U.S. dollars that I gave the airport manager each month, so they cleared us to leave straight away. I started the engines and beckoned our two passengers onboard. They scrambled up and climbed into the cabin, Paul closed the door and I opened up the throttles for take-off. Soon we were airborne and I set course for north, the trip would take us about six hours and we took turns at the controls. Using the auto pilot was an option we rarely used, this was a war zone and pilots needed to keep alert for the enemy, more than once a MIG 17 had wandered south bent on causing mayhem. Then there were the friendlies to consider, many of the South Vietnamese pilots were recruited more on family connections than skill, they were just as likely to shoot at us as the communists. Yet it was an uneventful journey, we landed on time at Lang Vei and a crew of Vietnamese immediately began to unload the crates. They were dressed in a rough approximation of paramilitary uniforms, no two were alike, but their faces were unmistakably Montagnard. The camp they were building was not impressive, I hoped they would develop some sort of effective well defended fire base before the Viet Cong attempted to overrun it, as they did with every camp that was built.

Our passengers had gone away when the crates were

finally unloaded, one of them returned to invite us to the mess for drinks.

"Hi, we were never introduced, my name's Ed, I guess you knew we were army."

I shook his hand. "I'm Jurgen, this is Paul. Yes, I'm afraid it was pretty obvious. If you're an American in civilian clothes in this country armed with an M16 it normally means US Army Special Forces. We've transported a lot of your equipment around Vietnam, and a few of your people."

We wandered into their mess tent, a bar was set up and one end and everyone was sprawled around folding chairs and tables, some were lying on the floor. Ed ordered us a cold beer each with condensation running down the outside of the glass, we drank it thankfully in the extreme humidity which was even worse here than at Tan Son Nhat.

"Someone said you were here before, Foreign Legion, right?"

I nodded to him. "Yes, it was before the country was partitioned."

"Well, we hope to do better this time."

I didn't reply. Paul looked away and took a deep sip of his drink. Ed looked at us intently.

"You don't think we will?"

"Ed, Paul and I were soldiers during the Second World War, on the Eastern Front."

"SS?" I nodded. "Waffen-SS. We were soldiers, like the French, like the Americans, like you. We went into Russia using overwhelming force, a mechanised army and air force the like of which the world had never seen before. And they beat us."

He listened intently. I noticed that heads had turned to listen too, well, let them. He had asked a question, I would give him a straight answer.

"They beat us because when our rear echelon forces were terrorising the population, stealing their land, enslaving them, the communists promised them everything if they would fight for Stalin. Land, wealth, food, freedom, everything a man could want. And of course, it they refused to fight for Stalin, there was a bullet for them. So they fought, in their millions and millions. The communists here are making a similar offer. While the government gives them nothing, no hope, only endless corruption so that everything they own is liable to be stolen from them by the officials, the Viet Cong offer them peace, bread and land," I smiled. "In fact, that was the slogan of Lenin, the architect of Soviet Communism. Peace, bread and land. Whoever can offer them that will win."

There was a silence in the mess tent. Then a voice came from a dark corner at the back of the tent.

"Ain't no fucking Nazi gonna tell the U.S. Army it's beat before we've even fought a battle."

We looked over as a tall man got up. He must have been six feet six inches tall and almost as broad, unusual for Special Forces who tended to be more conventional in appearance, often slight and wiry. He came over to us.

"You hear me, Nazi? Are you telling us that we're beat before we even start?"

"No, leave it Jerry," Ed said to him, "they're drinking with me."

"It's ok, Ed," I smiled. I believed I had the big guy's

measure, undoubtedly a bully, very strong but a heavy drinker and right now he'd clearly been indulging for some time.

"In the first place, my friend, I am not a Nazi. And in the second place I did not suggest that the Viet Cong would beat the U.S. Army."

He lunged forward, shouting, "You're a shitfaced liar, you fucking Nazi bastard."

He telegraphed his move very obviously. Even before he launched the blow I was ready for him. A huge fist came around that would have broken my jaw if it had connected, but I stepped slightly to one side and scooped his ankle away, chopping the side of his neck as he went down. He lay quietly, unconscious. The tent was silent, the other soldiers astonished that their huge comrade had been knocked out so easily. I looked around the room.

"Before I go, let me be clear. The American forces will probably beat the Viet Cong, but the day you leave Vietnam the Viet Cong will roll through this country like a knife through butter. Good night, gentlemen."

We walked back to the plane. The wind had risen and it had started to rain. Through the blackness we could see the trees bending in the wind. We checked the ground anchors to make sure the Douglas was securely tied down.

"What do you think?" I asked Paul.

"Monsoon," he replied, "it'll be here by morning, it's going to be a bastard to take off."

"We've done it in worse," I replied. I heard him grunt. He didn't sound happy.

As usual when we were away from Tan Son Nhat, we

took turns on watch. There was little to worry about, the Special Forces patrolled regularly, they were taking no chances this close to the DMZ. By morning the storm was just as bad and we sat in the cockpit to wait it out. We heard a noise at the door and looked around, a captain was climbing in. He walked through to the cockpit.

"Gentlemen, my name is Captain Forester, I'm in command at this base. We've has a message from Saigon, you're required to return immediately to Tan Son Nhat."

Paul smiled at him. "Captain, we'd like nothing better than to go home, but in this weather we have no choice but to wait it out."

The American looked cold. "Sir, you don't understand. You are to return to Tan Son Nhat, my orders are to make sure you leave immediately."

Paul looked at me. I tried to reason with the soldier. "Captain Forester, you can see the weather outside. If we try and take off now it is quite likely that we will not even clear the airfield. That won't help anyone if you have a crashed plane littering your field."

"Nevertheless, Sir, I have my orders. You will take off from this airfield within the hour or your aircraft will be impounded and become the property of the U.S. government. Either whole or in pieces," he smiled thinly.

I could see Paul beginning to glow bright red with anger and I hurried to head off a violent confrontation.

"Paul, leave it. Captain, we will take off as ordered."

"Very well, have a safe flight," he grunted ironically as he left the cockpit.

"What the hell, Jurgen, it's impossible, we'll never get off the ground, we'll lose the plane."

"Maybe. I've been watching the weather, it swirls in with torrents of rain, then the wind and rain eases for perhaps a minute or two, a tiny weather window. If we can catch that moment, we could make it."

"That's crazy," he said angrily.

"No, not at all. Would you have us walk home and give the C-47 to the U.S. government?"

He was thoughtful for a moment. "Ok, perhaps that's not much of an alternative. We'll need to be throttled up ready to go as soon the weather is about to ease, it'll be touch and go."

"When has that ever stopped us?" I asked him.

We pre-flighted the plane and started the engines. We taxied to the end of the short strip, head to wind, and waited with the brakes on. It was impossible to see more than fifty yards in front of us, the rain smashing against the windscreen. When I thought the window was approaching, we throttled up, the engines screamed and then nothing. The rain lashed against the aircraft, shrouding the field in wet mist. After a minute, Paul shouted across to me over the noise of the engines. "Jurgen, we're going to overheat, we'll need to throttle back."

"Another few seconds, just wait."

I could see him looking at the gauges, the starboard engine was already in the red, the port engine nearly there. The engines continue to scream, the gauges rose, and then something, some sixth sense, told me that the moment was about to happen.

"Go, Paul, brakes off, let's go!"

With a look of astonishment on his face as if I'd just told him to jump off a cliff, he released the brakes. The engines were still screaming and the rain beating down on us as we hurtled along the field, gathering speed. To his credit, Paul made no further objections, trusting in my judgement, but I wondered if his trust was misplaced. We reached takeoff speed, he looked over to me, but I kept going. Suddenly the wall of green jungle loomed in front of us, I wrenched back on the column, we left the ground and the rain suddenly, magically eased. Paul began retracting the undercarriage and added his weight to the control column as we fought to gain height to clear the trees. We weren't going to make it, then I saw a slight gap in the tree line, I banked the plane over and kicked the rudder bar to take us towards it. We edged nearer the tree line, I banked over more steeply and we were in the gap. We gained height and within seconds The C-47 was soaring over the jungle.

We flew on in silence, Paul throttled back slightly to stop the engines exploding and we continued to slowly gain height. We looked at each other and burst out laughing.

"Gott im Himmel, Jurgen, you've taken five years off of my life."

I laughed, we'd made it. At six thousand feet we burst out of the clouds and rain into clear sky. Provided we didn't run into a wayward MIG or trigger happy ARVN fighter jock, we'd be back at Tan Son Nhat by afternoon.

"How about some music?" I said as we eased the throttles back to cruising speed and the intense racket of the engines became more bearable. He turned on the radio already tuned to AFN. It was playing 'The Wanderer' by Dion and the Belmonts. It seemed appropriate for the two of us, lost forever to wander the skies over the dank, hostile jungles of Vietnam like the tale of the Flying Dutchman that became one of Wagner's most famous operas.

"What made you start the take off roll before the weather window arrived?" Paul asked.

I shrugged my shoulders, not wanting to share the moment with him. In truth, I didn't know for sure myself. We had faced death many times over the years, the grim reaper always seemed to be waiting for me with open arms. I could swear that at the blackest moments I'd seen him, hideous in his hooded black cape, grinning at me with his skull like face. So it was at Lang Vei, yet this time I'd clearly seen Helene standing next to him, her hand outstretched. If I told Paul, he'd have me checked out by a doctor, so I kept quiet. The mind played strange tricks on you.

When we landed at Tan Son Nhat, two American civilians, probably CIA, were waiting outside the hangar for us. As we taxied in and stopped, they walked over to the aircraft. Almost certainly they were behind our being forced out of Lang Vei, I wondered what the hell they wanted that was so important.

'A revolutionary must be thrifty, be resolute to correct errors, be greedy for learning, be persevering, adopt the habit of studying and observing, place the national interests above personal interests. . . be little desirous of material things, and know how to keep secrets'
Ho Chi Minh

The men glared at each other, Giap wondering how Pham Van Dong, Chairman of the Council of Ministers of North Vietnam, dared to criticise Ho. The President of the Democratic Republic of Vietnam had made it clear that they were becoming far too dependent on aid from China. Yet Pham Van Dong objected, coming out strongly on the side of the Chinese. Ho tried explaining once again.

"For a thousand years this country belonged to China. On a dozen occasions during that period, the residents of Vietnam attempted to expel the ruling officials and soldiers by force of arms. Many of the rebels had even been born in China or descended from Chinese ancestors, but they did this out of a desire for power or freedom from the oppressors. The final revolt in 939 ended with Vietnam receiving vassal status from its massive northern neighbour, which entailed the payment of tributes to China in return for our autonomy. They were replaced by the French, who we drove out. Now we have the Americans, who we will also defeat in the course of time. Are we to replace these invaders with the Chinese, invite them back for a further thousand years?"

Le Duan nodded emphatically to agree with the President's word, Giap added his own weight.

"Let the Chinese in, Chairman? That way is madness, we have fought hard for the first victory of our struggle for independence. Now, before we have beaten the Americans, you talk of opening the door to the Chinese once again. Would you have us paying tribute for another thousand years?" He sneered as he finished. He had not shed blood to forge his professionally trained army into becoming servants of China.

Pham was calm and refused to be flustered. "Comrades, all that you say is true. But listen, in the past we took arms from the Americans, has it made us vassals of America? No, they will suffer inevitable defeat at the hands of our loyal army," he nodded towards Giap. After Ho, Giap's favour was not to be discarded lightly.

"But listen, we already have the Russians on our side, even as we speak their guns and munitions are travelling down through Laos to reinforce the struggle in the South. Are we their vassals, their client state? Of course not. Is there any rule, any law that states that we cannot accept the generosity of more than one patron? I say take everything the Chinese have to offer us. They think we are fighting their war against the imperialists for them, as do the Russians. Let them think so, when our country is free of the foreign invader we will send them the bill for fighting their war. We will owe them nothing, they will owe us everything. But to achieve victory, we need guns."

They all nodded, it was a strong philosophy.

"So you make no agreements, Comrade Pham, no promises?" Giap asked.

The Chairman shook his head. "None, nor would I ever commit to making any kind of agreement."

Ho overrode them, it was time to move on.

"So it is agreed, we accept the arms from both China and Russia and make it clear they are all in our debt for fighting their war for them. Agreed?"

They all nodded.

"Excellent. Now what of these two Americans being

held at Son Tay? How can we use them to our benefit?"

Le answered him.

"Propaganda, Comrade President. One of them is certainly a CIA spy, we will put them both on trial. Perhaps the American public would like to see that their government is sending spies to invade foreign nations."

"I have heard there may be a rescue attempt," Giap said abruptly.

Ho looked at him sharply. "When is this due to take place?"

"It is being planned now, Comrade Ho. We had word from Saigon to expect someone to try and break them out of prison. As yet, we have no further details." Giap paused, as if he wanted to add something, but he continued. "I have sent a company of soldiers to reinforce the local militia, we expect to prevent any attempt at a break out."

"You have given orders to shoot the invaders on sight?"

Giap nodded slowly.

"Excellent, Comrade Giap, keep me informed," Ho said.

"Now, about the rice harvest for this year. How can we distribute sufficient to feed our army and yet prevent the peasants from starving?"

"Perhaps they will just have to starve, the army must take priority," Le Duan said.

"Will you then give them your rations, Comrade?" Pham Van Dong asked.

Giap let them bicker, he was thinking about the rescuer from the south, and one of them in particular. He made a note to get clarification from his contact in Saigon.

CHAPTER THREE

We believe that Communist progress has been blunted and that the situation is improving. . . . Improvements which have occurred during the past year now indicate that the Viet Cong can be contained militarily and that further progress can be made in expanding the area of government control and in creating greater security in the countryside.'

NIE 1963

We shut down the engines and slumped for a moment in our seats, still astonished that we had got off so lightly at Lang Vei and made it home safely. When I had drawn breath I got up and walked back into the cabin and opened the door. The two men were stood there waiting for us.

"Mr. Hoffman, we're glad you got back safely, could we talk to you for a moment?"

Paul and I climbed down the ladder to the ground. "You'd better come into the hangar and I'll find some cold beer," I said to them.

"That's ok, Sir, we don't need any beer, we instructed the base commander at Lang Vei to order you back so that we could have a talk, we have a new contract for you."

Paul spoke angrily to them. "Your stupid order to get us to take off from Lang Vei in a storm almost cost us the aircraft, we certainly do need a cold beer, so your business will have to wait a little longer."

He walked to the port wheel, there was a tangle of foliage around the leg. He looked at me and smiled, then pulled a small branch out from the leg and gave it to one of the men.

"Here, this is yours, government property, part of your field at Lang Vei."

They looked at it without understanding and followed us into the hangar. Johann was grinding pieces of metal, the broken wheel leg was on the bench. He waved to us and carried on and we went into the office. We took an ice cold bottle of beer apiece and sat down.

"Now, gentlemen, how can we help the CIA?"

Why were these people always surprised that they were so obvious. Just like Miles Anderson, these clean-cut American WASPs could not be anything else in their middle class American clothes and middle class American faces that were now looking at me with surprise. Perhaps they thought that ordinary well dressed American businessmen came to airfields in the war zone of Vietnam to charter ramshackle aircraft to carry anonymous cargoes around the country.

"We'd better introduce ourselves, I'm Milton Burns, and this is Robert Anderson."

We shook hands, I thought that Anderson looked familiar. "Mr. Anderson, are you by any chance related to Miles Anderson?"

He nodded, "Yeah, Miles is my older brother."

"So you both went into the same line of business?"

He smiled. "It seemed like a good idea, they were actively recruiting at Harvard, so when I graduated I just followed Miles into the Agency."

Milton Burns leaned forward. "And you, Mr. Hoffman, we understand you had a military career before starting your own airline?"

I waved my hand around the hangar. "Not much of an airline, I'm afraid. A Douglas C-47, a Cessna 170B and a tired old Junkers JU52. Hardly any competition for your Air America."

"It's not ours, Sir, Air America is a purely civilian operation, a commercial airline like yours."

Paul nearly choked on his beer, at least Anderson had the grace to go pink with embarrassment at the transparent lie.

"As you wish," I replied gravely.

"However," he continued, "I was asking about your military career. Where did you serve?"

"I was a Senior Sergeant in the French Foreign Legion, here in Indochina, or Vietnam, as it is called these days."

"So you've seen plenty of action against the communists?"

"Some, yes."

"And before that?" He was looking at me keenly.

"Mr. Burns, I'm sure you have a file on me, the CIA has files on all foreigners in Vietnam, does it not?"

"It is true, we do keep files, but they don't always tell the full story. You fought in the Second World War?"

"As you know, Mr. Burns, I was an officer in the SS, I fought on the Eastern Front."

"Yes, so I understand. Tell me about your service in the Foreign Legion, did it ever take you behind enemy lines?"

I was suddenly very wary. Paul and I looked at each other, we had both taken part in a highly secret mission up on the Chinese border, before partition. It was still classified secret by the French government, I didn't like the way this was heading.

"How can I help you, Mr. Burns?"

He sighed, understanding that I wouldn't discuss it with him. "Ok, it's like this. Miles, my brother, he's been captured. He was with Lieutenant Colonel Goldberg. They left Hue overland for Quang Tri to meet up with some of the ethnic tribes. They never reached Quang Tri and we had word yesterday evening that they were snatched by the Viet Cong. They've been taken to a small prison outside Hanoi, called Son Tay. Have you heard of it?"

I resisted the invitation to become embroiled. "That is most unfortunate. Are you planning a rescue mission?"

They looked at each other, Burns spoke first. "Diem's government won't agree to it, they're worried about upsetting Hanoi. Diem is looking pretty shaky at the moment, he won't do anything that may make things worse for him. So officially, the answer is no."

I knew exactly where this was going, we all did in this room. I looked across at Paul and he gave a small shake of his head. We both knew it would be absurd to even consider going on a military mission behind enemy lines.

"Well if there's anything we can do to help you, this side of the DMZ, of course, do let us know. North of the DMZ is of course a foreign country, that would be an invasion, as you are aware. Sorry, gentlemen, we cannot help you there."

Robert Anderson stood up, his expression so woebegone and desperate that it was almost a caricature. Almost. "Hoffman, they'll torture him, maybe kill him."

I inclined my head, "That does occasionally happen, yes, this is a cruel war."

"Cut the crap, Hoffman," Burns snarled, revealing his true colours. "You know what we want, there's no one else who can do it, even our black operations guys have to have some sort of official clearance and that isn't going to happen, Diem has closed the door. You've carried out missions behind the lines before, certainly in Vietnam, although we don't have the details. Probably in Russia, too."

So they didn't know about our assassination mission. At least that was something, they wouldn't be asking us to go and shoot the enemy generals in their sleep.

"Gentlemen, all that was in the past, I was younger then." I smiled and showed them my palms so that they could see how open I was being with them. "Now I have a business, this airline, as you call it, and a wife. It's just not possible, sorry."

"How much?" Burns asked abruptly.

"How much? There is no price because we will not be going," I replied firmly.

My refusal only seemed to spur him on.

"I am authorised to offer you one hundred thousand dollars, cash, half in advance, half on completion of the mission." He sat back, waiting for me to absorb the amount on offer.

"I'm sorry, but we cannot do it."

"Two hundred thousand dollars, and your commercial permit will be guaranteed to be renewed for the next five years."

"What the hell are you talking about, there's never been a problem with our permit before," Paul shouted.

Burns shrugged. So that was the way it would be, a large sum of money and our permits renewed, or the possibility of being grounded next year.

"A dirty trick, Mr. Burns," I said coldly.

"Maybe, but we're in a dirty situation. For Christ's sake, this is my brother you're talking about here, not some gook rickshaw driver," Anderson said loudly. "Mr. Hoffman, I'm begging you, will you at least consider it?"

I looked at Schuster. "Paul?"

He nodded. "We'll consider it, a serious look but no more, on condition that the threat of the permits being withdrawn is taken off of the table."

A clever move, they had little choice if they were not to look like cheap, bullying blackmailers.

"Very well," Burns said, "come over to MACV at 0900 hours tomorrow morning, we can go over the situation there with all of the intelligence reports. You'll be meeting the commander, General Paul D. Harkins, so try not to keep him waiting.

"It would help if you would send us out some transport,

our jeep was destroyed in a VC mortar attack, and we haven't replaced it yet."

It was all agreed, we'd be ready at 0830 and they would send transport to pick us up. We shook hands and they left.

"What do you think?" Paul asked anxiously. "It's a lot of money, it could be a simple in and out operation."

I laughed. "Paul Schuster, when have you ever know any military operation be either simple or in and out?"

He nodded and grinned. "You're right, they never are. No, this is one to give a miss to."

Helene came into the office, she'd walked out to the airfield when she heard us land. We embraced and kissed each other warmly.

"Darling, I was worried about you," she said, "The weather reports said that there was a monsoon over Quang Tri province, I'm glad you weren't caught up in it."

"We were glad too," I replied. Schuster kept a straight face.

"I've cooked up a late lunch, would you care for some, Paul?"

He agreed enthusiastically, he had a local Vietnamese girlfriend but she was more decorative, a typical Vietnamese pocket Venus in her Ao Dai, but she wasn't the domestic type like Helene. We walked over to our bungalow, as we got nearer we could smell the cooking. She had the radio playing, a haunting song called 'Stranger On The Shore', by and Englishman, Acker Bilk. We washed and sat down to eat. I went to speak, but Helene stopped me.

"Listen to me, you two. I'm not a fool, what were those

two CIA spies doing waiting for you at the hangar when you landed?"

We looked at each other. It was true that Helene had an intelligence gathering network that was sometimes the equal of the CIA.

"Just a job," Paul replied, "they wanted us to fly up north and make a collection."

"I see," she said, looking thoughtful, "so the CIA trains its Harvard and Princeton summa cum laude graduates to be simple messenger boys, do they? Why couldn't they just pick up the phone?"

I hadn't got a fool for a partner, she was highly intelligent, a doctor and an accomplished woman. I guessed that she already knew exactly why they had come, so we told her everything, including the hairy takeoff from Lang Vei.

"You're not going to accept, of course?" she said immediately.

"Well, it's not as simple as that," I replied hesitantly. "It's not just the money, if they pull our commercial permit, we're finished. We may as well pack up and leave."

"At least you will be able to pack up and leave. If you're dead or in a North Vietnamese prison, you won't even have that option."

It was a fair point. We argued backwards and forwards, but in the end there really was no way we could consider going, it was an operation best left to the military. We sat eating and drinking for the evening, it was one of those times when it was good to be alive. Vietnam could be a scented paradise, the sun shining and birds singing, when it wasn't hell on earth. Finally

Paul got up to say goodbye, he thanked Helene for dinner.

"You're welcome, but remember, no missions to the North, do you understand?" she said severely.

He looked at me uncertainly, but I didn't smile.

"No, my friend, she isn't joking."

When the car came to collect me in the morning, Helene came out and got in.

"What are you doing?" I said, aghast.

"Doing? I'm representing my interests as a part owner of the airline, darling. What else?"

I sighed and made room for her in the car. The driver, an elderly Vietnamese MACV employee, turned around and glanced at me and we both raised our eyebrows. Women!

The airfield was becoming busier with every week that passed. Our operation was conducted from what was little more than a field at the side, which kept us away from the hubbub of the stream of traffic that went in and out constantly. MACV had a satellite office situated in a building at the side of the airfield. We went through the door, Anderson and Burns were waiting for us, they raised their eyebrows at Helene but said nothing. We shook hands and went up the stairs and into a reception room outside the General's office. We only waited for a few minutes, then a tough looking major came out and called us in. The General stood up to greet us, he shook hands with me, Helene and Paul and the major seated us in chairs set before the desk. Looking every inch the professional soldier, Harkins sat down behind his desk and waited for the two CIA men to begin.

He was fifty eight years old, a soldier who had made his

name serving under General Patton in the Second World War when Adolf Hitler embarked on his final piece of idiocy, the Ardennes counteroffensive in the winter of 1944. As Patton's operations officer, he earned the name Ramrod Harkins for his constant efforts to press forward. Harkins had repeatedly expressed optimism about the course of the war, although I wondered if his optimism has been dented by the poor performance of his forces at Ap Bac.

Milton Burns, the CIA man, started the ball rolling.

"I've spoken to Mr. Hoffman and Mr. Schuster, so far I haven't managed to persuade them to give it a go, but I'm still hoping they may find it possible when they've seen the plan we've prepared."

"And Mrs. Hoffman is here for what reason?" Harkins asked.

Before Burns could answer, Helene spoke up. "General, Mrs. Hoffman is here herself, you can ask me personally. And the answer would be that she is part owner of the airline so she has a say in the decision of whether to go or not."

He smiled. "Very well, allow me to introduce Major Duane Brown."

We nodded to the Major, who gave us a quick smile. "Major Brown is a man of, shall we say, exceptional talents, he has led several teams on search and destroy missions against the Viet Cong."

"Does he have experience of North Vietnam?" I asked him.

"No, not as such, but we're confident he can do the job."

I wasn't. The culture, customs and everything about

North Vietnam was totally different from that in the South. But it was their business, not mine.

"The plan is to fly his men into the North, his team will parachute into Son Tay and break the prisoners out, then lead them back to safety. Right, let's have a look at the maps."

We spent some time going over the maps and charts of the area, intelligence estimates, reports, even some aerial photographs that the General told us were taken by a U2 overflight. We winced as he said it, almost three years ago the Soviets had shot down a U2 spy plane with an S-75 missile, it was piloted by Francis Gary Powers who was still serving a ten year sentence in Russia for espionage.

Russia, of course, was the country that was supplying Hanoi with most of their arms and equipment. I hoped for the U2 pilot's sake that they hadn't yet supplied Ho Chi Minh with the S-75.

The photographs were remarkably clear, they showed a village and a larger structure at one side which they said was a factory that had been converted into a prison. It was about twelve miles outside Hanoi. After surveying all of the maps, looking at the photographs and reading the reports, we sat back down to discuss it.

"Mr. Hoffman, what do you think, you've fought in that area, can it be done?"

"General, what you are proposing is to send a small team into the heart of Ho Chi Minh's territory, take on the guards of this prison and release the prisoners, who may be injured or wounded, then get them back hundreds of miles through enemy territory. The chances of success are very slim. If you fly them out, you'll be up against North Vietnamese MIG 17s and their air defence system, which has become quite sophisticated. It is definitely not worth the risk, unless one of these Americans had knowledge of your complete order of battle and the Commander in Chief's strategy for the next several years, which I assume is not the case."

There was a silence in the room. The General, the Major and the two CIA men looked embarrassed, and it suddenly stuck me in a blinding flash of comprehension. The extraordinary sum of money on offer to get them back, the threats, the personal interest of the MACV commander. Bringing them back was not a priority.

"It's not a rescue mission, is it, General? It's an assassination."

Helene went white. "Oh, dear God, like the Giap mission."

They all looked at her. "What was that," Burns said, "About Giap?"

"Something we heard, that's all, about a French plan to kill the commander of the Viet Minh during the French war," I said quickly.

"Oh, right, did it come to anything?"

"No," Helene, Paul and I replied in chorus.

"How would you know?" Burns asked suspiciously.

We would know because we were there, fighting through a hostile, inhospitable country on a virtual suicide mission. But it was a forgotten part of our past, sealed by order of the French government and mutual agreement.

"There was something about it in the local paper," I

replied lamely.

Burns nodded and lost interest so I tackled the General further. "So what exactly do these two men know? Am I to understand that you sent them into hostile territory with detailed knowledge of your military planning? That's why you're talking about coming out overland, you don't intend that they'll be with you, you're planning to silence them."

Harkins looked angry. "What knowledge they have is not your concern, Mr. Hoffman, but we consider it vital to our interests that they not be forced to tell the communists what they know."

He put emphasis on the Mr., underscoring my civilian status. "Neither did we send them into hostile territory, they were operating inside the Republic of South Vietnam."

I couldn't help laughing out loud. "You may not consider it hostile territory, General, but I can assure you that the communists do."

The office went silent, we were at an impasse. Major Brown made an attempt at a resolution. "Look, arguing won't make a dime's worth of difference. I propose we make a deal with Mr. Hoffman and Mr. Schuster."

We looked at him. "Go on, Major," Harkins said suspiciously.

"It's just this, they both have considerable experience of operating in the North. If they will agree to act as mission consultants, we'll offer them a reasonable payment for their services and no threats on their licenses. We'll get one of the company aircraft to take us, I'm sorry, Burns," he said, nodding to the CIA man, "that's the way it will have to be."

He looked hard at Burns as he mentioned the licenses and using the CIA's own aircraft, Burns glared back at him.

Harkins nodded. "That's sounds reasonable, Major. Mr. Hoffman, Mr. Schuster, what do you say?"

Paul nodded to me in the affirmative. "On one condition, that this mission is a rescue, and not an assassination, we'll have no part of that."

"Of course, we can agree to that. There never was a plan to assassinate anyone, so that's no problem," the General said. He had the grace to avoid my eyes as he said it. He rounded on Burns, who was trying to speak.

"Mr. Burns, just get me an aircraft, I don't care how you do it, clear?"

The man nodded resignedly.

"In that case we're agreed," I said, "we'll give you all the help you need."

We spent the rest of the morning going over their plans. Schuster and I checked and rechecked maps and reports and passed on our knowledge of the area around Hanoi, constantly reminding them that it was ten years out of date. The General had sandwiches and coffee brought in for lunch and we kept on working into the late afternoon. By six we still hadn't finished and they took us back to our hangar.

The following morning we were booked on a routine flight to Hue, taking regular supplies for a French exploration company. We agreed to meet the day after, which would be the final day before the actual mission began. Time wasn't on their side, if the communists found out about the information that their two American captives held, the mission would be over and with it a large part of American strategy for the foreseeable future in South East Asia.

Schuster and I took the C-47 to Hue in the morning. It was a milk run, as the RAF used to call their missions during the Second World War. We flew up, unloaded and started the flight back without any problems from the communist insurgency. On the way back the starboard turbocharger started malfunctioning again, we decided that we would have to import a spare from the US, expensive but the only way we would keep the aircraft flying. The radio crackled, it was Johann.

"Johann," I greeted him cheerily, "you're just the man I need, we're still having supercharger problems, we're going to need to source one in the U.S. if there's no other way."

There was silence. He came back after almost a minute. "Jurgen, we've got a problem. There's been another mortar attack at Tan Son Nhat."

"Damn, any damage to our hangar or aircraft?"

"It's not that, one of the shells missed the airfield completely, Jurgen. It hit your bungalow."

Helene! I couldn't ask the question, I felt as if I'd been punched in the stomach, I felt dizzy, everything started to go black. Schuster understood immediately and took over.

"How is she, Johann, is she alive?"

"Yes, she's alive," he said hastily, "but she's badly wounded. A U.S. officer, a Major Brown, found out and pulled some strings, he had her taken to Saigon Station Hospital on Tran Hung Dao Street, it's a naval hospital that serves the whole of MACV."

I cut in. "Johann, how is she, what are they doing to her?"

"She's not good, Jurgen. She took a splinter to her abdomen that went right through and is resting against some major organs, I'm not entirely certain what they are, sorry."

"Look, tell me the truth, is she expected to live?"

He was silent for a full half a minute, it seemed like an hour. When he spoke again, his voice was stretched and broken as if he had been weeping. "It's touch and go. We don't know, but a priest has given her the last rites."

I reeled and clutched at a metal stanchion for support. Once again I felt the blackness coming over me. Paul looked over. "Are you ok, Jurgen?" I nodded, took a deep breath to control myself and spoke into the microphone. "Thank you Johann, we'll be back as soon as possible. Would you have a taxi standing by in an hour?"

"Of course, I'm sorry, Jurgen."

"Yes."

Schuster had already throttled up to maximum speed, he flew the aircraft steadily on to Saigon while I sat in my misery. When we landed I bounded out of the door, the taxi had come up and I got in.

"You know where to go?"

"Tran Hung Dao Street, Saigon Hospital."

We roared off, I heard Schuster shout that he'd follow me when the plane was secured. The taxi dropped me outside the hospital, when I ran in there was the usual antiseptic smell, doctors in white coats walking past and nurses in white uniforms. It being a naval installation there was a pretty, uniformed chief petty officer behind the counter. She raised her eyebrows as I rushed in, dusty and dishevelled after my long flight.

"I'm looking for Helene Baptiste, she was brought here after the mortar attack this morning."

"Yes, of course, the French civilian. She's in the OR at the moment, they're working on her. Who are you?"

"Jurgen Hoffman, Miss Baptiste is my wife."

"Very well, if you would like to sit and wait we'll call you as soon as there is any news."

"Will it be long?"

She looked at me sympathetically. "She was seriously hurt, Sir. They're doing their best for her, but…"

She left it unsaid.

"Please call me if anything changes," I said to her.

I went to the waiting area at the side of the reception counter, but I couldn't sit. For over an hour I paced up and down, waiting for news. Both Paul and Johann joined me, they were immensely fond of her and I could see in their faces that they feared the worst almost as much as I did. I shook my head in response to their unasked question.

After two more hours of agonised waiting, a surgeon came to speak to us. His face was grave.

"She's very sick, Mr. Hoffman, a fragment of shrapnel is lodged against her spine. Did you know she was pregnant?"

Pregnant? I was astounded. After all this time, we'd hoped and prayed that a baby would come along. Now it had, only for this to happen. I felt even more numb with the enormous loss I was facing.

I went in to see her. She was covered in bandages, the

mortar had inflicted several small cuts to her face but the main damage was underneath the bedcovers. She was asleep, very peaceful under the effect of the painkilling drugs and the anaesthetic. I stayed with her for an hour, Paul and Johann spent a short time and then returned to the airfield, there were problems there that needed dealing with too. When I came out of the intensive care ward, I went and found the surgeon. His name badge identified him as Surgeon Commander Walter H Bloom, USN.

"Doctor, tell me, what are her chances?"

He hummed and hah'd the way all doctors do.

"Look, Mr. Hoffman, we have basic facilities here. Our hospital can only provide very limited care. This injury is far too serious for us to treat. Helene has shrapnel lodged in her spine and possibly spinal cord. Two vertebrae are damaged, L1 and L2. There are concerns that they could collapse further and cause permanent damage and paralysis."

He stopped to allow me to digest the bad news.

"Is she in pain?" I asked him.

He thought for a moment. "I'm afraid so, yes. She is in considerable pain, but it is controlled. Although she has feeling and movement in her legs, at times this movement is restricted and is replaced by a feeling of numbness. This is causing great concern as it suggests increased pressure on the spinal cord. She has no signs of infection, but this is also a major concern as is likely to develop if untreated and cause serious complications, including meningitis. She has had no major blood loss, but her blood pressure is slightly elevated, there could be kidney damage. It is also possible that bone fragments and shrapnel could be in the spine which may lead to further damage or infection. Bear in mind, Mr. Hoffman, she is about eight weeks pregnant. Before she became unconscious, she made it clear that under no circumstances will she consider an abortion, which the hospital also feels should be considered."

We stood in silence as he watched me carefully. Did he think I was going to become hysterical, I wondered? But I supposed I had every right to go crazy. "So what can you do?"

"She needs urgent surgery, you must understand how life threatening this is, a potential outcome of permanent paralysis, kidney failure, brain damage if untreated and…" He didn't say the rest, I understood.

"We may be able to save her and the baby," he continued, "but it's touch and go. If we were back in the States I'd say her chances were very good, but we're not. Our equipment and expertise here is mainly for dealing with less serious wounds, we patch them up and either send them home for more treatment or back out into the field to rejoin their unit."

"Can you get her on a flight back to the States?"

He smiled and shook his head. "They pulled strings from MACV to get her in here, but a medical flight to the States, well, she'd need to be service personnel, which she clearly isn't. I'm sorry, Mr. Hoffman, but we'll do our best."

I argued with him for a half an hour until I was almost thrown out of the hospital, but it was useless, they wouldn't allow it. Before I left they let me see Helene, she lay alone in a white room, covered in pipes, wires, drips, bandages and monitors. She hadn't recovered consciousness, her face was ghostly white with a stretched, clammy pallor that I had seen many times before in the field worn by heavily wounded casualties. Some of them never recovered.

I left the base, walking like a zombie, I was in a dark, damp fog of misery and despair. I eventually found a taxi to take me back to Tan Son Nhat. I didn't go to the hangar, instead I went to MACV and asked for Major Brown. Robert Anderson came out instead. He nodded to the sentry. "It's ok, he's with us." We went through and upstairs to an office I hadn't seen before, Milton Burns was sitting behind a desk. So this was where the CIA operated from.

"I came to see Major Brown, where is he?" Burns looked up.

"General Harkins asked for volunteers to go on a search and destroy mission to find that Viet Cong mortar team, he's out there now with a team of Green Berets. He thought it would be a good chance to get some field training prior to the mission."

I nodded. "You heard about my wife?"

"We did, yes, it's terrible news, Hoffman," Anderson replied.

"I want her on a flight back Stateside, she needs medical treatment and she won't get it here."

They both looked at me in surprise. "But she's a civilian, that kind of medical flight is impossible," Burns said.

"I'll do whatever you want, I'll do anything. You want me to transport your team into Hanoi, I'll do it, just get her to a U.S. hospital."

They both shook their heads. "It's impossible, not for a civilian, no matter what you are able to offer. We're truly sorry,

Hoffman."

Burns at least did look genuinely sorry, perhaps the CIA man did have a soul after all. I left the office in despair and walked back to our hangar. Paul and Johann were both waiting for me, but I shook my head, no news.

The evening dragged on and I went back to the hospital, but there was no change, Helene was still unconscious. I sat with her for several hours and went home. Half of our bungalow had been destroyed, but I managed to make up a bed in the undamaged part and I spent a few hours drifting in and out of sleep. In the morning I phoned the hospital but there was no change. I got dressed and walked to MACV, Paul was already there waiting for me.

"I can take care of the meeting if you wish," he said. "Why don't you go back and see Helene?"

"No, I'll go to the hospital later, let's get this done."

We walked in, the sentries were ready and let us through, and we went up the stairs and into the outer office of General Harkins. Burns and Anderson were waiting, they both looked grave.

"What's up?" I asked them. They shook their heads, tight-lipped spooks to the very end. The door opened and a different officer showed us into the office. General Harkins nodded a greeting.

"Gentlemen, this is Captain James Cady, Special Forces. He is Major Brown's replacement for Operation Reachout." He saw our looks of incomprehension. "That's what we've called the rescue mission."

"So where is Major Brown?" I asked him. "Why has he

pulled out?"

"Major Brown is dead, Mr. Hoffman, he was hit by a Viet Cong bullet last night while leading a search and destroy team to locate the mortar crew that did the damage on this base, your wife included."

It was a major blow to their mission. Brown had studied the plan for several days and he had at least a slim chance of pulling it off.

"How much experience does Captain Cady have of fighting the Viet Cong?" I asked him. They all looked embarrassed, eventually, the General replied.

"Captain Cady arrived in the country two days ago, he was unassigned and volunteered to take charge."

I felt chilled, a sense of déjà vu. While our Waffen-SS troops were bleeding and freezing to death on the Eastern Front, Heinrich Himmler sent out teams from his Ahnenerbe research institute to discover archaeological evidence related to the origins of the Aryan race. He had a bizarre mix of adventurers, mystics, and even reputable scholars to help rewrite all of human history. His expeditions went to Biskupice in Poland, Olympia in Greece, Slovakia, the Croat fortress of Surval, Serbia and Caucasia. Further expeditions made their way to Tibet to help find evidence to support his crackpot theories of the origins of the Master Race. This mission was of a different type, but it seemed just as ill-conceived, just as crackpot.

The office was silent for a moment. Cady broke it. "Mr. Hoffman, I may not have the experience of fighting these savages, but I've seen action and I'll see this mission through."

Harkins looked at me and Paul. "Well? What do you think?"

It was Paul who spoke up, angrily. "Is this the way the U.S. Army operates, sending ill-prepared, untrained men to carry out dangerous missions? Good God, General, it's crazy."

"Hoffman?" he asked. I shook my head. "Paul is right. Without the kind of expertise that Major Brown had as a bare minimum, the chances of success are zero."

"Hoffman," Milton Burns broke in, "that's not your call to make."

"Shut up, Milton," Harkins said. "There are only two people in room who have actually been there and know how the land lies, and you're not one of them." He looked at Paul and me. "What do you gentlemen suggest? We have to get them out, it is imperative."

"I'll take them in and bring them out," I said to him. He nodded thoughtfully. "I see. What's the price, Mr. Hoffman?"

"You get my wife on a flight to the States today, and get her wounds treated in a hospital equipped to deal with them."

"General, you can't..."

"Burns, I told you to shut up," he snapped. He picked up the phone.

"Get me the colonel in charge of logistics, I want him now, wherever he is. Get him in here, on the double."

We sat waiting for less than a minute before the door burst open and a harried looking colonel rushed in and saluted. "Yes, Sir, General, what can I do for you?"

"Colonel, there is a lady in the Saigon Station Hospital, Helene Baptiste. I want her on a flight tonight to Washington and a team standing by at Walter Reed Army Medical Centre to operate on her. Make it happen, Colonel, I won't take no for an answer."

"Sir," the colonel saluted and rushed out.

"Satisfied, Hoffman?" Harkins said to me.

I nodded. "Thank you, General. I'll get your men back for you." I felt an enormous weight beginning to lift off my head, but I knew this was only the start. It was a long flight Stateside and a lot of complicated treatment before she recovered. And there was the baby of course, Jesus Christ, I was about to become a father and now this.

"Good, then I suggest you make a start. Nice meeting you, Mr. Hoffman, Mr. Schuster."

He shook hands with us and we left his office, an aide was already announcing the arrivals for his next meeting.

"It seems we're going back to war," Schuster said grimly.

I nodded. God help all of us this time.

* * *

'A Communist land reform program in South Vietnam, begun by the Viet Minh, is still being carried out under the Viet Cong. Current reports also indicate that the Viet Cong provide assistance to peasants in land clearance, seed distribution, and harvesting, and in turn persuade or force peasants to store rice in excess of their own needs for the use of guerrilla troops. Controls are apparently imposed in Viet Cong zones to prevent shipments for commercial marketing in Saigon, or to collect taxes on such shipments. The Viet Cong themselves often pay cash or give promissory notes for

the food they acquire. Captured Viet Cong doctors or medical personnel indicate that dispensaries for treatment of Viet Cong wounded often are scattered inconspicuously among several peasant homes in a village, and that civilians are treated as facilities and supplies permit. There are also references to primary and adult education, much of it in the form of indoctrination, and to Viet Cong run schools operating almost side by side with government schools. The Viet Cong also promote cultural activities, heavily flavored with Propaganda, through press, radio and film media, as well as live drama and festivals.'

CIA Secret Memo

Eight new senior officers leapt to attention, all newly arrived in Vietnam to help lead the American 'Special Advisors' programme. Harkins looked at them one by one.

"The groundwork has been done, gentlemen. On every front our Vietnamese allies are fighting the communists and achieving good results. The Viet Cong is retreating and will eventually be defeated if we keep up the pressure. Your contribution will be invaluable to that success, as will the contribution of further American units that I expect to arrive in this country over the next few months. Questions?"

"Sir, there've been stories in the news that suggest that the ARVN is not committed to the fighting and they've taken some pretty good beatings from the communists, or that they've refused to fight at all." The newly arrived major could see the General's face darkening as he spoke, but it had to be asked, it was their lives that would be on the line.

"Is the ARVN a serious problem?"

Harkins looked irritably at the major then at Colonel Gia, the ARVN liaison officer, standing passively next to him. He had to defuse this potentially embarrassing question, for no other reason than the need to maintain good relations with the Vietnamese army, the ARVN.

"The ARVN is a well trained and equipped fighting force, Major. Nothing to worry about."

Most present looked satisfied, but the major was obviously puzzled at the General's inability to answer the question. One of Harkin's aides, a captain, looked up sharply as he heard what his general had said. But it was not for him to contradict his commanding officer, he had his own career to worry about.

Harkins looked down on the assembled officers. He knew that he was not giving them the whole truth, politics prevented him from giving them the real story. He recalled a recent meeting with Diem, the President of the Republic of Vietnam. He'd spoken to Diem directly, giving it to him straight.

"During the preceding week, all of your ARVN divisions, everywhere, it was reported that there was a serious shortage of company grade officers. In some cases, there were only six officers in a battalion. There were instances of companies commanded by trainees or sergeants. Leadership is lacking in platoons and companies, the very place where it is needed most, since these are the units which do the fighting."

He had recommended diverting officers from headquarters or logistical commands to combat units, shortening the training time at the officer school, and bringing more young professional men into the armed forces with abbreviated officer training.

Diem had nodded to Harkins.

"Of course, you are correct, General. I am concerned over the number of senior officers who have reached the height of their potential and who lack the education and initiative required in higher grades."

"Such men should be eliminated," Harkins replied.

Diem spread his hands wide, as if to say 'look how difficult this is, how my hands are tied.'

"One of the difficulties in identifying incompetent officers lies in the fact that my generals do not want to recommend the separation of officers who are old friends. But I am considering the thought of elimination."

But of course, none of this was for the consumption of these new officers, nor for his superiors back in Washington. He had a war to fight, sometimes that meant bending the truth a little to get people on your side, it was called politics. In the meantime, he needed men, both American and Vietnamese, who were on his side.

"Don't worry, men, although the Viet Cong is already beaten, there is still plenty to do. We're making history here, defeating the communists. For you officers that means promotions and medals, and there are plenty of both to go around."

The men cheered heartily. Now he had to get them and their ARVN counterparts to fight the communists.

CHAPTER FOUR

As you are aware, the great difficulties we had to live through last August and September resulted largely from a nearly complete breakdown of the Government's ability to get accurate assessments of the situation in the Vietnamese countryside. The more we learn about the situation today, the more obvious it becomes that the excessively mechanical system of statistical reporting which had been devised in Washington and applied in Saigon was giving us a grotesquely inaccurate picture. Once again it is the old problem of having people who are responsible for operations also responsible for evaluating the results.

Michael Forrestal, NSC 1963

Paul and I went into the city to see Helene. Still unconscious, she was already being prepared for a flight to the States. It was late evening by the time we got back to the hangar, I decided to sleep there, I was too sick with worry and grief to go back to the ruined bungalow. Besides, there was work to be done.

Johann Drexler was waiting for us, he seemed to live in the hangar surrounded by his beloved aircraft and tools. Strangely, he'd learned to fly during a period of time he spent in South America after the war, but he preferred spending his time up to his armpits in grease. He freely admitted that with poor eyesight he would be a danger to himself and to his passengers if he ever flew. He had gone through the war on the Eastern Front as a Waffen-SS Hauptscharführer in the Das Reich Panzer Regiment. Escaping from the Battle of Berlin with hardly a scratch, he made his way to Bolivia where he was hit by a shell fragment during one of the many upheavals that were a feature of that country's politics. Besides, he preferred the company of engines and tools, they were much more reliable and less fickle than the shadowy clients for whom we flew cargos and passengers around the country.

He asked about Helene and was visibly relieved that she would be receiving the best possible treatment.

"We had a Captain Cady called round earlier, he said he would be back in the morning to brief you."

Paul and I smiled at each other. So this fiery young Special Forces Captain with no experience was coming to brief us with his extensive knowledge and experience of North Vietnam. It would be interesting. We sat and drank our way through a few beers. Aircraft took off constantly from the main runway of Tan Son Nhat, Helene would be on one of them, it was reassuring. I thought of her as she lay in that hospital bed, so close to death, then I thought of the woman I knew, lively, vivacious, caring, warm, she was everything any man could want and more. She had to pull through, just had to. I vowed to do everything in my power to make that happen even if I had to go into Hanoi and murder Ho Chi Minh personally. Finally, I made up a camp bed in the office and slept. In the morning, I was drinking a cup of coffee and making some notes on a pad about maintenance schedules when I heard a series of shouts outside the hangar. I went outside and there was Captain Cady lining up his Special Forces troops, five soldiers, festooned with packs, weapons and a heap of stores they were unloading from a U.S. army truck. He was shouting orders at the top of his voice and it was obvious his men were unhappy, all Green Beret sergeants who were trained to act and fight independently. Cady spotted me.

"Good morning, Mr Hoffman, where do you want us to stow these crates?"

I nodded to Cady. "Captain, we are about to embark on a mission that is highly secret. I suggest you get your men and equipment inside the hangar immediately and send that truck away. You're advertising your presence to the Viet Cong."

His face darkened, stung by the implicit criticism.

"Hoffman, we are on a friendly airfield, are you suggesting that the communists are operating here?" he laughed. "Jesus Christ, are you gonna be the type that sees a red under every bed?"

I had misgivings before about working with an inexperienced officer, but now my confidence ebbed even further.

"Captain," I said gently, "in Vietnam, it is safer to assume that every single native is the enemy. That way, you tend to live longer, and I have lived here for almost fifteen years. Please, get everything inside the hangar."

He sighed and muttered something about "fucking krauts," but he shouted more orders to his men.

"And Captain," I continued, he looked at me, his face harsh, "please, a little quieter, let's keep this mission a secret for a little longer."

I thought he would explode. His men were grinning to themselves, but it had to be done, this inexperienced fool would get us all killed. They quickly stowed all the equipment inside our hangar and Cady called everyone around to go over the mission briefing. He had a packet of maps and intelligence documents in front of him.

"Ok, our reconnaissance shows that they are being held at an old rubber processing factory near Son Tay. My plan calls for us to go in during daylight, I'm unhappy about night actions. We'll make contact with elements of the Vietnamese resistance and use them to guide us to the prison. Any questions so far?"

I was astounded, what planet had this soldier been living on? "Captain Cady, tell me more about the 'Vietnamese Resistance'."

"Yeah, you should know more about that, Hoffman. When Vietnam was partitioned, a lot of anti-communists were left in the North, we just need to make contact with them to get help."

Paul and I looked at each other, this was going to be difficult. "Captain, when we cross the DMZ, you must regard every single Vietnamese as the enemy, period. Even south of the DMZ, as I have said, it is little different."

"Hang on there, pal," he said angrily, "we have made

contact with one of the resistance already, Le Van Tri. He's offered to help us, we won't be on our own."

He sat back, a 'so there' expression on his face. Paul and I laughed.

"Le Van Tri is a crook," I said to him. "We move his shipments occasionally, he's a smuggler, pure and simple. His main business is taking goods into North Vietnam to beat the communist blockade. I strongly advise you to be careful when you accept his help, there will be a high price."

He shook his head, he was a hard man to convince. "Not your worry, Hoffman, I'm expecting a message from him shortly, they'll forward it from MACV, the whereabouts of a good landing zone for our aircraft and his radio operating frequency."

I shrugged. "As you wish. Next, Captain, there will be no daylight landing."

He opened his mouth to object, but I hurriedly overrode him. "Captain, when we overfly the North every gun will be turned against us. The second we cross the DMZ during daylight hours, we'll start taking ground fire. As well as that, every single Vietnamese peasant will be alerting the local party HQ that an aircraft from the South is crossing their airspace. They'll scramble the MIGs and we'll be shot down before we even get near Hanoi."

Once again he opened his mouth to object, once more he was interrupted, this time by one of his own men.

"Cap'n, this guy's been here a long time, might be worth listening to him," he looked at me. "Pleased to meet you, Sir. I'm Master Sergeant Tim Beckerman."

I nodded to him, "Jurgen Hoffman. Captain, perhaps you would introduce your team before we go on?"

Cady wasn't happy about the interruption, but he gave in with bad grace. "Yeah, I was about to get to that. Hoffman, these are Master Sergeant Beckerman, Communications Sergeant Jack Bond, Abe Woltz, the unit sniper, Chief Warrant Officer Frank Burr, Weapons Sergeant Joe Russo."

I said hello to each of them. Now that the introductions had been made, they started to hit me with a barrage of questions about the North, but Cady cut them off.

"Can it, men, save it for later. Ok, Hoffman, you reckon on a night landing?"

"It's the only way, Captain. You can contact Le Van Tri and get him to light the landing field for us."

He nodded. "Yeah, we can do that. So what about getting out?"

"Preferably the same night, it's the only way to be certain. Remember, every single peasant is a potential enemy, it would be almost impossible to hide an aircraft during the hours of daylight."

"Why not fly it back out when we go in and return the next night for the pick up?" he persisted.

"Same problem, the whole North Vietnamese defence system will be alerted during the intervening time. No, it must be done in the same night, in and out."

He nodded slowly. He was obviously unhappy that his carefully drawn up plans were being torn to shreds, but he at least understood my reasoning. On top of that, his men listened alertly as I spoke, nodding when I made a point. He knew that these were tough, experienced soldiers, the best. He may have led them by virtue of his rank, but with men like these, consensus was just as essential to get them to follow orders. Perhaps more so. One of them spoke to me, a huge, black sergeant.

"Chief Warrant Officer Frank Burr, Sir, you obviously know what you're talking about," everyone looked at Cady, who reddened slightly. "What's gonna be our main problem, what do you see as the biggest obstacle to us successfully completing the mission?"

The men waited quietly for my reply. I considered carefully. "In the German army, we called it the 'Schwerpunkt', the hard point. Yes, a good question. The answer is communications. The communists have an extensive early warning and intelligence system. Every farmer, every village has a means of communicating enemy incursions with Hanoi. If one of them, just one, a farmer herding pigs on a hillside, a labourer digging a road, gets the word out, we're in trouble, we'll have the MIGs on our backs before we cross back over the DMZ."

Cady sneered. "You make them sound almost invincible, Hoffman, a bunch of commie peasants and guerrillas."

I smiled. "You haven't beaten them yet, Captain. These people have been fighting one oppressor after another for over a thousand years. Just think, hundreds of years before the Europeans discovered America, they were fighting the foreign invader. And they keep fighting, they beat the French and it is by no means certain that you Americans will do better. At Ap Bac they defeated a combined ARVN and American force ten times their size. Don't underestimate them. That way, we stand a good chance of getting in and out without undue problems. Avoid contact, that's the real trick."

The room was quiet, then a soldier rushed into the hangar clutching an envelope.

"Message from MACV for Captain Cady."

"I'm Cady."

He took the envelope, ripped it open and rapidly read the message. Then he looked at me meaningfully. "It's a message from Le Van Tri, did you know about this?"

I shook my head.

"Well," he continued, "it seems you were right, Le Van Tri has named his price."

The soldiers looked at me as if I was Merlin the Wizard, but the truth was, I dealt with these people all of the time, there was always a price.

"His son, Le Van Dao is down in the Mekong at a place called Soc Trang. He's staying with some people called the Binh Xuyen. We're to pick him up and take him with us and hand him over to Le Van Tri. What do you make of it, Hoffman?"

"Paul, would you explain to the Captain what this means?"

"By all means," he replied grimly. "Firstly, the Binh Xuyen is a criminal gang, no more, no less. They're rivals to Le Van Tri's outfit, both are always trying to carve out a bigger slice of the cake. If Le Van Dao is with the Binh Xuyen, he's a hostage being held for some reason, maybe ransom, maybe something else. Le Van Tri wants us to go down there and bust him out."

They all looked at him in amazement.

"Mr Schuster," Cady said contemptuously, "You're saying that this fucking smuggler wants to use an American Special Forces unit as his own private army?"

"It looks that way, yes."

He shook his head from side to side. "No way, no fucking way. We'll have to do it some other way."

We were all silent for a moment.

"Hoffman, do you have anyone who can light a landing field for us near Son Tay?"

"Only Le Van Tri, I'm sorry. And if there was anyone else, he'd only kill them to force us to get his son back for him."

"Jesus H fucking Christ," he snarled, "one fucking slope peasant holding the U.S. army to ransom. Is there no other way?"

I shook my head.

"What if I could persuade the General to pay this ransom?"

I shook my head again. "It may not be ransom, it could be something else entirely, a squabble over territory, anything."

Just then, Johann walked over to us, he'd been working on the C-47. "Bad news, Jurgen, that supercharger has finally given up altogether."

"How soon can you source a replacement?"

He looked mournful. "It's already on order. Three days, I'm afraid."

"Is he talking about our plane, the one you said you'd fly us in with?" Cady asked harshly.

I didn't answer him for a moment. I was sick of this

arrogant, corn fed American officer. His men were quiet, watchful, intelligent, obviously tough and competent at what they did. He was a product of wealthy parents, probably an Ivy League college and regarded anyone not as privileged as him as a lesser human.

"It's ok, we'll use the Junkers 52, it's not a setback."

"Are you talking about that piece of Nazi junk out there in the hangar?" he said incredulously.

I gave them a potted history of the 'Aunty Ju', as we called this stalwart of the German armed forces during the war. The Junkers Ju 52, a German transport aircraft, was manufactured from 1932 to 1945. It saw both civilian and military service during the 1930s and 1940s. In its civilian role, it flew with over twelve air carriers including Swissair and Lufthansa as an airliner and freight hauler. In a military role, it flew with the Luftwaffe as a troop and cargo transport and briefly as a medium bomber. The Junkers 52 continued in post war service with military and civilian air fleets up to the present day. Indeed, the Portuguese Air Force, already using the Ju 52s as a transport plane, employed the Junkers as a paratroop drop aircraft for its newly organised elite parachute forces, later known as the Batalhão de Caçadores Páraquedistas. The paratroopers used the Junkers 52 in several combat operations in Angola and other Portuguese African colonies before gradually phasing it out of service in the 1960s. The Swiss Air Force also operated the Junkers 52 from 1939 and was still using them. During the 1950s the Junkers 52 was also used by the French Air Force here in Vietnam as a bomber.

"She may not look much, but it's a thoroughly reliable

aircraft that will get us there and back," I finished.

I could see his point, looking across the hangar she did look outdated with the corrugated fuselage. But she was also the only aircraft ready to go and one that I would trust implicitly. Cady finally gave in. "Yeah, yeah, if that's all we've got, we'll have to use it, but I don't like it, Hoffman. Right, what about this kid Le Van Dao, what do you suggest?"

His men were looking at each other, realising uneasily that their captain was out of his depth. From that moment, he effectively lost control of the mission, although he was almost certainly too arrogant to either admit or even understand it.

"The Binh Xuyen has a warehouse next to the airfield at Soc Trang, it's almost certain that's where they'll be holding him. It should be possible to fly in with a couple of men and free him, they won't be expecting it. In the meantime, we can get the Junkers loaded, fuelled and ready to go."

"Yeah, ok, how many men can you carry?"

"It'll have to be the Cessna," I replied. "She'll carry a maximum of four, that's the pilot, two of your men and Le Van Dao on the way back," I replied.

"Very well, that's what we'll do. Take off this evening for Soc Trang, Sergeant Woltz, Chief Warrant Officer Burr, you will accompany Mr. Hoffman and bring this gook kid back here. Hoffman, I want to be ready to leave as soon as you get back. How long will it take to get us to the North?"

I looked at the clock. "Paul, you'll need to load extra fuel in the Junkers, we'll refuel on the ground in the North. We can get you there tonight, Captain, we'll time it to cross the DMZ soon after dark to give us the maximum mission time."

"Right, I'll get things organised here. Good luck, Mr Hoffman. Frank, Abe, you look after Hoffman and this gook, get him back safely."

Did he mean for them to get me or 'the Gook' back safely? Cady's men were open mouthed at his arrogance and stupidity, but had no choice but to ignore it and get on with their jobs. I talked to Paul about the load for the Junkers, and then set out across the field to the Cessna. Johann had already gone ahead and was unfastening the ground anchors. Burr and Woltz followed, the sniper was carrying a long rifle fitted with a sniper scope.

"That looks impressive," I said, looking at the rifle he held carefully, its stock was finished in a dull, matt varnish, the metalwork had that slight sheen of frequent but careful use.

"It's the Springfield Sniper Rifle M1903," he said proudly, he went on to describe what was obviously a favourite topic of his. The M1903 was officially adopted as a United States military bolt-action rifle in 1905, and saw service in World War I. It was officially replaced as the standard infantry rifle by the faster-firing, semi-automatic eight round M1 Garand in 1937. However, the M1903 Springfield remained in service as a standard issue infantry rifle during World War II, since the U.S. entered the war without sufficient M1 rifles to arm all its troops. It also remained in service as a sniper rifle during World War II, the Korean War and was still in service, particularly as a specialist sniper rifle in Vietnam.

"It ain't everyone's idea of the perfect rifle, but this baby shoots clean and straight every time," he added, as he wiped the action over with an oily rag.

I left him to clean his beloved rifle and checked over the aircraft, climbed in and the others followed, Woltz carefully fitting the awkward long length of his rifle in the cabin.

"Mr Hoffman, are you armed, you got anything to defend yourself with?" Burr asked me.

I smiled at him. "I have something, yes. Please, call me Jurgen, I didn't go to West Point."

He laughed. "Yeah, the Captain is a bit of a pain in the ass, but we manage to ignore him. It's Frank, this is Abe." They held out their hands and we shook.

"Frank, would you open the locker behind you, I'd like my weapons out ready to use." He opened the small door and whistled. "I see you're prepared for anything, Jurgen."

"Yes, it's the only way to survive in Vietnam. Would you pass me the Tokarev and an M2 carbine, there's a canvas satchel with clips for both guns, I'll need that too."

Johann waved all clear, and I started the engine and called the tower for clearance. Cady had already alerted them and they cleared us straight out. I throttled up, let off the brakes and taxied out to the main runway. Then I throttled up all the way and we accelerated down the runway and took off. Another mission, I wondered if I was too old for this, then I thought of Helene, whatever it took I would do it.

We set course for Soc Trang, it wasn't a long flight. I described the layout of the airfield for them. Neither soldier was in army uniform, indeed, they looked just like two of the thousands of foreign mercenaries that operated in Vietnam offering armed protection to the highest bidder. We discussed the best way to carry out the rescue. In the end it was decided

ERIC MEYER

that Woltz, the sniper, would remain hidden inside the aircraft to provide fire support. It would be difficult for him to hide his sniper rifle outside of the aircraft before the time came to use it, but when it was needed the need for secrecy would be gone. Burr and I would go into the warehouse with pistols only, concealed inside our shirts. I had a cardboard box of old aircraft parts waiting for Johann to get around to reconditioning them, it was stowed behind the seats next to the weapons locker. I got Burr to remove the parts and put in two MP38s that we carried with several spare clips, just for insurance. He would carry the box as a pretext for delivering a shipment of drugs to the smugglers.

After an hour we came up on Soc Trang and I got clearance to land. It was the airfield that served a small tourist destination with a number of historic sites nearby. It was also strategically positioned in the Mekong Delta, a place where deals were done and cargos shipped through with few questions asked. I dropped the Cessna onto the runway and taxied over to the Binh Xuyen warehouse. There was nobody to be seen anywhere, either around the airfield or near the warehouse. Woltz had already ducked down low, he had a blanket over his head to hide him from a casual observer. There was no reason for them to be alerted, two civilians flying in a Cessna usually meant a straightforward drug shipment, something they were used to all the time. Frank opened the door and climbed down with the cardboard box, I climbed down after him and we walked casually over to the warehouse and opened the door. Two Vietnamese were inside, one sat behind a desk, the other sprawled on broken couch reading a comic book. A local radio station was playing softly, I recognised the song, 'Telstar', a haunting instrumental piece played by a band called The Tornados.

"Hey," I greeted them, "where do you want the shipment? We'll need to see the money before we leave it."

The guy behind the desk looked puzzled. The other guy on the couch was disinterested, he looked up for a moment and then back at his comic. He was the guard, we'd both noted his well worn shoulder holster with a large automatic, his AR15 rifle leaning against the wall nearby.

"We're not expecting any shipment. Who sent you?"

"Le Van Tri," I said softly.

The one on the couch looked up sharply as he heard the name. Burr had his silenced pistol hidden under the cardboard box in his hands, he brought it out in one fluid motion and shot the guard between the eyes, he slumped down on the couch without a word. The man behind the desk reached inside a drawer, I stepped to one side and Burr's pistol coughed again, he was thrown backwards out of the chair and fell to the floor in a bloody heap. We heard someone call out through a partially opened door at the rear of the office. Burr opened the cardboard box and tossed me an MP38, took one for himself and we waited.

Four Vietnamese came hurtling through the door, we hit them with short bursts from the machine pistols and then ran through the door into a narrow passage. Two more Vietnamese were standing with pistols pointed towards us, we cut them down with short bursts from the MP38s. A side door was open and we could hear footsteps running away from the building.

"They'll be going for reinforcements, we need to hurry, let's find Le Van Dao."

Burr nodded, we started checking the doors that led off the passage. He opened one and a Vietnamese aimed a pistol at him, I cut the guy down with another burst and we ran in. Dao was there, tied to a wooden chair. He was in a bad way, bruised and beaten, but at least he was alive. We untied him and almost carried him out of the building. We ran across to the Cessna as several bursts of automatic fire sprayed over our heads. Woltz was prone on the ground, sheltering behind the wheel of the aircraft.

He took aim and fired several times, the gunfire stopped.

"We've got him, get in the aircraft, we need to get moving," I shouted.

We climbed aboard, I started the engine and began taxiing to the downwind end of the strip. A voice was shouting in my headset that we had to wait for clearance, meanwhile, a Toyota truck with half a dozen heavily armed Vietnamese was speeding towards us. I estimated our speed and distance, we weren't going to make it.

"Guys, you need to deal with that truck," I shouted.

They nodded. Burr used the butt of the MP38 to smash two of the back windows of the Cessna to give them a firing slot for their guns.

"Sorry, Jurgen," he shouted.

"I'll put it on your bill, now finish them, they're coming in fast."

Burr hosed the truck down with the sub-machine gun,

emptied the clip and snapped in another. Woltz poked his rifle out of the broken window and took careful aim, the truck lurched as one of the tyres was hit. He fired again, and again. The incoming fire that threatened to overwhelm us had slackened, finally the sniper hit the driver and the truck slewed around and tipped over, throwing dead and dying to the ground. We reached take-off speed and I rotated the Cessna off the runway, we were airborne. The headset still babbled incessantly, the controller outraged that we had taken off without clearance. I made a note to telephone him in the near future and find out how much he wanted to forget it. I still had an airline to run after this operation was over.

It took us just over an hour to get back to Tan Son Nhat. I landed and we taxied to the hangar. Cady came out and peered in.

"Good work, Hoffman, we're all ready to go, you can transfer Mr. Le to the Junkers."

"Certainly, Captain, your two men had something to do with it as well, you know."

Oh, yeah," he looked at Burr and Woltz, "good work men, let's snap to it, we've got a way to travel."

I don't know who he was trying to impress, but he was failing dismally with his men, already I could see he was becoming a laughing stock. That could be a liability in a dangerous situation, but in the meantime dealing with it was going to be difficult. The ideal situation would be for him to break a leg before we started, but that was not likely to happen, I'd dealt with officers like him before, no doubt his men, all Sergeant's and Warrant Officer's ranks had experience of officers like

Cady too. We helped Dao over to the Junkers, it was still inside the hangar. Paul had packed it with enough fuel drums to top up the tanks when we got to the North, enough at least to get us back south of the DMZ, where we could refuel at Hue. The wooden crates that Cady's men had brought were there too, they were all marked, AR15 assault rifles, two Browning M60 light machine guns, grenades, demolition explosives, even food rations. Another large crate carried a single Browning .50 calibre heavy machine gun.

"He thinks he's going to fight a war," a sergeant with the name Russo on his breast pocket said to me with a smile. Weapons Sergeant Joe Russo, the man who would be responsible for taking charge of this arsenal.

"Yes, it seems that way," I replied. "We'll have trouble getting off the ground with all this lot. Sergeant, doesn't he realise that if we have to use this amount of weaponry, we'll have lost already? How are we expected to carry it if we have to abandon the aircraft?"

Russo shrugged. "I know that, you know that, but he doesn't. The name's Joe, by the way."

I shook his hand. "Jurgen."

Joe Russo was a wiry, slightly built man of about twenty seven. Cropped hair, almost bald, like most soldiers in the U.S. army his small build concealed a body that was all muscle. He was dark, betraying his Mediterranean ancestry.

"Don't you worry, Jurgen, we'll manage to keep him in check, we've had worse," he hesitated. "We've had better too, most of our officers are good men, this one, well, I think his daddy is related to a congressman or something. He wants this tour to put on his resume for when he goes back Stateside."

There was the noise of a diesel engine, Johann drove our old John Deere farm tractor into the hangar, jumped down and hooked the hitch up to the drawbar of the Junkers. Paul sat in the cockpit as Johann slowly towed it out of the hangar and turned it to face the runway.

I found Cady going over his mission plans in my office. "We're ready to go, Captain."

"Uh, yeah, ok, Hoffman. I'm going over the mission brief one last time. Do you want me to run you past everything?"

"Captain," I replied gently, "Paul and I have been there before, we're fine. When we get near, we'll call Le Van Tri on the frequency he gave us and he'll give us further coordinates for the landing field. As soon as we're overhead he'll light it up for us. I think it might be a good idea to load the men and go."

"Right, yeah." He seemed oddly hesitant, not something I would have expected in a Special Forces officer.

"Look Hoffman, I think I'd better go over to MACV and see if any last minute changes of plan have come in."

I had it now. He was scared, terrified of going behind enemy lines for the first time. Maybe that was understandable, but a lot of people were depending on him to see this mission through, my wife Helene included.

"Cady!" I spoke to him as loudly as I dared. He looked up at me. "Look, we go now or not at all, if you waste time going over to MACV it'll be too late, you'd better have your excuses ready for General Harkins. What's it going to be, do we go or not?"

His men had come into the office and were watching

him curiously. He stared at them and back at me. Then he squared his shoulders, as if something had clicked in his brain. "Let's go then, mount up."

Paul already had the three engines running, I distributed the soldiers around the cargo bay and went forward to the captain's seat. Paul looked over at me.

"A heavy load with all of that junk, we'll need a good take-off roll."

"Yes, you take her up, Paul. I'll take a look at the charts for the Hanoi district."

I flicked on the tiny map light and began poring over the maps even before the aircraft took to the air. There were only a limited number of fields we could land on, I hoped that Le Van Tri had chosen a good one without too many potholes and obstacles. Still, we were carrying his son and the Junkers was a sturdy aircraft, built for operating out of rough, temporary fields, so I saw no reason for concern on that front. We droned north towards Hue and the DMZ, by the time we reached it the sky was dark.

* * *

'I refuse to play the role of an accomplice in an awful murder. According to a few immature American junior officials—too imbued by a real but obsolete imperialist spirit, the Vietnamese regime is not puppet enough and must be liquidated.'

Madame Nhu
'The Dragon Lady'

The room in the Saigon Presidential Palace was magnificent, furnished in the most expensive and exquisite manner. The short man looked around the room and thought for the thousandth time how wonderful were the trappings of power. He could and did have the ear of the most powerful man in the free world. At a word from him armies marched and people quaked in fear. Especially the traitors. Who could he trust here? Madame Nhu, his brother's wife, known to many as The Dragon Lady, was the official First Lady of the Republic of South Vietnam. But she had enemies, so many enemies, she seemed unable to adopt even the most basic understanding of world politics. Ngo Dinh Thuc was the Archbishop of Hue and also his brother. Carrying the torch of his beloved Catholicism throughout Vietnam, he also had amassed enemies, not least amongst the country's majority Buddhists. Ngo Dinh Nhu, another brother, head of the Republic's Secret Police. Was he planning a coup? Already, Diem had survived two coup attempts, who would be next to try it? And Nhu, of course, was a known opium addict, patently unstable. Lastly, there was ARVN General Duong Van Minh, his most trustworthy general. Diem had bowed to demands to allow the ARVN to avoid the most dangerous contact with the rebel Viet Cong. As Duong has pointed out, what was the point of defeating the Viet Cong if the army was so demoralised and alienated that it turned on its leaders, including Diem himself. They all needed watching, Diem knew, every single one of them.

"Mr. President, the Americans are protesting that our army fought like cowards at Ap Bac," Madame Nhu snapped out suddenly.

General Duong looked sullen. Everyone here knew why the ARVN was encouraged to avoid military contact, even if it could not be openly admitted. "There were Americans there too," he said, "it made no difference."

Nhu giggled suddenly, Diem made a mental note to speak to him about his opium consumption. He rang the bell and a servant came in quietly. "You may bring my jasmine tea now."

The servant bowed and left, he came back within moments carrying the President's tea on a silver tray.

"Two Americans were captured in the North recently," Madame Nhu continued.

Diem took his tea from the servant and looked up at his first lady. "Were they soldiers or spies?"

"Hanoi says they were spies," Nhu giggled again as he spoke, "but they always say that, they'd have said that if they were nuns," he giggled yet again. Diem became more irritated.

"What are the Americans doing about it?"

"I understand they're sending in a rescue mission tonight," Madame Nhu said.

The servant bowed and left the room. Back in the kitchen, he hurriedly wrote a note and gave it to a maid who was about to go off duty.

"We must pray for their success," the Archbishop of Hue said pontifically.

"Yes, yes, of course," Diem agreed.

He wondered when it would be time to speak to his brother about the armed Catholic militias that were reportedly terrorising the Buddhist population of the Republic. Still, many of his people were converting to Catholicism, so perhaps it was best to leave things as they were. A Catholic South Vietnam would be a magnificent legacy to leave, especially if it meant the end of these hideous Buddhists and communists.

"Nhu, find out what you can about this American rescue mission, find out what would benefit us most, success or failure," his brother nodded.

Diem continued, "General, there will be no change to our strategy for the time being, if the Americans are not happy, let them deal with it, they have plenty of troops, they can always send more. Our army needs to be protected and nurtured against the day when they are really needed."

General Duong bowed, "Yes, Mr. President, very wise."

"Good, that's settled," the President looked harsh. "Now, I hear that the Buddhists are still refusing to pay their taxes and are even disobeying orders to show more respect to Catholic shrines. It must not continue. Nhu, see to it."

The head of the secret police smiled and looked at his wife, the Dragon Lady.

"It shall be as you say, brother, Mr. President."

CHAPTER FIVE

"It seems, on the face of it, absurd to think that a nation of 20 million people can be subverted by 15–20 thousand active guerrillas if the Government and people of that country do not wish to be subverted. South Vietnam is not, however, a highly organized society with an effective governing apparatus and a population accustomed to carrying civic responsibility. Public apathy is encouraged by the inability of most citizens to act directly as well as by the tactics of terror employed by the guerrillas throughout the countryside."
Joint Statement - Robert McNamara, Secretary of Defense and
Dean Rusk, Secretary of State

"Gentlemen, we are now leaving the DMZ, you may like to know that you are now overflying the Democratic Republic of Vietnam."

A few minutes before we had taken the Junkers down to five hundred feet, crossing the DMZ as low as possible and hopefully out of sight of North Vietnamese radar. We were flying on instruments, almost blind, relying on pinpoint navigation to thread our way between the hills and valleys of North Vietnam. I'd gone back into the cabin to alert the men. Russo had a transistor radio playing, turned up loud over the noise of the engines. A song called Soldier Boy, by the Shirelles was playing. I wondered if that boded well for the mission or not. He turned down the volume and they all looked at me as I explained our situation.

"Although we're off their radar, we need to be ready for anything. Remember, the peasants like to take pot shots here at low flying aircraft, they usually assume that they are from the South. We don't know about the possibility of the North Vietnamese Air Force flying night fighter patrols, so we need to stay alert. If we have to make an emergency landing, well, bear in mind that everyone in this country will be more than glad to turn us in to the local militia, that's if they don't shoot us first. I need to get back to the cockpit now, we're entering a mountainous region and the navigation is going to be tricky."

"Try not to fly us into a mountain," Frank Burr joked. No one laughed.

"I'll bear it in mind," I said as I went forward.

It had started to rain heavily, visibility was becoming extremely poor, the wind had also come up strongly, the windscreen wipers were struggling to keep the screen clear. Schuster was flying the plane with one eye on the instruments and the other trying to catch glimpses of the terrain below us when the sheets of rain cleared for a few moments, although there really was little to be seen. Occasionally we came out from under the cloud base and the wan moon tried to light up the countryside, so that we could just make out grey shapes of mountains slipping by us. We took advantage to drop even lower and navigate through the valleys, below the height of the surrounding hills. Then the cloud came over and we had to ascend. I checked the chart.

"You need to take her up to three and a half thousand feet, Paul, the mountains here start to get higher."

He nodded and pulled back on the stick. The aircraft pointed her nose steeply upwards as we quickly gained height to clear the nearby hilltops. "We'll show on radar at this height," he said to me quietly.

"Yes, but we've no choice if we're to avoid flying straight into the mountainside," I replied.

We flew on for another fifteen minutes, I checked the chart and looked down, the cloud had thinned.

"You can take her down again, we passed the mountain range, five hundred feet should be fine."

He pushed the stick forward and we descended rapidly. "I can see lights up ahead, we're coming up on some sort of town."

The Democratic Republic of Vietnam was a dark country at night, most of the countryside without electricity, even the towns were limited in their use of power and there were no street lights. The sight of half a dozen lights almost certainly meant a good sized town or a military installation. As we neared the lights, I saw a stream of fairy lights twinkling towards us. Tracer.

"Paul, bank right, take her up higher," I shouted, but he'd already seen it and was hauling on the control column.

We went back up to two thousand feet and disappeared in a bank of heavy cloud. But we were now visible on radar. We flew on, hour after hour, playing cat and mouse with the North Vietnamese defences. So far, we'd not seen the lights of any other aircraft, a night fighter would finish us.

I checked the map again, we were coming up on Hanoi. We were down to treetop level again, so we couldn't see the lights of the city, but I knew we were quite close. I had Le Van Tri's frequency so I warmed up the radio and called him. He answered straight away, after all, we were carrying his son, he wouldn't be taking any chances. He gave us a map reference and told us to look for nine lights arranged in an arrow. That would be the leading edge of our landing field. I told him about twenty minutes, then the radio went quiet, neither of us wanted to be picked up by the North Vietnamese. We were heading for a field midway between Hoa Binh and Son Tay, normally used by smugglers, twelve miles outside Hanoi. As we were well within range of their inner air defences, I knew that we'd only have a limited time to find the airfield before they picked us up and came to investigate.

"There," Paul pointed ahead, about a mile away. Nine lamps, laid out in an arrow, by a rare streak of luck we had flown straight to our intended destination.

"A good omen," I said, but I was thinking of Helene. This needed to work for her, somehow I knew that if I could pull this off she was going to recover. It was a weird feeling, as if I was a psychic, but I knew in my guts, in the blood of my Teutonic ancestors, that somehow it was true.

Paul looked at me briefly but didn't reply, he was

concentrating on preparing the Junkers for landing. I ran back to tell the soldiers to prepare for an imminent landing, then back forward to assist. There was a strong crosswind blowing, the aircraft rocked from side to side. I called out the altitude and air speed, he had to keep his attention focussed totally on the lights.

"Two hundred feet, flaps down, one hundred knots," I said.

He nodded. The Junkers had a huge wing flap that gave us a low stalling speed, he was bleeding speed off quickly to lower our landing speed on the unknown field.

"One hundred feet. Eighty knots."

We crossed the lights and almost simultaneously hit the field with a bump. Paul throttled right back and I hit the brakes hard. The field was still wet, we slewed at an alarming angle, but he corrected with a touch of throttle and rudder and we eventually came to a stop. We had landed in North Vietnam, there was no time to celebrate. I rushed back into the cabin.

"We are in Le Van Tri's field, we need to get out fast and establish a perimeter, watch out for his people, we don't want anyone getting shot accidentally."

Cady looked at me resentfully for shouting the orders, but I didn't give a damn, this was bandit country, we had little time for niceties. I wrenched open the door, dropped the ladder to the ground and climbed down into the field. Several shadowy figures surrounded me, all armed with a variety of weapons, I recognised Soviet or Chinese AK47s and a couple of American M1s. An elderly Vietnamese walked through them and came face to face with me.

"Mr Hoffman, do you have my son?"

"Yes, Mr Le." I called through the aircraft door, "Dao, come out, your father is here."

He came to the door, Tim Beckerman jumped down and helped him down the ladder. His father gave a small smile of relief.

"I am pleased you are back safely, my son." Dao nodded. "Thank you father."

At a nod from Mr Le two guards helped him away and across the field, I assumed they had some kind of transport waiting. The rest of the Special Forces were unloading their equipment from the aircraft. Le frowned when he saw the huge quantities of weapons. "I thought this was a simple rescue of two men, Mr Hoffman. Is it wise to carry so much weaponry?"

At that moment Cady jumped down into the field. "Mr Le, this is Captain Cady of the U.S. Army, he is leading this mission." They nodded to each other. "Mr Le, pleased to meet you. How far away is this prison?"

A younger man stepped forward. "This is my other son, Bao," Le said. "He will guide you, it will take about half an hour to get there."

"Form up, men, we'll be leaving soon," Cady shouted. They all looked around in alarm. "Captain, I would suggest you keep it quiet, we are in enemy territory," Le said respectfully, but the scorn in his voice was there for all to hear.

I couldn't see his face in the dark, but I was certain it reddened. "Yeah, well, there's no one around," but he kept his voice lower, "let's move out."

Paul was at the door of the plane. "I'll go with them,

Paul, I suggest you get the aircraft refuelled from the drums, can you manage?" He nodded grimly. "It'll be a long job with the hand pump, but yes, I can do it. That fool Cady will need you along, he's going to get everyone killed. Good luck, Jurgen."

"You too," I replied.

We walked along a mud track for almost half an hour until we saw a few hundred yards away the looming shape of a concrete factory. Bao stopped us. "They're being held in there, Mr Hoffman. We understand that there are eight guards, four will be on duty and four asleep at this time. There is no rear entrance, only one double door at the front with a smaller door to one side. The double door is rarely opened since the factory became a prison."

"Are there any more prisoners being held?" I asked him. He shook his head, "no, only the two Americans."

Cady came up to us, clearly he was irritated that we were excluding him from the conversation. "Right, Hoffman, here's what I propose." I held up a hand. "Captain, please. Save it for later, let's just go into the prison, bring out your two men and go home."

He glowered at me. "Damnit, Hoffman, this is a military mission, if we encounter a North Vietnamese Army unit..." "Then we're finished, Captain. If we do run into the communists, they'll just call up reinforcements we'll find ourselves in a battle we can't win. Let's get in and out without stirring up too much fuss, ok?"

He looked furious, but his men were making encouraging noises, "makes sense, Cap'n," and more like that. In the end he gave a curt nod. "Have it your way, Hoffman, but God help you if it all goes wrong."

I didn't add that if it went wrong we would be beyond any help. Bao crept forward and then held up his hand. We stopped. Outside the building we could see the glow of a cigarette and the vague outline of a helmeted soldier became apparent, the strange pith helmet favoured by the North Vietnamese regular army. Thank God they all smoked so heavily.

Woltz was already bringing up his rifle. It was fitted with a huge silencer, making it look as if it had part of a cannon on the end of the barrel. There was a faint thud and the guard crashed to the ground. We ran forward, Burr checked his pulse and shook his head, he was dead. Woltz stayed back with Jack Bond, the communications sergeant, as the rest of us waited outside the door, there was no other sentry outside. The rest of us, Burr, Russo, Beckerman and Cady waited either side of the door. I spoke quietly to Bao. "Tell them you've brought women up from the village, do they want any."

He nodded, and then knocked on the door while I waited to one side. After a few moments a suspicious looking guard opened the door a crack and looked out. Bao spoke to him quietly, I saw the man's expression change. They negotiated for a few moments, then the door opened wide to let Bao enter. He moved to one side, the four Americans stepped around the door, a knife flashed and the guard was carefully lowered to the ground. They dashed in and I followed. Two soldiers were sitting at a desk reading magazines, two shots coughed out from silenced pistols and they crashed to the floor. The Americans rushed over and checked that they were dead, I went past them and opened a door at the back of the room. There was a long corridor with more doors leading off it. I heard one of the doors opening and ducked back out of sight, a sleepy Vietnamese voice shouted something. I pointed to Beckerman, who was holding a silenced pistol, he jumped through the doorway, another cough and a clatter as the man dropped to the floor.

I looked around, he was in his shorts and t-shirt and probably had got out of bed to go to the bathroom. We ran down the corridor, a door was partly open to sleeping quarters with eight bunk beds. Three were occupied, the Americans went to work, the pistols coughed and they all died without even waking.

"The officer," I whispered to Beckerman and Burr. They nodded, there were two more doors both closed. One was reinforced steel, that had to be the cells. The other was a normal wooden door. They burst through, both pistols coughed and another crash. They came back out.

"That should be the lot, let's see if our boys are in here." Cady came up and gestured for them to cover him while he opened it. There was another corridor with three barred cells, Miles Anderson and Aaron Goldberg were in one of them. Their faces lit up when they looked through the bars and saw us.

"By Christ, are we glad to see you boys," Goldberg said. I rummaged through the keys on a panel on the wall and found the one that opened their cell. "Miles is in a bad way, he's got a broken leg and some cracked ribs," Goldberg warned.

"Can you walk, Mr Anderson?" Cady asked. He looked

dazed, I looked at Goldberg. "Hard interrogation," he explained.

"Shit. Russo, Beckerman, give him a hand, we need to get back to the aircraft," he looked at me, "do we have much time left?" I shook my head. "We need to be airborne within the hour, Captain."

"Right, men, let's go," he called out.

When we got outside the building, there was no sign of Bao. "Where'd the gook go?" Cady asked me. I shrugged. He asked Woltz and Bond but they hadn't seen him slip away in the darkness. He looked irritated. "Fucking natives, never trust them. Right, let's move."

We stumbled back along the path to our landing field. I had memorised the path and managed to guide us back. When we got to the field I put up a hand to stop them. "What's up?" Cady asked. "Schh. We've got trouble." "Yeah? What kind of trouble?"

"Can't you smell it, Captain, cigarette smoke?"

"Maybe it's Schuster," he said, "No, he doesn't smoke," I replied. "One of Le's men, then?"

"I don't think so. Stay there, I'll go and check." I skirted the field and looked closely. Nothing. In the cockpit, I could make out the figure of Paul Schuster sat at the controls. Then the clouds slid away from the moon and in its dim light I could see another shadowy figure behind him, holding something to his head. It was enough. I crept back to the Americans. "North Vietnamese, they've taken Paul and are holding him in the cockpit. Somehow they found us."

"Damn," Cady looked flustered for a moment, "we'll

have to go in and take them out, we need that plane to get out of here."

I shook my head. "Captain, you can forget the plane. They'll have heavy machine guns set up around the field, the minute they see us they'll open fire. Besides, they could have twenty men hiding in and around the plane." "Shit. We can take twenty of these bastards, no sweat," he said cockily.

His men looked concerned at his stupidity. "Captain, even when American and ARVN forces outnumbered the Viet Cong ten to one at Ap Bac, they couldn't beat them. I suggest we use a little caution." He didn't like me correcting him, but the alternative was this officer getting us all killed. A shadowy figure ran up to us and gun barrels swung around to cover him, but it was Bao returning, Le's son. "I'm sorry, we didn't know they were coming," he said.

"Not your fault, thanks for coming back. What do you know? How many of them are there?" I asked him. "It looks like a half-platoon, about twelve men. They're from the local barracks in Trung Chau, about twenty five kilometres from here."

I felt strangely alone without Paul Schuster to talk things over with, we'd been together for so many years that it seemed second nature to turn to him and say, 'What do you think, Paul?' But this time, he needed help and I was determined that I wouldn't leave this Godforsaken country without him. I spoke urgently to Bao.

I heard Cady giving orders to his men, preparing them for an overland trek to the South. "Captain, could I have a word with you?" I said. He looked annoyed at the interruption.

"Yeah, what is it, Hoffman?"

"You'll never leave North Vietnam on foot, it's virtually impossible." He was too angry to be told how to do his job.

"Mr. Hoffman, I can assure you that we'll walk out of here and kill any sonofabitch that gets in our way. What the hell do you mean, we'll never leave?"

I sighed, he was going to be difficult, and I needed him, or at least, his men. I explained about up to a million North Vietnamese Army regulars, the guerrillas, the Viet Cong, and the peasants, every hand would be turned against them and every eye would be watching for them.

"The problem is they know we're here, Captain. It'll be the biggest manhunt in their history, no matter what you do they'll find you and probably sooner rather than later. Your mission will all be for nothing."

"So what do you suggest? I assume you do have a suggestion?" he sneered. "Certainly. We can fly out, after we've picked up Paul Schuster, of course."

"But you said that reaching the aircraft would be impossible, it would bring down the Viets and we'd be blown out of the sky."

"True, it would be inevitable in that plane, now that it's compromised. I'm suggesting that we go elsewhere and take a different aircraft, we steal one."

He was interested, so were the men and they clustered around while I outlined what I had in mind.

"There's an airfield twenty miles from here at Bach Mai. These troops will give up at dawn when they know we're not coming back and return to Trung Chau. If we move quickly we can be there before dawn and ambush them when they get there. We release Paul and head for Bach Mai, Le says that there are at least two transport aircraft stationed there. We simply take one and fly home, their air defence system will be looking at the Junkers. With any luck we'll get away before they know what's happening."

Cady looked sceptical. "You and I both know it won't be so easy, Hoffman. What do you plan to do about the survivors of the ambush? Take them with us?"

"That won't be possible," I replied. A silence descended on the group. "For God's sake," Frank Burr protested, "you're saying we'd have to kill them all, aren't you? Jesus!" I heard someone say the words 'goddamn Nazi' quietly.

"There's no alternative, if we leave them alive they'll raise the alarm. If we tie them up and one escapes, we're finished. We have to kill them all. It's either that or we die here, those are the choices.

You need to decide quickly, we'll need to get in position before dawn." Across the field, we could see two of the Viets had climbed out of the aircraft and were pouring petrol into the ground to make sure it never took off.

They talked among themselves. I heard some arguing, but I knew from past experience in Russia that when a man is thousands of miles from home, those kinds of decisions preyed less heavily on conventional morality than when safely within the borders of your own country. I told them that Paul wouldn't admit to carrying American troops, at worst he'd spin a story about Vietnamese smugglers trying to earn a few extra dollars. The prison guards were all dead, there was no one there to sound the alarm about an American led rescue mission. So far, we had a few things in our favour. If we could release Paul and steal an aircraft, we had a good chance of getting home. Otherwise, we may as well hand ourselves into the waiting North Vietnamese Army unit.

"Ok, we'll do it your way, Hoffman. God help you if you're wrong," Cady whispered. "If I'm wrong, Captain, I'll be beyond God's help."

He nodded and quietly gave orders to the men to form up. Bao had offered to lead the way and we marched away in the darkness towards Trung Chau. According to Bao there was only one viable route to Trung Chau and we were on it. I looked at the sky, the glow of dawn was just over the horizon. I didn't think we'd make it in time, but Bao had been scouting ahead with Abe Woltz and they came running back.

"Sir, the Viets have set up a checkpoint about half a mile up the road from here, there are four Viets guarding it, a sergeant and three soldiers," Woltz said to Cady. "It'll be a bitch to get past it unnoticed." I asked him to describe it for me, it sounded exactly like the small fortified posts that the French built during the first Indochina war. "This could be useful to us. If we can kill the garrison, we could set the ambush there and catch them by surprise. I don't think we have sufficient hours of darkness left to get to Trung Chau, this would be perfect."

Cady saw the sense of it, I think by then he realised that he was out of his depth and welcomed the advice. We put together a simple plan and Bao agreed to act as a decoy. Woltz went off the path to get his sniper rifle into position while remaining hidden, Tim Beckerman went with him as his number two. We gave them ten minutes to get into position, and then started towards the checkpoint. Bao ran ahead, he'd torn his clothing and had prepared a story about being attacked by bandits who'd stolen his money belt. It was thin, but the guards would be tired and we had a good chance of making it work. He hurtled around a bend in the path and we heard shouts in Vietnamese as they ordered him to stop. He was good, playing his part to perfection. I understood him pouring out his indignant story of being robbed under the noses of these guards, what were they going to do about it? They barked a series of questions and it sounded as if a row was developing.

We got to the bend in the path and stopped, peering through the undergrowth to see Bao arguing strongly with the soldiers. I couldn't see Woltz and Beckerman but I knew they were there. The argument peaked to a shouting match, they were angry, Bao was virtually calling them cowards for not keeping the roads clear of thieves. Then he stomped away up the track. The sergeant shouted to him to stop and he ignored him, turning his back and making a rude sign as he walked off. The sergeant shouted louder, gave an order and one of his men cocked the bolt of his rifle. That was enough, Bao darted off the track and threw himself flat, the soldiers looked bemused, then two shots cracked out and the sergeant and the soldier with the loaded rifle were flung to the ground. The other two looked panicked and quickly chambered rounds into their rifles, but Cady's men hit them with a barrage of sub-machine gun fire that almost sliced them in two. We walked warily up to the checkpoint but they were all dead and no more soldiers waited to ambush us. Cady gave orders and the bodies were dragged away into the jungle and the path cleared of any evidence that there had been a slaughter. We looked at the building, it was quite small, maybe fifteen feet square with just one door at the front and two windows. There was an observation slit at each side of the building as well as two at the front on either side of the door and another at the back. There was only one room, it stank of cigarette smoke, sweat and urine. We prepared the area as best we could and settled down to wait. Frank Burr and Bao retraced out steps back down the path to watch for the Viets, the rest of us set up the ambush. The key to it was Abe Woltz, he was hidden with Beckerman behind fallen tree trunks that looked as if they'd been cut down for firewood, opposite the checkpoint. I went inside the evil smelling room with Cady, Joe Russo and Jack Bond setting up a position twenty yards from Woltz so that they could catch the Viets in their crossfire. We all had grenades, although I spoke sharply to them about using them.

"If you throw one of those near Paul Schuster, you'll kill an expert pilot and maybe the only chance you have of getting out of here." Cady looked amused. "Hey, Hoffman, we've got you, you're the pilot. We'll take care of Schuster, of course, but he's not vital to the success of the mission."

"Isn't he?" I said harshly. "Let me make this clear, without Paul, I won't fly you out of here, period. We helped each other through the Eastern Front and through the French Indochina war and I'm not leaving him now."

He was silent for a moment. Then he looked across at me. "Don't sweat it, Hoffman, my men know what to do," he said. "They'd better, Captain," I replied.

He gave me a nasty look and then focused his binoculars on the path. We waited there for two hours, the sun was high in the sky and we were as much worried about peasants coming past as we were about the arrival of the Vietnamese troops with Paul. Cady and I looked at each other, they'd fired the Ju52 to make sure we didn't ever use it again. It wouldn't be long. Another hour passed and we heard the sounds of Vietnamese voices chattering and grumbling as they finally arrived. Soon they were in view, a lieutenant, a sergeant and ten men, with Paul in the middle of them, looking bruised and bloody. They approached the checkpoint carefully, I could see their faces clearly, they were puzzled that there were no guards outside the post but not unduly worried. This was North Vietnam, party officials giving unexpected orders was by no means unusual and they doubtless assumed that the guards had been moved elsewhere. We peered through the slits, I had my M2 carbine trained on the officer, Cady was looking through the other slit with his M16 pointed at the enemy. They were almost abreast of us when I heard the soft 'pop' and the lieutenant crumpled into the dust. The sergeant ran forward to pick him up, undoubtedly assuming he was ill and was thrown to one side by the second of Woltz's bullets. There was no question now, they were under attack and they hurriedly unslung their rifles and worked the bolts to begin firing.

The need for stealth was over, we hit them with everything we had. Woltz kept firing, Beckerman joined in with his assault rifle firing single shots and I saw Paul dive off the track in the confusion and crouch down in the undergrowth.

Cady was firing single, well spaced shots into the panicking crowd of men when Russo and Bond stepped out, with Paul under cover they hosed them down with sub-machine gun fire. It was over, I went out of the door and began checking the bodies, one twitched slightly and I put a round through his head from the M2. I heard another shot crack out. Then there was silence, abruptly broken by the sound of Paul's voice calling cheerfully as he ran towards us. "Christ, am I glad to see you guys. Jurgen, I knew you wouldn't abandon me."

"I was tempted," I replied, "but you still owe me money, Paul, so I didn't have a choice." He laughed and we hugged each other. In truth, we both knew it had been a near thing. He went and shook hands with the Americans and Bao.

"You know about the Junkers?" he asked. I nodded. "We saw the smoke, but we couldn't have used it anyway, they'd be on to us before we'd gone a hundred miles."

"Shit, we're stuck. What do we do?" I smiled at him. "We're going to steal another aircraft, the Viets have got plenty, they won't miss one. Besides, they owe us one for destroying the Junkers." He grinned. "You're serious?" I nodded. "We're heading for Bach Mai. Bao says they have transport aircraft on the ground there and not too much security. Bao," I said, turning to the Vietnamese, "what kind of aircraft have you seen on the ground, could you describe them to me?"

He thought for a few moments, then spoke rapidly and described what could only be the Ilyushin Il-14. Codenamed 'The Crate' by NATO, it was a Soviet twin-engine commercial and military personnel and cargo transport aircraft that first flew in 1950, and entered service in 1954. The Soviet equivalent for the Douglas C-47 it seated up to twenty four passengers and would be perfect for our uses. Provided that we could steal one, of course, and provided it had enough fuel, and provided that they didn't shoot us out of the sky before we crossed the DMZ. I looked around, Cady's men were dragging the corpses away from the checkpoint and into the jungle. Then I made a last sweep of the checkpoint to hide any evidence of our being there.

Finally, we were ready to move out. Bao agreed to come with us as far as the airfield. Cady came over to where Paul, Bao and myself were checking our packs. "I estimate we can reach Bach Mai in three or four hours, Hoffman. Let's move." I smiled. "Captain, travelling to Bach Mai during daylight would be suicidal. We need to get clear of here and find somewhere to rest up until nightfall."

He was obviously annoyed at having his orders questioned yet again. "Look, we came here in daylight with no problem, why would getting to Bach Mai be any different?"

"No problem? We had to kill the troops at the checkpoint and ambush and kill the troops that were holding Schuster. Are you planning to kill every single person in this part of North Vietnam? Why not telephone party headquarters in Hanoi and tell them we're here, it would be just as quick?" He gave a huge sigh. "Yeah, ok, we'll do it your way. Ok, men, we'll head out and when we're clear of here find somewhere to rest up for the day."

Woltz and Beckerman took the point, we moved off with Jack Bond guarding our rear. Burr and Russo helped Goldberg along, Paul and I lent our shoulders to helping Anderson. Cady strode out in front as if to give a demonstration of how Special Forces officers led from the front. With his head up, his back ramrod straight and his gaze looking unwavering ahead, he was the very model of a military commander. Look out George Patton, I thought, you've got a potential rival. Paul and I smiled at each other and swallowed the laughter that tried to leave our throats.

* * *

By 1964, the CIA's clandestine service was consuming close to two-thirds of its budget and 90% of the director's time. The Agency gathered under one roof Wall Street brokers, Ivy League professors, soldiers of fortune, ad men, newsmen, stunt men, second-story men, and con men. They never learned to work together - the ultimate result being a series of failures in both intelligence and covert operations. In January 1961, on leaving office after two terms, President Eisenhower had already grasped the situation fully. "Nothing has changed since Pearl Harbor," he told his director of central intelligence, Allen Dulles. "I leave a legacy of ashes to my successor." '

Tim Weiner - Legacy of Ashes: The History of the CIA

General Paul Harkins glanced across at the two men who with himself made the crucial decisions about who would live and who would die in Vietnam. A West Point graduate, he instinctively distrusted the CIA Chief of Far East Division,

William Colby, the Princeton boy who had previously served for a period as station chief in Saigon. He distrusted the Ivy League man, disliked the numerous unsanctioned missions that he knew the CIA had launched both north and south of the DMZ and found it difficult to believe much of the so-called intelligence that his office received from the CIA Chief. Colby's boss, Director of Central Intelligence John McCone gazed coldly into the distance, it was difficult to fathom his thinking.

"General, have you had communication with your people on the ground in the North?" Colby was asking about Cady's mission, Harkins realised.

"No, we're still waiting but it's early days yet, they've only just arrived. We understand unofficially that the prisoners have been broken out and we assume that Cady will get them back to the South very soon." McCone cleared his throat. The other two looked up at the man who had the ear of the President. "You are quite correct that the two officers, Anderson and Goldberg, have been sprung from a North Vietnamese prison. You are incorrect when you say that they will be back in the South very soon."

"How can you possibly know that?" Harkins asked.

"Let's just say that we have aerial intelligence to that fact," McCone replied.

The U2 spyplane overflights, it could only be that. The Lockheed U-2, nicknamed "Dragon Lady", was a single-engine, very high-altitude reconnaissance aircraft operated by the United States Air Force and flown by the Central Intelligence Agency. It provided day and night, very high-altitude all-weather surveillance.

"Do you have photos on which to base your assumption?" Harkins asked him. Without replying, McCone took a packet of photos out of his briefcase, they showed a burnt out aircraft in a field.

"That's the aircraft they were using, Hoffman's JU52. It looks as if the Viets destroyed it."

They studied the images. "Casualties?" Harkins asked. McCone shook his head. "Not on site, anyway. No sign of any bodies."

"Look, I'm working on the plans for an extended programme of infiltration," Colby interrupted. "I'm talking about sending teams into the North to disrupt their leadership, demolition, that kind of thing. Can we liaise on this Cady operation, General, maybe we can even assist?" "I thought you were already sending people into the North, William?" Harkins said wryly.

Colby shrugged his elegant shoulders. McCone interrupted. "General, William is working at putting together a new operation that could change the course of the war. It's important that he has access to the Cady operation at all levels, can you sanction it?"

"I'll ask my people in Saigon to put something together," he said grudgingly. The CIA men knew they had gone as far as they could.

"The President has agreed to a preliminary study on a bombing campaign in the North to advance our campaign," McCone added, "that alone could tip the balance in our favour. If we could synchronise it with William's raids and your own conventional forces, it could hit them hard enough to finish them."

Harkins grimaced.

"Director, you should read your history. They tried it in the First World War, in Spain they wiped out a whole town, every single building was destroyed, thousands dead. During the Second World War we bombed Nazi Germany with the British, as well as bombing the Japanese. The Germans bombed England too, it all had one result. Nothing. Except, of course, for Hiroshima and Nagasaki. I assume the President isn't contemplating a nuclear strike on Hanoi?"

"No, nothing like that," McCone said quickly, "our technology is different these days, General. We could hit them hard enough to really make a difference." Harkins looked across at the CIA men. Hadn't he heard them and their predecessors saying exactly the same thing last year and the year before that? He thought about Cady's mission to the North. He wisely said nothing, this Vietnam business was difficult enough without upsetting men who had the ear of the President. He realised that Colby had been talking to him. "Sorry, William, what was that?"

"The programme to convert the C-47 into a gunship is going well, we hope to have it operational next year."

"Yeah, I heard about that. You realise that a cargo aircraft is totally unsuited to accurately aiming a rapid fire weapon at a single target?"

"That's the conventional wisdom," Colby continued. Harkins noted his emphasis on the word 'conventional', of course he was the soldier with his boots firmly planted in the tactics of the previous war and the CIA man was the forward thinking planner who would amaze everyone with his new ideas. That was the theory, at least. He'd seen his share of theories during his career, most had one thing in common, they were either useless or downright dangerous.

"So what's the unconventional thinking, William, what does your military wisdom say on this one?"

Colby smiled, acknowledging the swift riposte. "We're perfecting the aiming systems so that the aircraft will circle the target while the Gatling gun is kept pointed at a single target." Harkins grunted. "It sounds interesting, you'll keep me informed about it?"

"Of course, General."

McCone moved to wind up the meeting. It was a quid pro quo, the CIA would be more forthcoming about the gunship programme and the Army would cooperate on the Cady mission. "Are we all agreed, gentlemen?" They nodded and shook hands.

Both knew that neither would fully keep the bargain, and each would do their best to give the very least in return for as much as they would get from the other.

CHAPTER SIX

'We must face the fact that the United States is neither omnipotent nor omniscient, that we are only six percent of the world's population, that we cannot impose our will upon the other ninety-four percent of mankind, that we cannot right every wrong or reverse each adversity, and that therefore there cannot be an American solution to every world problem.'

John F Kennedy 1961

We rested up several miles away from the checkpoint, Paul, Bao and I grabbed some sleep while the sergeants looked after the rescued men and maintained a sharp watch. Cady was restless, patrolling around the area, giving unnecessary orders and generally making a nuisance of himself. As night fell we pushed on and were lucky to get all the way there without sighting a local. Electricity was almost non-existent in these rural areas and nightfall meant home to family and bed.

The airfield at Bach Mai was in darkness. The only light

came from a low building the other side of the field across from where we crouched at the edge of the jungle. We could see the glowing tips of the guards' cigarettes as they ceaselessly patrolled the area. I doubted they'd heard about us, this country was a communist bureaucracy where no one made a decision or even a phone call without going up through the chain of command. But petty theft from the locals would be a problem, as well as larger scale raids from Vietnamese tribesmen who were still opposed to the communist regime, hence the guard presence.

The airfield probably had landing and take-off lights, but they would only be switched on when necessary, the possibility of raids from the South was always a very real danger. Across the field I could see several aircraft, including a MIG that appeared to have crash landed, lying abandoned just off the main runway. Near the control tower was a light aircraft, difficult to make out in the dark but it was similar in size to a Cessna 170, quite possibly that's what it was. The other side of the control tower two larger aircraft were parked near to each other. Ilyushin IL14s.

"Are those what we're here for?" Cady asked me. His face was stretched with tension, I got the impression he wasn't coping well with leading this mission into enemy territory. In contrast, his men were relaxed and quietly checking their equipment. I nodded. "Yes, exactly what we need. The question is which one will have enough fuel to get us south of the DMZ? We need to find out."

"I'll get two of my guys to take a look. Tim, Jack, check out those two IL14s, Hoffman needs to know the fuel situation.

Abe, cover them all the way, if they're spotted by the Viets, we won't get home."

They nodded, I gave instructions on what to look for and Beckerman and Bond disappeared into the shadows at the side of the airfield. Abe Woltz set up his sniper rifle with the silencer and waited while Joe Russo kept a constant watch on the field with a pair of night glasses. I kept checking my watch, we had to get off the ground before midnight to cross the DMZ before dawn. Any later and we would be ducks in a shooting gallery. They all knew that, there was no need to remind them. At one time a soldier came close, we could smell the smoke from his cigarette quite strongly. Mingled with the aromatic smells of the jungle edge it left a slightly sour smell. He didn't see us and walked on, avoiding the two silenced pistols and three combat knives that were waiting to take him out if he came too close. Beckerman and Bond suddenly came out of the darkness.

"The aircraft look good, Jurgen," Bond said. "Both seem to be operational. As for fuel, we've no way of estimating what they have in the tanks. The gauges are broken."

"On both aircraft?"

Beckerman nodded. "I checked out the second aircraft, no dice, the gauges are out."

I checked my watch again, it was five minutes to twelve, and we were already out of time.

"Captain, we'll have to take one aircraft and hope for the best, we need to move right now."

Cady nodded and signalled for his men to help Anderson and Goldberg to their feet. Beckerman and Bond led off, taking the point as they had already covered the ground. They crossed the perimeter and disappeared into the darkness. A Vietnamese voice called across to where they had gone to earth.

"Ngung lai! Stop!"

We hadn't noticed the sentry walking back on his route, he'd seen the movement as the two men ran across the field, or thought he'd seen something.

Cady opened his mouth to give an order, but Russo has already crawled away to get behind the sentry. Cady closed his mouth and we waited. There was a slight noise, the rustle of clothing, a muffled grunt that was quickly cut off and silence returned. Russo crawled back to us.

"All done, Cap'n, I can't see any more of them, we can go when you're ready."

"Ok, Russo. You men all ready? Let's go."

We darted across the field towards the waiting aircraft. Anderson and Goldberg were helped and five minutes later we were under the wing of the nearest Ilyushin. Beckerman and Bond were waiting for us, a metal ladder hung down from the cabin door to the ground. Woltz set up a sniper position to cover us as two men climbed into the aircraft and helped Anderson and Goldberg up the ladder. I turned to Bao.

"I think this is goodbye, maybe we'll see each other again. Thank you, Bao."

"Goodbye, Jurgen, Paul, you have a safe trip."

He disappeared into the blackness and we climbed the ladder and walked through to the cockpit, behind us we could hear the last of the soldiers boarding. The aircraft was the cargo variant so there were no seats in the cabin, just piles of straps and cargo nets strewn over the floor.

The cockpit was depressingly Soviet era style, cheap red plastic upholstery and black plastic control wheels. Even in the semi-darkness everything was obviously much worn and badly maintained. Beckerman and Bond had said the fuel gauges were not working, what they hadn't said, perhaps hadn't even noticed, was that several other gauges were missing. They had been removed from the aircraft. The only good sign was the smell of aviation fuel, suggesting that it had been refuelled recently. Behind the pilots' seats was a tiny radio cabin, barely large enough for one man to squeeze in and sit on the ripped upholstery to operate the radio, which I imagined was working. Paul and I checked the operation of the controls, the rudder, elevators and flaps all seemed to be ok. I went to get up and go back into the cabin to speak to Cady but when I glanced around he was standing in the doorway, waiting.

"Captain, would you get the chocks removed from the wheels, we'll be taking off shortly. Can you withdraw the ladder and close the door?" He nodded curtly and disappeared.

"I'm not happy about taking off without knowing the fuel load, Jurgen," Paul said.

"Think of it as a gamble, Paul. Hopefully we'll get lucky," I grinned.

"And if we don't?"

I laughed. "Then maybe we should say goodbye now, before we dive into the jungle, although we might land this thing without engines if we find a suitable strip."

"Might, if. That's not usually the way we do things," he sniffed.

"How many times have we charged the Soviets or the Viet Minh, hoping that we didn't take a bullet before we killed them?"

He was thoughtful for a moment. Then he smiled. "Ok, I see your point. Nice knowing you, Jurgen."

"You too. I'll see you in hell."

We shook hands just as Cady came forward.

"All done, Hoffman, the men removed the chocks, the ladder is stowed and the door shut."

"Ok, Captain. Would you get your men to hold onto some of the cargo straps, this take-off is going to be touch and go."

"Yeah, I'll tell them. Hoffman?" I looked back to him. He was holding out his hand and I shook it, Paul did the same.

"You're a pair of Nazi bastards, but before we crash in some Vietnamese jungle shithouse, thanks for what you've done."

I shrugged. "It's no problem. Why the problem with the Nazis, the war was over a long time ago?"

"My grandmother, she was Polish, she died in Auschwitz."

"I'm sorry, Captain. For the record, I was never near any prison camp and we didn't even belong to the Nazi Party. I agree with you, they were bastards. Hold tight, now." He went back into the cabin and we primed the engines and switched on ready to start. I looked at Paul.

"Hals und Beinbruch!"

He grinned. "Du auch!"

I hit the start button on the port engine and it whirred slowly, picked up speed and burst into life. Then the starboard engine spooled up and shortly we had both engines running. A light came on in the control tower, then several buildings lit up and a flood of light spread over the field as the overhead security lights were switched on.

"Time to go," I said to Paul.

I throttled up and taxied onto the runway, heading for the end to turn into wind for take-off. Across the field, a Soviet built GAZ jeep had turned on its headlights and I saw soldiers jumping into it. It started towards us, bumping on the uneven field at the side of the runway. I put on the headset and heard the North Vietnamese controller shouting in French at the unauthorised Ilyushin 14 to halt immediately or they would open fire. Another set of headlights switched on and a ZIL-157 lorry, another gift from the Soviet Union, started towards the runway, we could clearly see a dozen armed troops sitting in the back. More ominously, the passenger side of the cab had a mounted light machine gun, the gunner was pushing up through the roof hatch preparing his weapon to fire.

"They're going to block us, Jurgen," Paul said.

"I can see that, it'll be touch and go. If Cady's men could open the cargo door and return fire when they start shooting, it would be a help, would you give him a shout?"

While I concentrated on getting the aircraft to the end of the runway, Paul turned in his seat and shouted for Cady. When the Captain came into the cockpit, he explained to him what we needed. Cady nodded and went out. We reached the end of the runway, I spun the aircraft through one hundred and eighty degrees, lined up on the runway and opened the throttle wide. The aircraft picked up speed but it was too slow, much too slow. The GAZ was almost alongside us, keeping pace and the ZIL was halfway down the runway, manoeuvring to block it and prevent us from taking off. The voice in the headphones was screaming at me now but I had to keep listening, I needed to know when they decided we were an enemy. Which wasn't long in coming, I heard him shout 'Trier' into my headphones to be picked up by the Viets on the airfield frequency. Paul heard it too. He shouted back to Cady.

"Open fire, Captain, now!"

There was a single muzzle flash from the GAZ, then it veered off the runway as the Special Forces peppered it, Woltz's rifle cracked first to hit the driver and then the others open up with sub-machine gun fire. I could see an anti-aircraft emplacement across the field, men were running towards it but they would be too late, our problem now was the ZIL.

"Call Cady back up here," I shouted to Paul.

He called out and the Captain appeared in the cockpit. I explained what I wanted, he nodded and went back into the cabin. The ZIL grew nearer and nearer, a soldier with a rifle fired three shots but they went wide, I ignored them.

"Three seconds," I shouted to Paul.

He called back to Cady, we were almost on the ZIL when I wrenched the aircraft to the right and onto the rough grass at the side of the tarmac. The IL14 had a reputation for being able to operate on rough fields, I was about to test it to the limits. As we shot past the ZIL the soldiers in the cabin opened fire again, I didn't have time to see the effect of their gunfire, we were past. I swung back onto the runway, the aircraft lurching to one side and then righting itself.

"Rotate," Paul called across to me.

We hauled on both control columns, the aircraft was a heavy bastard as it took to the air, climbing slowly. I kept her at treetop level, they'd get that anti-aircraft gun working soon enough and we'd have been a sitting target at high level. At five hundred feet we levelled off and set course for the DMZ. Paul took over and I went back into the cabin to check the passengers.

"A bit of a hairy one, Hoffman," Cady said.

I looked at him closely, he'd acted well during the take-off but I was still worried about his ability to lead men under battle conditions. I smiled.

"Hannah Reitsch would have done it with half the Vietnamese Army shooting at her."

"Who's Hannah Reitsch, does she work for you?"

I laughed. "No, Captain, she does not. On Hitler's orders, she took off from the Tiergarten in Berlin with von Greim, the newly promoted chief of the Luftwaffe, during the evening of the 28th April 1945. She flew the last German plane out of the city shortly before it fell by climbing out through heavy Soviet anti-aircraft fire. The Soviets were in the city at the time, it was an incredible piece of flying."

He was silent for a moment, digesting my little piece of history.

"Well, yeah, but they were Nazi's, weren't they?"

He didn't get it, just didn't get it.

"That's true, Captain, they were Nazi's, fighting the same enemy that shot at you and your men out there on the airfield." He looked puzzled and I didn't pursue it.

"Were there any casualties during the take-off?"

He shook his head. "None, but Anderson and Goldberg don't look too good, we need to get them medical attention as soon as possible. They took a good beating back there."

"I'm doing my best, Captain."

"Yeah. When will we cross the DMZ?"

"If we don't run out of fuel, and if we're not shot down, I would hope we should reach it in about three hours."

"No way to check the fuel situation?" he asked.

I shook my head. "In situations like this one they would top the fuel tanks up before every flight so that they know they always start with a full fuel load. We don't know of course if they did that or not before we took the aircraft."

I noticed the other soldiers looking at us intently. Of course, they wanted to know their fate as much as I did.

"If we run out of fuel, what then?" Cady asked.

"Then we land. Crash land, that is. If we can find a flat piece of ground we may get down in once piece, if not, who knows?" I shrugged.

"Fuck it," he said abruptly, "if only…"

"If only what?" I asked him curiously.

"Nothing," he answered.

We droned on for two hours, our spirits lifted and somehow Russo managed to tune in the antiquated Soviet built radio to receive a South Vietnamese channel, they were playing an Elvis Presley song, 'Good Luck Charm'. That was something we sorely needed, a good luck charm, somehow I doubted we were going to get one on this mission. In my experience you made your own luck and the more enemy you killed the luckier you became. It was a simple equation of war.

Cady smiled after a few minutes. "I reckon we might actually make it, Hoffman."

I shrugged. Ideally we would have called for an escort from the South, possibly from an American aircraft carrier off the coast, but the second we used the radio they would triangulate on us and we'd become the target for every MIG they could send to shoot us down. Besides, the American military had made it quite clear that we were on our own. I looked out of the window, they would be hunting for us now, of course, but flying at low level made it difficult for them to find us. Difficult, but not impossible.

The first burst went just wide of the port wing, the sound of the gun coming just after the fighter shot past us, one cannon round even went through the wingtip but failed to explode.

I banked hard to port, guessing that the attacker was crossing port towards our starboard. Sure enough, a MIG 17 flashed past the cockpit as Paul shouted for the passengers to hold on tight.

"That's something new," he said, "I'd heard about the MIG 17 but it's the first one I've seen in the flesh."

His voice was oddly calm, he was making an effort to keep relaxed and not do anything that would panic the soldiers in the back. Cady had come up to the cockpit again and was peering silently out of the windscreen.

"It could be the last one, my friend," I said to Paul, "Unless we can lose him, can you see any cloud we can disappear into?"

He was looking out of the window at the sky, but it

was clear and blue. A mountain range loomed in front of us, maybe five minutes flying time away. Too long. I could see the MIG turning in for another attacking pass and I pushed the control column forward just as another burst of fire came towards us, this time we weren't so lucky, it stitched across the fuselage causing chaos in the cabin. Cady rushed back to check the damage while we concentrated on keeping the aircraft alive.

We reached the jungle canopy flying literally feet above it, if we'd lowered our wheels they would probably have touched it. We flew on, but I wasn't in any doubt that it was a matter of seconds, minutes maybe if we were lucky, before the MIG came in again and finished us.

"He doesn't know his business, that pilot," Paul grinned.

"Let's hope he's not a fast learner," I replied grimly.

Cady came back into the cockpit. "No injuries yet, Hoffman, what do we do next?"

"I'm trying to find somewhere to put down, Captain, before we're blown out of the sky."

He looked down at the unending jungle canopy and shook his head. "Any other options?"

"Pray he runs out of ammunition," Paul said with a grin.

The smile was wiped off his face as the MIG came in again, I was ready for him and wrenched the rudder, turning the aircraft sharply to starboard to vector away from the cannon fire, but it was hopeless. Another burst hit us, this time it was the port wing that took the brunt of the attack, the engine erupted in a cloud of smoke and oil and caught fire as the propeller began to feather.

"Get your men ready, Cady, we're going down," I shouted.

He went back in the cabin and I heard him shouting orders to them to find something to hold on to. We were almost on the ground anyway, there was no room to manoeuvre when I saw a small clearing in the jungle and pointed the aircraft at it.

"Landing gear?" Paul shouted.

I shook my head. "No time and anyway, the gear could topple us if it tangles with any branches or roots. Feather the starboard engine."

The first of the trees rushed past the cockpit window and we hit the ground with an enormous crash, the Ilyushin bounced back into the air and came down again as we slid along the clearing. We bounced up and down as we hit fallen trees and small mounds of earth. The sea of foliage hurtled towards us as we rushed along, then we came to the end of the clearing and the Ilyushin buried its nose into the first of the trees. We instinctively threw up our arms to cover our eyes as the windscreen burst in and shattered glass showered the cockpit and the aircraft rolled to a halt.

"Get everyone out fast and undercover," I shouted to the men in the cabin. "Paul, we've done what we could, let's go."

He nodded, picked up his pack, we grabbed our weapons and rushed into the cabin and I followed him with my pack. The cabin was in chaos as the men scrambled to get out of the crashed aircraft, they had the door open already and were helping Anderson and Goldberg down to the ground.

"You need to move faster," I shouted to Cady, "the MIG is still around and there may be several hundred gallons of aviation fuel that could catch fire."

He nodded and started to urge them on but they had

heard me and were already throwing their gear out and jumping clear as if their lives depended on it. Which of course, they did.

When they were all out Paul followed them and I left last, jumping to the jungle floor. Paul was already urging them to get away from the aircraft and they were running for the shelter of a huge, fallen tree that looked almost like the body of a giant dinosaur that had lain there for centuries, millennia even. I followed them and looked up at the sky from behind the giant tree trunk. The MIG was circling, almost certainly using his radio to ask for instructions. In a communist North Vietnam everyone had to wait until orders were relayed from someone at the top. Apparently this time he didn't have to wait long. Abruptly he banked and turned towards us at high speed, then fired his cannons at the crashed plane. Someone would be in serious trouble for that order, I reflected. This was North Vietnam with a chronic shortage of everything. A crashed aircraft could be retrieved and repaired to fly again, one that was destroyed with cannon fire was useless. Then the Ilyushin exploded as the cannon shells hit the fuel tanks, sending a ball of flame shooting up in the sky that we could feel behind the shelter of the tree. Before he completed his attack his guns suddenly stopped firing, he was out of ammunition. I turned to Cady.

"Captain, we need to move, fast, away from here."

He was mystified. "Hoffman, we're ok, he's out of ammunition."

"And calling in reinforcements and ground troops to catch us here. Round up your men and get moving."

His expression changed as he realised the danger we were in. He started giving orders and we struck out under the jungle canopy, out of sight of the MIG. We came on a game trail that looked passable and almost ran along it for a mile before I called a halt.

"We need to move east or west, the Viets know we're heading to the South and they'll be hunting for us in that direction. What do you think, Paul?"

He was looking at a map he'd brought from the Ilyushin. "We're a few miles away from the village of Dong Hoi, I think. If we head due east, we can swing south when we're further away and cross the DMZ near an old French fort just south of the border called Lang Vei, it's near the village of Khe Sanh."

"So we'll be as good as home when we get to this Lang Vei place, yeah?" Cady asked.

"No, we won't be. There's over a hundred miles to travel to get to the DMZ, the area will be thick with Viets searching for us. Once we're over the border, the Viet Cong will still be hunting us down, we won't be safe until we get back to Tan Son Nhat. Let's move."

We hacked our way east through the thick jungle, eventually we hit another game trail and the going got easier. As far as we could tell no one had passed this way recently but we couldn't allow ourselves the luxury of jumping to conclusions. Cady put out a rearguard, Russo and Beckerman, to stop us being attacked from behind. There was little point in sending out a point guard, we could barely get through the jungle as it was. We travelled that way for fifteen hard, brutal miles until the light was fading. Goldberg and Anderson looked all in, as if they were about to collapse unconscious.

"We'd better stop here," I said to Cady. "We can't go on any further and neither can they."

Cady nodded and gave orders to make camp. It started to rain and we sat miserably under our waterproof shelters to try and keep dry, but it was hopeless, the rain seemed to get through everything and we spent a miserable night listening out for the enemy. In the morning we were a sad, sorry group, cold, wet, tired and hungry. Frank Burr went to each of us and put together a collection of rations from which he produced a breakfast that tasted like decaying rat, but we wolfed it down, it could be the last food we would eat in a long time.

I was discussing the direction we would be heading in when Beckerman came up to us.

"Captain, Goldberg and Anderson, they're not looking too good."

We went over to inspect the two men. Goldberg had an obvious fever, he was hot, his eyes unfocused and he had been unable to eat any food. Anderson was no better, apparently his ribs had been broken and his right knee smashed with a blow from a pistol, he said he was in a great deal of pain. They wouldn't make the entire trip, of that I was certain. I nodded to Cady and we moved away to discuss it out of earshot.

"What do you think?" he asked me. "They don't look as if they'll travel a hundred miles through this jungle." I nodded in agreement, it would be impossible.

"We need to get them evacuated. Do you have a working radio?" I asked him.

"Yeah, Jack Bond our comms guy has been working on

the surviving set, the other was smashed during the escape. But you know that the second we transmit they'll home in on us like flies around a stale turd?"

I grinned, it was an apt analogy. "You'll need to move the party on at least ten miles. I'll remain here with your communications sergeant and contact my people at Tan Son Nhat. What about the military, will they help?"

He shook his head. "My orders were clear, Hoffman, no involvement of any U.S. forces north of the DMZ. It's not negotiable."

"I thought not," I replied. "In that case I'll contact my people, we've got a light aircraft on the field, a Cessna, big enough to carry out Goldberg and Anderson. If we can find a field or even a road we can get it down and back off again. May I suggest we move out and travel until we find a suitable landing area, then I'll return with Sergeant Bond and try the radio."

"That sounds okay to me. You're a good man, Hoffman."

"For a Nazi," I smiled.

"Yeah, I guess."

We started out, this time the two casualties had to be completely carried in litters made from branches with our waterproof shelters stretch over them. Two men carried each of them, it was hard, heavy and slow going. Paul and I took a turn when they tired and I was impressed by the sheer strength of these Special Forces men, the task of carrying the litters through the jungle was an act of torture. We'd travelled about seven miles when we came to an open space. I asked Cady to halt the men while Paul and I went to check the clearing. It was feasible, just. Barely six hundred feet long, it was strewn with broken trees, low hillocks of earth thrown up by some sort of subterranean creatures and a variety of rocks and debris deposited over hundreds of years. But it was flat, it would have to do. We took the map coordinates and I explained to Cady that his men would need to set to work to clearing it as much as humanly possible. Then I set off with Jack Bond to make contact with Tan Son Nhat, leaving Paul to supervise the runway clearing.

We hiked back the way we had come, it took us three hours to travel the seven miles through dense jungle. Finally we arrived at the tiny clearing where we'd camped the night before. We'd tried to camouflage it but I guessed it was obvious we'd been there, it seemed unlikely that we could mask our stay sufficiently to fool the noses of the Viets that would be tracking us. Bond got the radio out of his pack and switched it on to warm up, I checked my watch.

"When you start transmitting, we have a maximum of three minutes, then we cut the transmission and head out fast."

"They're that quick are they?" he said to me surprised.

"This is their country, Jack, not ours." I replied softly. He nodded and bent to the radio to dial in the frequency of my Tan Son Nhat radio. Then he turned to me. "That's it, Jurgen, she's all yours."

I picked up the telephone style handset and pressed the send button.

"Hoffman for Drexler, do you read?"

I waited as the static hissed back at me, and then called again. Still no reply.

"Are you sure the radio is okay, Jack?"

"Certain, yeah, it's working one hundred percent."

Then a voice crackled out of the earpiece. "Jurgen, is that you?"

"Johann, listen, and listen fast, we only have a little time before they triangulate our position. I need the Cessna brought to the following coordinates to bring out two casualties. Can do?"

"Of course, Jurgen. Where are you?"

I'd already calculated our position and worked out how to encode it. "Can you look up my birthdate in the files?" I asked him. There was a brief pause. "Of course."

"Good. Add that to our business bank account number, that's where we are."

There was a hesitation, then his voice came back, uncertainly. "Roger that, I'll do my best. I'll get the plane moving straight away, I prepared it ready, I suspected it might be needed."

"Don't leave today, you won't be here until after dark and we can't light the landing strip. Leave at first light and time your arrival for mid-morning. We'll put down a smoke marker. Is the C-47 operational yet?" Another pause. "Yes, I think so."

What wasn't he telling me? Presumably that he wasn't confident about making it, but there was no time to discuss it.

"Johann, you are able to make the flight, aren't you? "Er, sure, I think I'll find it."

I checked my watch, time was up. I desperately wanted to ask about Helene but it could endanger our mission even more. "Hoffman out."

I cut the transmission and gave Jack the handset.

"That's it, we need to move fast, they'll be searching for us and we need to be as far away as possible."

He nodded and stowed the radio in his pack and we set off. When we reached the track that led back to our group we continued for another mile laying a false trail. Then we cut back to the original track and went on to find our group.

Through the rest of the day we waited under the shelter of the jungle at the side of the field. From time to time aircraft buzzed overhead, hunting for us but none came near enough to have seen us. When night fell we tried to get some sleep, the rain had stopped and we were exhausted after the previous sleepless night. I woke up at dawn, as I usually did. Two of the men were already moving around, Cady and Woltz, the others were still fast asleep. Paul woke up and together we went to make a final check on the landing field. It was the best we could do under the circumstances, Drexler wasn't an expert pilot, he had a pilot's license but only used it to enable him to maintain and test fly the aircraft if he was working on. He wasn't good enough, but he was all we had. Helene had a license too and she was a far better pilot than Johann, but she was in a hospital in the U.S., several thousand miles away and even if she wasn't I would never have suggested her coming this far north on a risky rescue mission. It was all up to Johann Drexler.

The rest of the men gradually woke up and the camp came alive as they busied themselves readying for the pickup later that morning. We brought Goldberg and Anderson to the side of the clearing on their litters. When the aircraft landed they needed to be loaded and sent away almost before the wheels stopped turning. Even if we allowed ourselves the luxury of a short break for the pilot, the Viets would definitely not. Their air patrols had increased and I became increasingly nervous that the Cessna might be detected and blown out of the sky.

"He'll get here," Paul said, seeing my nervousness.

"I hope so, sometimes he doesn't seem to be able to find his way back to Tan Son Nhat." He laughed and clapped me on the back. "He'll be here."

An hour later there was still no sign of the aircraft, then suddenly we heard a low buzzing in the distance. I looked up and made out the shape of the Cessna flying just above treetop height, it was nearly on top of us.

"Smoke!" I shouted to Cady.

Someone popped the smoke marker and a plume of smoke rose into the air, bending to show the direction of the wind. The Cessna banked and went around again and lined up for a landing. Then it came over the treetops and dropped onto the field in a perfect three point landing. I was impressed, Johann must have been taking lessons. The aircraft expertly taxied to the end of the field and turned into the wind ready to take off as the men ran out with Goldberg and Anderson. The aircraft door opened and a man stepped out. It wasn't Johann Drexler.

The man that was piratical in appearance due to the black eye patch, collected during one of his numerous crash landings. Ritter von Schacht. I must have looked like a goldfish, my mouth opening and shutting. "Ritter, what the hell are you doing, where's Johann?"

He laughed. "Did you want an amateur flying over the DMZ, Jurgen? Johann came to see me, said that he didn't think he'd even find you let along land the aircraft. Naturally I offered my own expert services."

"So he's ok, Johann, no problems? He should have run this past me, Ritter."

"Of course he's ok, he's fine. He's just not a pilot, Jurgen, a fair engineer, maybe, but hell, did you want Johann to pilot this plane so far north? You know he'd never get here."

I grinned and we shook hands. "No, you're right, poor old Johann, he's not the best pilot or navigator in the world. Thanks, Ritter, I appreciate this." He shrugged. "Any time, my friend."

I could smell alcohol on his breath, but that was the man, he drank heavily though never when he was flying.

A shout came from the men, they'd loaded the casualties, Frank Burr was going to care for them on the long journey back to Saigon.

"You'd better go, Ritter, I'll see you back in Saigon."

"Take care, my friend. Johann is worried about you."

"Half the North Vietnamese Army is worrying about us, Ritter."

He looked worried. "Will you get back ok, do you want me to get Johann to prepare the C-47 and we could fly back and pick all of you up?"

I grinned. "I've always got back in the past, haven't I? Don't worry about us, we'll be fine." He nodded. "Don't be overconfident, Jurgen. Be very careful. Use the radio if you need me again. Where are you headed?" I told him about the old airfield outside Khe Sanh.

"Could you bring the C-47 to pick us up there?"

I could have asked Harkins to provide transport within South Vietnam, but his headquarters was riddled with leaks and I preferred to keep the operation to ourselves.

"Of course, just call up and I'll come and get you, Johann can take the right hand seat." I nodded and he climbed through the door of the Cessna, it seemed overcrowded already with the three men inside the tiny cockpit, Frank Burr sat in the front seat."

"Can you fly, Frank?" I asked him as Ritter strapped himself in. He shook his head. "Sorry."

I slammed the door, another pilot would have been welcome but Ritter was more than capable. He throttled up and the Cessna began to roll, he saluted and I waved back. Then it picked up speed, took off and headed due south, barely clearing the treetops as it left the clearing. I looked around, Cady was standing beside me.

"Captain, we need to move, fast. They'll be down on us now, we don't have long."

"We're all set, Hoffman." He turned to his men, they were waiting expectantly.

"Let's go."

* * *

"Everything depends on the Americans. If they want to make war for 20 years then we shall make war for 20 years. If they want to make peace, we shall make peace and invite them to tea afterwards."

Ho Chi Minh

People's Army of Vietnam Militia Self-Defence Force Headquarters, Hanoi

It was a smoky room, windows grimy, the furniture worn and repaired many times. Quan glanced up at the two junior officers standing before his desk. One was Nguyen Minh, nephew of his sister's husband. His uniform was smart, polished, his attitude suitably deferential in the presence of his commanding officer. But he was useless, weak, despised by his men for his reluctance to take tough decisions and lead from the front as was normal in the People's Army. Sub-Lieutenant Van Thanh, standing next to him, ten years older than Nguyen, a tough, competent veteran who had fought in the French war as a private soldier but without connections would find it hard to advance beyond his lowly rank.

"You know about the Americans that have illegally crossed our border and kidnapped two prisoners of the State?" Both men nodded.

"These criminals should be hunted down and shot," Nguyen broke in enthusiastically.

Quan looked at him for a moment. "I totally agree, Lieutenant Nguyen, what are you doing about achieving that very desirable end?" Nguyen reddened and stammered. "Well, Sir, I am of course awaiting your orders."

"You mean you've done nothing?" Quan asked him.

Nguyen nodded.

"Sub-Lieutenant Van?" Quan asked the older man. "My men are all standing by for your orders, Sir. I've personally drawn weapons and ammunition from the armoury and rations for five days."

Quan nodded. "Excellent. Lieutenant Nguyen, perhaps you could follow Van's lead, if it's not too much trouble?"

"Yes, Sir, immediately. Nguyen inwardly cursed the junior man, he'd lined up a good night of cards in the city for tonight and his favourite girl would be waiting for him when he finished.

"Very good. You will leave in one hour." Nguyen felt his stomach lurch, it was a disaster.

"I want both of you in Dong Hoi as fast as possible," Quan continued. "Make yourselves available to the local militia commander, he is expecting you. Dismissed."

"Colonel," Van said suddenly. Quan looked at him irritably. "What is it, Sub-Lieutenant Van?"

"The Americans, if we find them, what do we do with them?"

"When you find them, Lieutenant, I want them dead. Is that clear?"

Both officers saluted and left the office.

CHAPTER SEVEN

If a free society cannot help the many who are poor, it cannot save the few who are rich

John F. Kennedy 1961

We pushed on fast, turning south to head for the DMZ, we were climbing now into a low mountain range. When we stopped for a rest Paul checked the maps and talked to Beckerman, we had less than seventy miles to travel. We were about to cross a rough track that led into the foot of the mountains when we heard the sound of a vehicle. Cady signalled for the men to take cover and we waited while the Russian built Zil came into view. We waited for it to go past but the vehicle stopped fifty yards from our position and the soldiers dismounted. We counted eighteen NVA regulars in all, fifteen privates, two NCOs and a lieutenant. The officer barked orders and the men began unloading their equipment from the lorry, a medium machine gun, a Soviet SG43 Goryunov and a mortar that they started to assemble on a stand. I looked across at Cady, he'd gone white, frozen into almost a statue. I inched over to him. "We have to take them out, Captain, we won't get past them," I murmured. "Either we kill them or they'll kill us."

He shook his head. "Christ, I don't know, there are a lot of them. An SG-43, a mortar, shit, I don't know."

His men looked across at him, they'd faced odds as bad as this earlier. The unstated feeling was like an axe hanging over us. He'd lost his nerve, bottled it. The taut infiltration and desperate fighting withdrawal from Son Tay had finished him, probably the forced landing was the end. But we had to deal with the soldiers or die here.

"Captain, if I may, I've been in this situation many times before. If you would maintain the perimeter, I'll organise the attack."

He looked bewildered, but after a few moments nodded. "Yeah, you do that Hoffman, you do that." I wormed across to where the other men were crouching down behind some rocks, Paul was peering through a narrow fissure to keep an eye on the Viets. "The captain has asked me to organise an attack on these soldiers, does anyone have any problem with that?"

They grinned and shook their heads. "He's calling his broker to check his options, is he?" Woltz murmured. We all smiled politely.

"We need to destroy the mortar and the machine gun, we can't get any further while they're intact. What's the grenade situation?"

They pooled their grenades, we had a total of seven. I explained my plan of attack, it was simple. Russo and

Beckerman would take the machine gun, two others would hit the mortar, and in each case the second man would give covering fire as the grenades were thrown. Paul and I would pin down the rest of them with sub-machine gun fire.

"Is that clear, any questions?"

"Yeah. Jurgen, were you an officer once, you seem to know what you're doing?" one of them asked.

"I was an SS-Sturmbannführer, that's a major, I commanded a company and later in the war a full regiment of the SS-Das Reich Panzer Infantry. I served on the Eastern Front and later in the French Foreign Legion as a Senior Sergeant."

"Yeah, I reckon that qualifies you to take the lead. What about Paul?" Beckerman asked.

"He was also an SS-Sturmbannführer in SS-Totenkopf, after that we served together in the French Foreign Legion where he was also a senior sergeant. A company, Second Battalion, 13th Half Brigade, if you're interested."

"Right, so you've both seen some action?" I grinned. "Some."

"And the lorry, what do we do about it?"

"Ride back across the DMZ on it, if we can deal with the soldiers."They looked across at me. "They don't look like beginners," I warned them. "There are no guarantees on this one. We just don't have a choice. We fight or we die."

They crawled into position, Paul and I loaded our sub-machine guns and made ready with a pile of spare clips next to each of us. I wistfully thought about the old days when we'd have an MG34 general purpose belt fed machine gun in close support. But we were well armed, it would have to do. I looked around, they were ready. I nodded at Paul and we poked the barrels of our guns over the rocks and pulled the triggers.

The first bullets smashed into the Viets, they scattered instantly. Loud explosions sent shock waves back towards us, hurting our ear drums. The machine gun and mortar disappeared. The surviving Viets had taken cover back in the rocks and began returning fire. I admired their skill, they were damned good to have recovered so quickly. Eight of them had fallen in our ferocious ambush but that still left ten to fight back, ten skilled and hardened communists who would probably be veterans of the Indochina war with the French. More to the point, they outnumbered us.

"We'll have to destroy the lorry," I shouted across to the men. It was not the way I'd planned it, but if they got away in the lorry we would be in lot more trouble. Two of our men shifted their aim and the lorry sagged on its springs as the bullets hammered into it. Every tyre was riddled, it wouldn't follow us south.

"Paul. Get Cady, we're pulling out," I shouted at him. He nodded and crawled away and came back with the Captain who looked almost as if he was sleepwalking. I gave the order and we retreated towards a gap in the rocks that led away from the battle, still firing at the Viets. We conducted a fighting withdrawal for half a mile, pursued by the vengeful Vietnamese. "What the fuck went wrong?" Russo asked as we ran.

"They outnumbered us three to one, that was the first problem and they were also very lucky. But we could have dealt with it if they weren't so good. They were veteran troops,

Russo, you saw how quickly they responded when we opened fire. They still outnumber us two to one and will have called for reinforcements, possibly even air support. It was a risk worth taking and it didn't pan out, so we're running."

We dashed along the track and over the top of the low mountain range. The valley below us stretched far into the distance, a sea of thick, dense greenery that would help us to disappear from our pursuers. Bullets clipped rocks as we tumbled down the steep path, it was fortunate that Ritter had taken the casualties, if we were carrying Goldberg and Anderson we would have been finished. We reached the bottom and fought our way into the jungle along a small trail. After half a mile I saw a tiny opening in the jungle and told Paul to lead them away while I took Russo further along to lay a false trail before doubling back and following our group.

It was getting dark by the time I called a halt, we hadn't heard any sound of pursuit for over an hour and I assumed we'd lost them. We'd also lost our way. We made camp and spent a miserable night listening to the sounds of the jungle, the occasional roar of a wild animal, a shriek as a creature was taken for food and the incessant buzz of thousands of crickets. They were the primeval sounds of the forest, no different to what they had been thousands of years ago. It was broken suddenly by the sound of Abe Woltz singing softly, a pop song called 'Duke of Earl' that had been on the radio stations recently. He had a surprisingly good voice, I think it cheered us all up, until Cady snapped at him to shut up in case the enemy heard us. We all looked at the officer sceptically but said nothing, his authority was slipping badly enough as it was. In the morning we prepared the last of our food and got ready to move out.

"You know where we're headed?" Beckerman asked me. "South," I replied. When I didn't say any more he shrugged and picked up his pack.

We pushed east through dense jungle for several hours, it was midday by the time we came across a trail that intersected out path heading towards the south. We took a short break and sat quietly, hungry and miserable, depressed by the unending green of the jungle that seemed to claw at our boots, our bodies and our very souls for every step of the way. Water was a problem and when we found a stream that looked less dirty than some Beckerman used water purification tablets to sterilise some water and we were at least able to fill our canteens. It was almost dark when we abruptly came out of the jungle and saw a road in front of us, by European standards it would have been a farm track but here in Vietnam is was something akin to an autobahn. I went forward cautiously with Russo and Woltz while the others followed at a distance. The road looked clear but after we'd walked along it for several hundred yards we nearly stepped into a roadblock.

It was only the smell of tobacco smoke that alerted us. We melted into the jungle and set up camp a mile away and settled down to wait for dawn. Cady insisted we mount a night attack on the roadblock, until I gently reminded him that we had no way of knowing where the Viets were deployed and that we could run straight into a much larger force. He persisted that we could get around them, until I pointed out that a large force of infantry in our immediate rear was not good military tactics.

We awoke at first light and crept forward. Two lorries were parked across the track to block it, soldiers were everywhere, possibly two platoons of them, with a pair of lieutenants in command. One of the lieutenants seemed to be more senior but oddly he was much younger than the other man, when I looked through my binoculars I could see the men looking at him with thinly disguised contempt. Half of them were to the east side of the track, the other to the west. The senior lieutenant joined the men to the east. They were poorly deployed, lounging around and smoking as opposed to the older lieutenant's men who were skilfully deployed in good positions, alert and watchful. We doubled back to our group and explained the situation.

"Couldn't we go around them?" Jack Bond asked the question they all wanted answered.

I shook my head. "If they know their business, they'll have patrols out in the jungle and further down the track, we've no way of knowing who we're going to run into."

"We're fucked," Cady said loudly, "totally fucked. We should have attacked last night." We all looked at him, shocked by the deterioration in him over the past twenty four hours. He was unshaven like the rest of us, but his eyes were red rimmed and blazing, his skin pallid.

"Not yet, Captain, not yet, we've still got some options." He seemed to retreat into some kind of trance. I turned back to the men.

"We need an inventory of our weapons and ammunition. Let's see what we've got."

"You mean you think we can take them all?" Russo asked.

"Unless you have a better plan, I don't see any alternative. Even if we crept around them we'd have no way of preventing them from pursuing us if they found out. Believe me, they always do find out, this is their country, we are just the visitors. A passing peasant would sound the alarm, a hidden checkpoint, an unexpected overflight, we've no way to tell. They're fully mobile, they'd be on us in no time at all."

They looked at me for a moment, obviously wondering if I was making the right decision. All except Paul, who had been in this situation many times before and Cady, who was unable to fully reason things out.

We took stock of our weapons and ammunition. We had six sub-machine guns between us, as well as Woltz's sniper rifle and an assortment of handguns. There were two AR15s, early versions of the M16 and about a hundred rounds for each of us. The grenades had been used up in the previous attack. I outlined a simple plan, ideally we would use one of their vehicles but taking one might prove to be impossible.

"The platoon to the east of the track appears poorly led and I doubt they'll be effective when it comes to a fight. They've got a light machine gun each side of the track, a Degtyaryev DP. If we can take the platoon to the east we can turn the Degtyaryev on the platoon the other side, I'm hoping they'll be less than enthusiastic about firing on their own positions. But it'll mean a long crawl to get behind them and we'll need to take them in total silence."

"That's what we're trained to do, Hoffman," Russo said.

"Very well, Joe, it's time to earn your pay."

We left Cady ostensibly to guard our packs, in reality to keep him away from the action. I took Russo and Beckerman and Paul took the other two, I intended to hit them from south of their position, Paul from the north and work towards the middle of the platoon. If one soldier cried out, fired a shot or shouted a warning, the plan would go awry. We crawled past them, about fifty yards back in the jungle. The smoke alerted me first, a hidden sentry was enjoying a cigarette behind a thick bush. I nodded to Beckerman and he drew his fighting knife and crawled around the other side of the bush to take him from behind. I heard a slight rustle of clothing, otherwise it was a totally silent kill. Beckerman crawled back to us and we continued towards the main group. As I had anticipated, they were poorly deployed, the two men at the most southerly end of the line were murmuring quietly to themselves. While I waited, Russo and Beckerman crawled quietly forward and I saw each of them put their arm around the neck of one of the soldiers and drive the points of their knives through the eye and straight into the brain. They pulled the bodies down and laid them out of sight. I heard another soldier whispering to his comrades, calling them and I crawled forward. His voice grew louder and he stupidly stood up and walked towards their position. As he came up to where he probably assumed his comrades were sleeping I stood up, clamped my hand over his mouth and slit his throat.

We crept quietly towards the officer and left two more Viet soldiers bleeding into the damp soil of the jungle. So far, none of the troops the other side of the track appeared to have noticed anything. The lieutenant our side of the track suddenly shouted across to the other officer, who hissed at him, I didn't need to speak Vietnamese to know he was telling him to get out of sight and shut up. But it made no difference, the lieutenant, smartly dressed but soft and oily looking, spoke more sharply to the other officer who shrugged and ran across the track towards him. It was too good an opportunity to miss, I'd warned Woltz to hit any target of opportunity that presented itself. The two officers were stood together with three of the soldiers from our side of the track. I prayed that our sniper would recognise the chance. There were five soft 'thunk' sounds, they couldn't have been more than a second apart. All five men dropped and lay still. There was an outbreak of confused shouting from both sides, three more men stood up on our side of the track and also half a dozen from the other side who looked suspiciously around the greenery that embraced them. The three men on our side went down, three 'thunks' in quick succession. Woltz switched aim to the soldiers the other side of the track and five of the six who had stood up went down, the sixth man scrambled away before Woltz could move his aim.

I heard the Vietnamese soldiers shouting to themselves and across to their comrades our side, but there was no answer, we'd got them all. Shots cracked out and a bullet whistled close to my head. I crawled away and came across the Degtyarev, Russo and Beckerman had already secured it and were checking the magazine. More shots cracked out from across the track, several sustained bursts of AK47 fire spattered around us, then Russo and Beckerman opened up with the Degtyarev. It was a slow rate of fire but devastating, they'd aimed at the Degtyarev opposite and hit it with several bursts. The two man crew, scrambling to bring their weapon to bear, went down in a hail of bullets, several of which smashed into the machine gun and I saw the pancake magazine spin away into the foliage as it was hit. The gun was out of use, we'd reduced the odds. The Viets had recovered well now and were pouring fire into us, so far no one had been hit but it was more by luck than skill. The Degtyarev kept firing, Russo furiously changing magazines as they emptied. I estimated that we'd killed or wounded around twelve of the enemy, which still left a good number to return fire. Then the Degtyarev jammed. They banged furiously on the breech to try and free it but I could see it was useless. They abandoned the gun and started using their sub-machine guns to continue the fight. We were outnumbered by perhaps three to one which was not healthy. Even worse, they only had to hold on for reinforcements to arrive which they inevitably would. We needed a miracle to turn this fight to our advantage and Cady gave us one. He ran onto the track, his hands in the air clutching a white cloth, I could hear him shouting "I surrender, don't shoot."

We all ceased fire, both sides, astonished by the incredible spectacle of an American officer wild and dishevelled, running towards the Viets. Several of them stood up, I assumed they thought that we were all giving up. It was too good an opportunity to miss. I stood up and ran, shouting, "Charge!"

The others needed no more encouragement, they rose up and ran towards the enemy only a few yards away across the jungle. The Viets looked towards us, alarmed as it dawned on them that we weren't surrendering and they started to aim their weapons at us, some dived for cover, but it was too late. As I sent a burst hammering into them, I saw Cady go down under a long burst of AK47 fire. Then we were amongst them and it was fierce, bloody work that we had all been trained for. Woltz was still firing, knocking down the enemy one by one as they came within his field of vision. Beckerman screamed and fell as a bullet hit him, but the rest of us crashed into the enemy and it took little more than a minute to scythe them down with sub-machine gun fire. Two of them threw up their hands to surrender, but Russo hit them with another burst. A sergeant loomed out of the scrub in front of me and I shot him as I moved past. The jungle went silent, we'd finished them all. We hoped that none had escaped into the jungle but we couldn't do anything about that, time wasn't on our side. The Special Forces men looked around, awestruck by what we'd achieved.

"Damn, if that don't beat all," Jack Bond said as he looked around at the carnage.

"Did anyone check Captain Cady?" I asked.

Woltz was walking towards me. He nodded. "Yeah, he's dead, that burst ripped him apart."

I came across Beckerman, he was lying against the trunk of a tree, blood stained his combat jacket. Bond had gone over to him to dress the wound.

"How is he?" I asked him. "A shoulder wound, he'll be ok."

"Paul, would you check out the trucks, see if they're useable. Joe, could you take a look too?" They nodded and quickly went to check them over. I heard the rumble of an engine starting, Paul came back to me shortly after.

"One of them is useable, Abe and Joe are changing a tyre that got shot out. The other took several bursts into the engine compartment, it's useless.

"Right. Would you help me to get Cady's body into the truck and we'll see how far we can drive towards the DMZ. I don't want to bury him here, we'll find somewhere quiet along the way."

We hoisted Cady's bloody body onto the bed of the truck and covered it with a tarpaulin. The men were gathering as much ammunition and weapons as they could find and they threw them in the back beside Cady's body. Finally they climbed aboard and Paul drove us along the track. We were back on our way to the DMZ.

We travelled for another fifty miles without incident, as we passed peasants along the track the men in the back put their heads down and Paul and I covered our faces with our hands. It may have fooled one or two, maybe more, but not all of them. It was all we had. I told the men in the back to watch for aircraft and we continued along the track, lurching and bumping on the ruts. Beckerman's wound re-opened but although he was in pain he gritted his teeth and didn't cry out as Bond re-fastened the dressing.

"Why do we always wind up fighting wars in these sub-human countries, Jurgen?" Paul said abruptly.

I started. I was miles away, I'd been thinking of something else, my mind had wandered to Helene. She'd smiled at me in that beautiful, sensuous way as I came to her and started to remove her blouse. Her breasts were still firm, the skin smooth and creamy. I was touching them gently, when Paul spoke I realised that I had begun to get an erection. I brought my mind back to the present with an effort, daydreaming would get us all killed. I had to survive, had to get back to Saigon and do everything in my power to help her. I focussed on what Paul had been saying to me.

"Germans have been fighting other people's wars since the beginning of time, almost. Even these Americans used our Hessians during their war of independence. I think it must be our destiny to be the world's military reserve, to be called on when anyone needs us."

Paul grunted. "Maybe we're just too stupid to stay at home when the bullets start flying." I grinned at him. "You'd prefer that, married to a fat Bavarian farmer's daughter and rearing a brood of little Schusters?"

He shuddered. "A good point, Jurgen, the Viet Cong sound positively inviting compared to finishing up like that." I laughed, about to make a reply when someone shouted from the back. "MIG coming in!"

The pilot must have been flying at low level, they hadn't seen him until the last moment. His aircraft shot past us and climbed ready to make a banking turn in the sky. He may or may not have identified us as the stolen lorry but I didn't intend discussing it. I saw a gap in the jungle and pointed it out to Paul, he swerved off the track just as a stream of cannon fire erupted on the part of the track we'd just left. As the MIG banked again for another attack run, we jumped out and scrambled to escape into the deep jungle.

I crouched behind a clump of trees as the MIG roared in again, this time the cannon fire riddled the lorry and it erupted into a ball of fire.

"That's Cady's funeral pyre taken care of," Paul said grimly. I nodded. The MIG came around yet again and gunfire smashed into the jungle all around us, he couldn't see us but was saturating the area with gunfire to try and hit some of us. Or contain us, of course, until the North Vietnamese army could reach us.

"We need to go deeper in the jungle, he'll have called for ground troops to surround us. Call..."

As I spoke there was a renewed burst of firing. A second MIG had arrived and came directly in for a strafing run as the first one circled overhead. Then a third one screamed in to attack and the jungle erupted once more all around us. I shouted for the men to regroup five hundred yards to the east and we crawled away. Behind us the MIGs were still searching, firing occasional bursts to remind us that they were still around. We didn't get five hundred yards, after two hundred yards the jungle petered out and we were left standing on the edge of a deep ravine, the cliff top dropped several hundred feet to a swirling river below. A circling MIG spotted us and roared down into the attack, we jumped for cover as the cannon fire shredded the jungle over our heads. The river meandered sharply to the west and curved out of sight two or three hundred yards away from us, I realised there had to be a bridge for the track we had been following, it would of course be guarded. We were trapped in a pocket, the only direction we could go was back to the north, which was not an option.

We pulled back into the dense jungle. The MIGs had stopped shooting up the jungle, presumably to save their ammunition until they could see us. We were a miserable group, crouched under the jungle canopy out of sight of the MIGs.

"Any ideas, Jurgen?" Russo asked me. I shook my head. "It's a tough one, we can't go east or south, if we go west they'll shoot us up on the track and if we go north we'll run straight into an ambush party, they'll have a regiment on the way already, we've stung them pretty badly."

They all laughed. "That's one way of putting it," Jack Bond said. He looked at the sky. "Anyone know how long we have to go until dark?"

"About four hours, I think," I replied. "They'll be here before then."

"You're sure about that?" Abe Woltz said. "Isn't it what you would do?" He shrugged. "I guess so. How far to the DMZ?"

"Maybe fifteen, twenty miles. I think the best move for us is to head south for the bridge, it can't be far away. At least we can see what we're facing there. Who knows, it might be possible to get across if it isn't too heavily guarded and if it's not too visible from the air."

"And if the MIGs don't see us," Bond added unhappily. No one replied, everything depended on the Viets not getting a battalion to the bridge before we crossed it, assuming that there was a bridge and it was even still standing.

We crept through the jungle, careful to keep under the overhanging canopy. It took us half an hour before we came back to the edge of the foliage. The river was in front of us, curving around as I'd thought. At this point it was about fifty yards wide, not a huge distance and it was spanned by a rickety looking wooden bridge. We could see four guards the other side, they had a Degtyarev light machine gun set up pointing towards the track that they expected us to travel along. Woltz came up to me.

"I can take them, Jurgen, at this range it shouldn't be too much of a problem." I looked at the other men. "What do you think? If Abe takes out the guards we'd have to rush straight over the bridge, if the MIGs see what we're doing they'll be waiting for us so it would have to be straight away."

We got as close to the edge of the jungle as possible and crouched in our jumping off point. Abe had positioned himself with a good field of fire, he was as confident as he could be of taking out all four of the enemy.

"I'm ready," he said, "just say the word." I looked up at the sky, there was a MIG near enough to spot what we were doing. "Nearly there, hold tight, Abe." I jerked around at the sound of an engine coming from the other side of the river. A ZIL was slowing to a stop by the bridge and as we watched, an officer climbed down and spoke sharply to the guards. He shouted and waved at the MIGs, at the track that led north from where we had come and then swept his arm over the expanse of jungle that hid us. His meaning was obvious. He inspected the Degtyarev, barked some orders at the soldiers and they unloaded six small wooden cases from the vehicle. Then he mounted the lorry and it drove across the bridge.

We almost held our breath, praying that it would pass our position and our prayers were answered as it continued up the track and we heard the sound of its engine receding into the background. Their intention was clear, they were to be the beaters that drove their quarry, us, down onto the machine gun waiting at the bridge. It was a simple plan but it could be effective. The problem we faced was that when the MIGs noticed their guards shot up on the bridge, they'd call the troops in the lorry back to pursue us and they'd run us down like dogs.

We slumped down again, the obstacles were getting worse and worse.

"We could set fire to the bridge," I said absently. "Christ, you never give up, do you Jurgen?" Joe Russo said. "Give up? Why would I do that?"

"Jurgen, admit it, we're fucked. Totally fucked. What's the alternative?"

I looked at the others, all except Paul were hanging on my every word. I felt angry, what the hell was the matter with these supposed elite troops. I tried to imagine them in the snows of the Eastern Front, fending off countless Soviet attacks, counter-attacking to regain lost ground. Did they think this was some kind of game, to be played until the other side appeared to have gained the upper hand then tamely surrender, hoping for a warm bed and hot food in a prison camp?

"If that's the way you think, that's your choice. But I strongly suggest you consider shooting yourselves in the head first, it'll save them the trouble of doing it afterwards. Don't you realise, they're going to kill us all? These people are savages, we've hurt them badly, not just militarily but their pride, the invincible People's Army of North Vietnam. There's only one way they can get that reputation back, it's time you men understood that. They want us dead."

They were shaken by my words, but they heard the truth

in them. We had to escape or die, there was no third option. We made plans to rush across the bridge as soon as Abe shot the guards. Once across, we'd try to set fire to it, but it seemed unlikely under the noses of the MIGs. Either way, we could dive into the jungle and set a course to the DMZ, away from the direct line of travel that they would be watching. Bond watched the track to see if the motorised infantry returned. Abe sighted on the guards once again. I opened my mouth to give him the order and another flight of fighter jets flew across. They disappeared out of sight and I shouted the order to go. Shots cracked out of the sniper rifle and we were up and running. Ahead of us I could see the guards were all down, crumpled into heaps on the ground. We hit the start of the bridge and ran onto the first wooden section. Then the roaring sound came back, the sound I'd hoped and prayed we could avoid with good timing and a little bit of good luck. Whatever else, our luck had run out as a stream of cannon shells sprayed the woodwork.

* * *

Should I become President...I will not risk American lives...by permitting any other nation to drag us into the wrong war at the wrong place at the wrong time through an unwise commitment that is unwise militarily, unnecessary to our security and unsupported by our allies.

John F. Kennedy

MACV Main Headquarters, 137 Pasteur Street, Saigon

Major General Victor H. Krulak, the special assistant for counterinsurgency for the Joint Chiefs of Staff, looked around the smoky room with distaste. He noted that the sole Vietnamese present, Madame Nhu, President Diem's sister in law, was smoking cigarette after cigarette, indicating how nervous she felt. That was surprising, the Dragon Lady normally exuded confidence. Madame Nhu's brother-in-law, Diem had been appointed Prime Minister of Vietnam by her mother's distant cousin, Emperor Bao Dai after the French had been defeated at the Battle of Dien Bien Phu. When French Indochina was dissolved Diem was left in control of South Vietnam and became President. She was regarded as the First Lady of South Vietnam, her mother, a former beauty queen, was South Vietnam's observer at the United Nations and two of her uncles were cabinet ministers. Some said that Diem and Nhu would have invented the word nepotism if it hadn't been invented.

So why was she so nervous? Certainly not with the company present. Colonel Ted Serong, a guerrilla warfare expert who headed the Australian training mission in South Vietnam, General Harkins, the supreme commander in Vietnam and American Ambassador Nolting were all giving optimistic reports about the conduct of the war. If they were to be believed, they were winning. It certainly wasn't a clear picture, but CIA led actions that included organising the Montagnards into fighting units had done well. The Australian Colonel Serong had reported that "the big success story in

Vietnam was the strategic hamlet program and this story has not yet been fully told."

It was clear for everyone to see that offensive operations against the Viet Cong were widespread and were growing steadily in intensity. True, the communists were infiltrating men into the South at an alarming rate, CIA estimated over five hundred a month, although Krulak had seen intelligence that put the figure higher, much higher. Some said that the monthly infiltration average was closer to fifteen hundred men. Chinese heavy weapons, including recoilless rifles and .50 calibre machine guns, were popping up throughout the country. Some of this ordnance had been carried overland through Laos, while other weaponry had been moved either by sea or other routes to South Vietnam through Cambodia.

So it was a mixed picture, but not one to be especially concerned about. Even the ARVN, shocked after the disastrous action at Ap Bac, were regrouping and beginning to show a more aggressive fighting posture that was showing results. No, there was something else. Diem, her brother-in-law, of course. A Catholic, there'd been a great deal of publicity describing how Diem's brutal treatment of the majority Buddhist population had caused the latest outrage. Quang Duc, a seventy three year old Buddhist monk had set fire to himself in the street by the Xa Loi pagoda. The newsmen alerted by the Buddhists covered the event in lurid detail, sending reports and film of the suicide for the world to see. Many of the Vietnamese military were Buddhist, in fact the overwhelming majority, in spite of Diem appointing Catholics to the most senior positions. If Diem fell, of course Madame Nhu, the Dragon Lady, would fall with him. Ambassador Nolting was on record as being vigorously opposed to the Americans becoming involved in any plot to oust the South Vietnamese leadership, including Madame Nhu and her husband Ngo Dinh Nhu. The Dragon Lady would know this through her spies. He shrugged mentally, it was an internal matter and they'd have to resolve it themselves. Krulak just prayed that they weren't aware of how enthusastic some of the Washington people were for a change at the top in South Vietnam.

"Colonel Serong," Madame Nhu said abruptly, "you have reported that the Strategic Hamlets plan now numbers a total of three thousand five hundred villages, is that correct?"

He nodded his head. "It certainly is, Madame. A very successful programme that has denied the enemy access to food and supplies."

"Good. Things have changed, Colonel. My brother-in-law, the President of South Vietnam, now requires the strategic and military emphasis to be switched to internal security. There is no point in defending our country against the communists when the real enemy is already here."

"You mean the Buddhists?" General Krulak asked her.

"That is correct. Their demonstrations are becoming dangerous and rock the very stability that we are fighting for."

And of course, they were not Catholic, Krulak thought. President Diem had effectively raped the population of Buddhists to distribute the plum jobs and plantations to his Catholic cronies. No wonder the Buddhists were up in arms. He sighed.

"Madame Nhu, to shift resources away from the Strategic

Hamlets Program now would be a disaster. You mention that over three thousand of these hamlets are in existence, well, that's true. But my staff reports that barely six hundred are in fact fully operational. The rest balance on a knife edge until they are fully established."

"Fuck the hamlets, General, my brother-in-law wants measures taken to control the Buddhists. Maybe you can put them in hamlets and surround them with barbed wire."

Her eyes were blazing, her voice slashed across the calm of the room, the atmosphere had changed to one of crackling tension. No wonder she was nicknamed the Dragon Lady, Krulak reflected.

"Madame, what you describe is concentration camps, I hardly believe the President wants…"

"I'll tell you what the President wants, General. He wants these heathen priests, these bonzes stopped. If that means putting them all in concentration camps I don't care."

The men in the room looked at each other, embarrassed by her outburst.

"Madame Nhu," General Harkins interceded, "we are fighting the communists from the North, if we dilute our forces to support the President's internal struggles, we'll have no chance of beating the communists. Can President Diem not make some kind of peace with the Buddhists?"

"Peace with those heathens, is that what you are suggesting? Perhaps they are working with the communists, we should treat them all the same, fight them as one enemy."

Ambassador Nolting leaned forward. "The Buddhist populist population of South Vietnam constitutes the majority of your people, Madame. Surely it is unrealistic to expect to be able to contain them all. There really does have to be some kind of dialogue with them," he said.

"Dialogue? I'll give them dialogue, we need to send troops into the monasteries and kill some of these traitors who undermine the lawful authorities. They don't need dialogue, they need the leaders to be taken out and shot. Kill them, kill them all!"

She'd totally lost control, flecks of spittle came out of her beautiful mouth. The door flew open and one of her bodyguards rushed into the room, his hand drawing his weapon. She looked up.

"Get out, get out, you fool. If you want to shoot someone, go find some fucking Buddhist priests."

She stood up. "The Buddhists, they must be dealt with. Perhaps you can send some of your precious bomber aircraft to destroy their monasteries."

"Madame, I hardly think," Nolting said placatingly. But she slashed him down.

"I don't care what you think, Ambassador. The President is threatened, these people should be killed. Kill them!" she shouted as she stormed out. They looked at each other, there was little to add to her tirade.

"Well I guess that screws our South East Asia program," Colonel Serong muttered. He got up and left.

General Krulak turned to Harkins. "General, any news of our people in the North? Washington is interested in the progress of your rescue mission."

Harkins winced. It was now 'his' rescue mission. Well,

that was the way Washington worked. He shook his head.

"Nothing concrete, I'm afraid. Their aircraft was destroyed on the ground, we've had some intelligence that suggests they escaped from Hanoi and were making their way south, but the communists know they're there, of course. I guess it's just a matter of time."

"So you don't hold out any hope?"

Harkins smiled. "There's always hope, who knows, maybe they'll pull it off. But no, I'm not optimistic."

"No chance of sending them any help?"

"Does Washington specifically want me to invade North Vietnam, then?"

Ambassador Nolting looked up sharply. "What, what was that? Did you say what I thought you said?"

Both generals laughed.

"Don't panic, Ambassador," Harkins said, "we've got enough problems in South Vietnam. No, I think the Nhu's want us to widen our war here to include the Buddhist population."

As they walked out, Krulak spoke quietly to Harkins. "I need an answer for Washington, General Harkins, about that rescue mission."

Harkins thought for a moment. "You can tell them that if they're not already dead, they're probably back in custody. Personally, I would think they're dead. Once the Viets destroyed their aircraft, they were finished. Sorry, General Krulak, but that's the truth. They only ever had a slight chance, and that chance has gone."

Krulak nodded and they went out.

In the long history of the world, only a few generations have been

CHAPTER EIGHT

granted the role of defending freedom in its hour of maximum danger. I do not shrink from this responsibility - I welcome it.

John F. Kennedy

"Keep running, faster!" I shouted at them.

But they could see the shells taking huge splinters out of the woodwork, and hear the noise of the three MIG 17s, their Klimov VK-1 engines roaring as they screamed out of their dive ready to turn and bank for a second pass. So far not one of us had been hit, but it was only a matter of time. They'd have time for at least one more pass before we got into cover and their formidable array of cannon would shred us, it was only because we had caught them unawares that they had missed on the first pass. There was the sound of more jet engines and we knew then that it was the end of the road. The thunder of the jet engines mixed with the whoosh of multiple missile launches, yet no missiles hit the bridge. I looked up to see the most wonderful sight I'd ever seen, a flight of four F-102 Delta Daggers, pouring missiles down onto the MIGs. Two were hit immediately and went down trailing smoke and flames. They hit the jungle almost side by side and there had been no ejections, just a pall of black smoke to mark their funeral pyre. The third MIG switched on his afterburners and rocketed north, pursued by two of the F-102s. Then there was an explosion less than five miles away and another plume of black smoke soared over the jungle canopy.

We were so stunned by our miraculous escape that we stood, mouths open, looking up at the sky. Then I remembered the troops that were coming up behind us.

"Run, get across the bridge and under cover, they'll be along any second," I shouted.

We ran off the end of the bridge, skirting the bodies of the machine gun crew and took cover in the jungle to the side of the track. Overhead the F-102s came back, circled for a few moments and roared off, the leader waggled his wings and the back marker did a three hundred and sixty degree roll that I was certain would get him grounded if the flight leader had seen it. Maybe not, fighter pilots were notorious show-offs. But every one of us would gladly have stood their drinks' bills for the next month. I only wished we could have communicated with them, one well aimed missile would have totally destroyed the bridge. With the bridge left standing the enemy would be after us in minutes and they had a vehicle whilst we were on foot.

Paul was checking our map. "The jungle looks bad, Jurgen, it's thick foliage, it'll take us forever to hack through. The track would be faster."

"Faster for them too and they've got the Zil."

A shout from Joe Russo distracted us. "Hey, take a look at this." He was standing next to the boxes we'd seen unloaded from the lorry. We went over and looked at the one he'd opened. Hand grenades, Soviet made, twenty of them. If the other boxes held the same, and it looked as if they did, we had a hundred and twenty small bombs.

"Can you do anything with those on the bridge, Joe?"

"You betcha ass, Jurgen. When those Viets come back they'll be in for a shock."

"Why not blow it when they're on the bridge?" Paul asked. We looked at him, of course, it was the obvious answer. If they were all dead, blown into the river below, there'd be no one to report that we were still at liberty, it could buy us a little time.

"If it doesn't work we'll be sitting ducks, Joe," I said to him.

He grinned. "It'll work, I've done it a few times before."

I nodded. "Let's make it work then."

He started modifying the grenades, linking their fuses together. He had his own electrical detonator and thin cable in his pack and he planted the remote detonator in one of the boxes and we carried them out onto the bridge. Joe climbed over the wooden struts and balanced on the cross beams below the roadway. One by one we passed the boxes down to him and he tied them firmly to the bridge support structure. Lastly, he passed up the cable and we took it to the side of the bridge and out of sight to the trigger that was hidden at the side of the track. Joe climbed back underneath the bridge, taking loops of the cable from us and fixing them to the woodwork out of view, then he crawled back onto the bridge and we ducked into the jungle.   The men had cleared the bodies of the enemy from the bridge and hidden the machine gun, now it all looked innocent. We didn't have long to wait. We all heard the engine of the Zil and then it came into view. They didn't even stop at the start of the bridge, the officer waved to the driver to proceed to our side, obviously he wanted to know where his troops were.   Joe let them get to a point a few feet before the explosives and hit the switch. He was true to his word, the bridge exploded with a huge roar, sending a shock wave that hurtled towards us and almost threw us to the ground. The troops in the lorry never knew what hit them, they went crashing to their doom into the river below, body parts mixed with fragments of metal and wood. Thousands of birds took flight as the jungle all but emptied of wildlife.

We stood up and took a look at the river. There was nothing to be seen, most of the bridge, the lorry and its troops had disappeared into the torrent. Of the bridge itself, all that was left were the wooden stanchions either side.

"Let's move out," I called.

We kept up a good pace down the track, confident that at least for the time being there would be nothing coming behind us. When we stopped for a break Paul checked the map, we were less than ten miles from the DMZ, although we had no way of knowing whether we were being pursued or from which direction the enemy might come. We rounded a bend in the track at the top of a low hill and saw stretching before us the long silver ribbon of the Ben Hay River marking the centre of the DMZ, a strip of land that extended from the Laos border to the coast, roughly three miles either side of the river. We didn't stop, there was a palpable feeling of excitement that surged through our group. We'd done some bitter fighting, had some good luck and some bad luck, but the payoff was staring at us only a few miles away. We started off again and got barely four hundred yards before a stream of machine gun fire spat out towards us. We jumped to the side of the track and kept our heads down while more bullets rattled overhead.

"I doubt that it's North Vietnamese regulars, although it's hard to tell," Paul said quietly. "Probably Cong, they're not very well trained, they could have taken us all if they'd waited a few moments."

I nodded. Abe Woltz had already prepared his rifle and was lying prone, looking for targets. He was almost completely hidden in a clump of bushes. The other men were lying close to the ground within a few yards of where we lay.

"Russo and Beckerman, would you circle around through the jungle and try and get behind them. Are you good to go, Tim?" It wasn't long since he'd taken the injury to his shoulder, but he nodded. "No sweat, I'm good."

"Ok then. See if you can pick them off one by one with the knives or silenced pistols." They waved acknowledgment and crawled away. All we could do now was wait. We lay there for almost half an hour, popping up every few minutes to keep their minds occupied and let them know that we were still pinned down. I knew it was time in which the enemy could be bringing up more reinforcements, but Russo and Beckerman knew their business, they would be as fast as the job allowed.

Abe was still sighting along the track to the estimated positions of the Viets when suddenly two of them leapt out into the open and turned to fire back into the jungle. The sniper picked them both off instantly and they were thrown to the ground. Russo and Beckerman stepped out and waved. We rushed forward as they were pulling the bodies off the track.

"Eight of them, Jurgen," Russo said, "We got them all except for those two that ran out."

"Well done, Joe, you and Tim did a good job. Let's push on to the river." We picked up the pace once more and in less than an hour were standing on the bank of the river. We had arrived in the middle of the DMZ. Not home yet, we still had a long way to go, but we were out of North Vietnam. Technically. The reality was that the communists in Hanoi regarded all of Vietnam as their territory, the government in the South and the Americans were just unwelcome visitors. What wielded authority in this land broken by constant war was the gun and the bomb, the tank and the fighter bomber.

Beckerman came up to me. "Jurgen, how the hell do we cross this river? I can't see any sign of a bridge."

"The bridges were all destroyed, Tim. The communists have tried once or twice to build temporary structures to ferry men and supplies across to the South, but the American and South Vietnamese aircraft always find them and destroy them. We'll need a boat, it shouldn't be a problem. There will certainly be fishermen who make their living from the river, we'll need to buy a passage across. I suggest we head west until we find someone with a boat, we'd better get moving before more Viets turn up with reinforcements."

We picked up our packs once more and pushed on, I led the way back to the high ground so that we could keep alert for the enemy. We travelled for hour after hour, eventually the light faded and we had to make camp, there'd been no sign of any kind of fishing village or boat. I discussed crossing the river on some makeshift raft with Paul, but we concluded that the risk would be too high, we'd be sitting ducks for any Viet that fancied taking a pot shot at us while we slowly crossed.

"There's a village marked on the map several miles to the west, when we cross over we can make our way south to the village of Khe Sahn. There's a Special Forces camp nearby with some kind of an airstrip, those camps always have provision for flying in men and supplies. Johann and Ritter are expecting us to call to be ferried out, they'll bring the C-47 out to pick us up."

"What about the military?" Paul asked. "These are Americans, after all. Why not contact them and get them to arrange transport back to Saigon, why risk our own aircraft?"

"Why indeed? I've asked myself that question a hundred times since we were at Son Tay. They knew we were coming, Paul, there's no doubt about that," I replied.

That night was even more dismal than the night before, we were in sight of friendly territory yet were still inside the danger zone. In the morning we hid all signs of our camp and pushed on. We were increasingly hungry, the food had run out and it started to rain again. It was cold and miserable, but at least the going was easier as there was a clearly marked path alongside the river bank. A river mist was swirling around us that at least partially hid us from enemy surveillance and we all silently thanked whichever Gods we prayed to for that useful cover. Then we saw the village. A typical Vietnamese fishing village with wooden huts that extended down to the river bank and some even overhung the river itself, supported on sticks. On the river several boats sat serenely in the water. I was nominally in charge now and there were no questions when I detailed Abe Woltz to cover us with his rifle, then sent Paul Schuster and Joe Russo on point to check out the village for any signs of the enemy. The rest of us followed at a distance of a hundred yards. We needn't have worried, Schuster and Russo entered the squalid collection of huts, while we lingered outside, and emerged a few minutes later with an elderly Vietnamese.

We followed them into the village, a sad, poverty stricken place. A few men and women emerged from the huts to look at us, then several children. All were ragged and filthy and covered with sores. We managed to make them understand that we wanted to buy passage across the river and when we gathered together a few valuables to show them as payment, they nodded their heads in ready agreement. Paul parted with a folding knife he'd owned for many years and Russo found a pair of gloves he carried in his pack. Jack Bond had a gleaming combat knife to throw into the pot and they seemed happy with the price on offer. I got out my wallet and showed them an American ten dollar bill, but they shook their heads, unable to fathom what it could be. Two of the women brought out some food which we fell on immediately, some kind of foul tasting stew with pieces of fish floating in it. It was the first food we'd tasted in a long time and we ate it ravenously, trying to ignore the rancid aftertaste and the stench coming from the pot. Then we boarded two of their boats and they poled us across. At last, we were in the south, the Republic of South Vietnam. Friendly territory, at least in theory.

We followed a direct route towards the Special Forces base at Khe Sanh, I estimated we were within two or three miles of the base when a soldier stepped onto the path.

"Halt! Stop there and identify yourselves."

We breathed a sigh of relief at the American accent. Tim Beckerman pushed to the front and explained who we were and where we were headed. As soon as he heard Beckerman's explanation he lowered his rifle, simultaneously three more American soldiers stepped out of the jungle, all Green Berets. One of them, a corporal, carried a backpack radio with a long aerial.

"Corporal, would it be possible to patch us through to Saigon on your radio?" I asked him. He looked at the master sergeant in charge who nodded.

"I can get you through to anywhere in the world if you like, well, normally anyway. What did you have in mind?"

I told him that I needed to make contact with my operational base in Saigon, at Tan Son Nhat Airfield. He thought for a moment.

"Will they be monitoring their radio, do you think?"

I nodded. "Certain to be, they'll be waiting to hear from us."

"In that case we'll give it a try." He took details of our call sign in Saigon and warmed up the radio set. In less than a minute he was through to Khe Sanh and five minutes later I heard the voice of Johann Drexler.

"Jurgen, it's good to hear your voice, we were beginning to worry."

"They've been trying to kill me for a long time, Johann, they haven't succeeded yet. Any word on Helene?"

"Nothing yet, Jurgen, sorry."

"Never mind, I want a pick up. Is the C-47 operational?"

"She's all serviced and ready to go, Ritter is waiting to fly out? Is this to bring you all home?"

"It is, Johann. I don't want to involve MACV, they don't seem to be very secure. Too many things have gone wrong with this mission and I don't want any more accidents.

"Where exactly are you?" he asked. I hesitated. This was an unencrypted radio channel and the Viets were sure to be listening in. I had the map coordinates of the airfield supplied to me by the radio operator, I had an idea.

"Johann, here are the coordinates. Remember last time, my date of birth?"

"Yes, I do, Jurgen. It's..."

"Do not say it over the air, this time I want you to subtract the day, month and year from the figures I give you, that's all. That will be the map coordinates for where we are."

I gave him a set of figures. "Is that clear to you, Johann?" The radio was quiet for twenty seconds, and then it crackled back into life.

"I've got it, I'll make a start straight away. We'll see you in a few hours."

"Very good, Hoffman out."

I handed the microphone back to the operator and

thanked him.

"That's no problem..." He didn't finish, toppling into my arms as a red hole appeared in the middle of his head. I heard the shots almost immediately, several of them went through his radio as he fell, smashing it beyond repair. A burst of gunfire crashed through the jungle and we dived for the ground. Beckerman was hit, riddled by a machine gun burst, and then the rest of us were in cover. We looked around for targets, but there was nothing to see, whoever had organised the ambush knew their business. All was quiet for a few minutes, almost as if whoever had fired on us had disappeared, but of course they hadn't. Joe Russo peeked out from behind the log he was sheltering behind and ducked back as a volley of machine gun fire rattled around him. He turned to speak to me.

"Any ideas, Jurgen? They seem to have us pinned down, we don't know how many of them there are, or what weaponry they have."

I shook my head. "None whatsoever, they've caught us with our pants down," I replied. I could have kicked myself. Although these were Special Forces, Paul and I were the old Vietnam hands, we'd thought ourselves relatively safe when the American Special Forces had appeared and for once I'd neglected to put out point guards. But once was all it took.

"It's a long time until darkness falls so we need to work out how to hit back quickly." I squinted from the side of the tree I was sheltering behind, my flesh crawled as I waited for the sound of a hail of gunfire. What I heard was far worse, the whistle of a mortar.

"Incoming," I shouted and threw myself flat on the

ground.

I hoped the others had followed suit, the bomb exploded with a shattering roar that stripped much of the foliage from the trees. I could hear screaming, they'd certainly hit one or more of us. Then more mortar rounds started exploding, one after the other. I could see Russo and Schuster, but of the others there was no sign. After about fifteen mortar bombs ceased as quickly as they had started. There was a silence for a couple of minutes, then the electric 'click' as a loudhailer was switched on.

"American soldiers, we know who you are. You must surrender immediately or we will continue sending in our mortar bombs until you are all dead. If you surrender you will become prisoners and will not be badly treated. You have five minutes to decide. Then we will continue firing. That is all."

Paul and Joe Russo crawled over to where I was sheltering.

"Any thoughts, Jurgen?" Paul asked me. I smiled. "I think we're in trouble, my friend. We know they have mortars, but the real question is how many of them are there? If there are only a dozen we might be able to do something, but if they're in company strength or more, we could be better off surrendering." They both winced.

"Surrender to these fuckers, are you serious?" Russo said with a grimace. "You said they'd hang us from the nearest tree and gut us too. Personally I'd sooner go down fighting."

"Point taken, Joe. Do we know how many of our people there are left?" I asked him.

"One of those mortar rounds hit those three Green Berets, a direct hit, must have shredded them, poor bastards."

I reflected that it was too late for them to learn lessons about posting adequate sentries.

"What about our people?"

"Abe Woltz is okay, he's behind those trees about ten yards away. Jack Bond is on the other side of him, as far as I know he's unhurt too. You know about Beckerman."

"I know." I had an idea, the chances of success were remote, but anything was better than nothing. "I need to get to Abe and have a word with him, can you cover me?"

They both looked puzzled, but nodded. I crawled away quickly and they kept a sharp eye for any enemy, but there was no more gunfire. I reached Abe and explained it all to him. Jack Bond looked sceptical. "It's a bit of a long shot, Hoffman. Not much chance of bringing it off," he said.

"Jack, I totally agree with you. If you have a better idea, now is the time to spit it out." I waited for him to respond, but he was silent.

"Well?" He shook his head. "I guess not."

"You'd better be ready then, about two minutes and I'll tell the Viets we're surrendering," I whispered.

"We'll be ready," Abe said. I crawled away, back to Paul and Joe. I explained my plan to them, we went over the details and then I stood up, threw down my rifle and shouted that we were surrendering.

"All of you, come out and throw down your weapons," a strongly accented voice called out.

This was the moment, would they fall for it? Joe and Paul warily stood up and tossed their assault rifles to one side, then Jack Bond stood up and followed suit. They waited patiently, their hands in the air. Around us, a dozen Viets came into view, their rifles pointed at us. Was that all of them, I wondered, did this include the mortar crews, or were there more waiting under cover of the trees? Then a man stepped into view who was obviously their leader. He wore no badges of rank, but his clothes, unlike those of his men, were of much better quality. A smart olive green military shirt and matching trousers, all immaculately pressed. I wondered how the hell he kept things looking like that in the jungle guerrilla war these people were fighting. His boots looked new, high, lace up jump boots, almost certainly American airborne issue. He carried a Soviet automatic, a Makarov, this guy was much too conscious of his position to carry an assault rifle like his men. On his head he wore the solar topee of the North Vietnamese Army, around his waist a highly polished Sam Browne leather belt with a pistol holster. And on his face the sneering smile of the bully, one who knows that he is about to deliver a good kicking to his victims and is relishing every moment of it.

"My name is Phan Trong. I am the People's Commissar for the Khe Sanh region. Is this all of you, only four?"

"My name is Jurgen Hoffman, Commissar. What you see is all of the survivors of your attack, the rest are lying dead in the jungle," I replied, allowing a depth of bitterness into my voice. He smiled broadly.

"You Americans think you can come to my country and walk unmolested, but you are mistaken. Wherever we find you, we will harass and kill you all until you are driven into the sea," he said.

He peered suspiciously at my tattered jungle greens. "I

do not recognise your uniform, which American unit are you from?" he asked.

"I am not a soldier, Commissar. I run a small airline, our aircraft crashed and I was leading these men to safety," I replied. I could see him thinking. "So you are a spy," he said abruptly, "anyone carrying a weapon out of uniform inside a war zone is to be shot as a spy. Those are the orders of Comrade Giap."

"I am not a spy, Commissar, I am a pilot. This is not a war zone, it is the Republic of South Vietnam and I am not American, I am German." His eyes shot up. "German! Where have you come from? From the North, yes?"

I looked at him steadily. "Yes," I replied.

"So, you're the ones we were told might be coming this way. You illegally entered The People's Republic of North Vietnam and helped convicted war criminals to escape. You!"

His voice was harsh and withering, but his eyes gleamed with satisfaction. "My orders are to apprehend you and sentence you all to death. Have you anything to say?" he asked.

"Do you mean about the fairness of communist justice?" I said. He didn't understand my sarcasm. "Very well, comrades," he shouted, "prepare to execute the prisoners."

He looked at me again, obviously waiting for signs of terror, the fear that would sate his bullying lusts. I ignored him and looked at his men, lining up in some semblance of a firing party.

"You men, get into line," he barked at us. "Fuck you," I replied.

His eyes bulged with rage and astonishment that his

victim has dared to insult him. He stepped forward and his hand swung across to punch me in the face but I was ready for him and I grabbed him and twisted around so that he was between me and his men. It was the signal for Abe to open fire, we had other arrangements if I couldn't grab their leader, but this was the best chance. As the startled Viets swung their weapons up to point at me, too confused and frightened to fire in case they hit the Commissar, Woltz fired his first silenced shot. It was an amazing pieced of shooting, the soft sounds went unnoticed in the jungle, especially when the Viets started shouting for orders, their frightened voices echoing along the track. But it made no difference, it was as if they had been hit by some deadly gas, they had no idea where it was coming from. One by one they dropped where they stood, twelve dead Viets until there was only one, Commissar Trong. As I relieved him of his pistol, he started to shake violently with shock and terror, as is the way with bullies all over the world.

"How...?" was all he could gasp. He went even paler when Abe stood up, almost like a ghost, covered in jungle greenery so that it was like a jungle spirit that suddenly sprung up where nothing had been before. A jungle spirit with a hot, silenced sniper rifle. I ignored him.

"We'd better destroy those mortars, I don't want the Viets coming to retrieve them and using them again. Get any weapons and ammunition you need from the dead bodies, then smash or destroy anything we can't carry. Commissar," I turned to the shocked Viet, "how far is it to the Special Forces base at Khe Sanh?"

"I, I, I, can't give information, it is..." He stopped when I screwed the pistol barrel, his pistol barrel, into his balls.

"Commissar, you've seen what happened to your men. If you want to join them, that's fine with me. If you prefer to come with us as a prisoner, I need to know how far it is to the Khe Sanh Special Forces base." It only took another couple of minutes of coaxing. His world had been destroyed and like all bullies, when his power had evaporated so had all his strength and bluster.

"It is approximately three kilometres," he said abruptly, "the track forks one kilometre further south, you take the right fork. The Special Forces base and airfield will be visible to you almost straight away." That made sense, a clear field of fire and a flat base of operations on which to position a remote airstrip. I gestured to Jack Bond.

"Tie his hands, would you, Sergeant. We'll hand him over when we get there." Bond nodded and rummaged in his pack for some electrical cable to secure the Commissar. I looked around at the remnants of the short action. It was sickening, the twelve Viets lay close to each other, reminding me almost of old photographs of the First World War, when men were mown down in lines as they left the trenches. I also recalled the Duke of Wellington's famous quote after Waterloo, 'Next to a battle lost, nothing is so sad as a battle that has been won'. Sad indeed.

The Americans were shredded heaps of flesh after the mortar hits, unknown to us and unnamed. We would need to collect their tags and I asked Abe Woltz to do the job. Beckerman's body lay where it had fallen and I asked Paul Schuster and Joe Russo to take his tags and bury him. The

Viets we left where they were, their own people would be along to deal with them soon enough, they usually came. I remembered battles from the Indochina War when we would leave a battlefield with a hundred or more Viet casualties, the following morning they would invariably have disappeared. It wasn't altruism, they merely hated to let anyone know that the invincible communist fighters had suffered so badly, it was bad for morale.

We advanced along the track, forked to the right and before long we were walking towards the barbed wire fence that marked the boundary of Khe Sahn Special Forces camp. I thought of the idiotic French policy of small, armed outposts, and how each had slowly fallen to the Viet Minh forces, finally ending with the disastrous defeat at Dien Bien Phu. How long would it be before this camp was finally abandoned I wondered, and how many bloody battles would be fought until that day dawned?

Half an hour later we went into the radio shack. The operator had AFN radio tuned in, it was playing 'Hey! Baby', the Bruce Channel smash hit. The operator turned it down and shortly I was on the radio to Tan Son Nhat, talking to Johann. Ritter von Schacht was almost sober, which was a miracle, and they were already fuelling and pre-flighting the C-47 to fly out and pick us up. We could expect their arrival within four hours, maybe five.

Most importantly, the report from MACV about Helene was positive, she was showing signs of responding and had regained consciousness. I thanked all the Gods for the news, it made everything worth it. We walked out of the radio shack and while we waited, the Special Forces made us welcome and treated us to a meal of C rations. It was delicious. At last, I thought, we were going home. How many men had died to get us here, to effect the rescue of the two Americans? Probably hundreds, we would never know. And there were of course questions to ask when we reached Saigon, the answers would be very interesting.

* * *

The ARVN soldiers themselves are good fighters, but they are very underpaid, and poorly led. Their morale is poor, and this brings about the biggest problem in the Army AWOLS [soldiers absent without leave] and deserters. The Government just doesn't look after their soldiers well enough to keep them happy. All soldiers' housing is terrible, dependents are not thought of in the least - they have no provisions for getting pay home when the husband is off on a big operation, maybe for over a month. Next - poor leadership. The commanders of the Army units are usually inexperienced, and only worried about staying alive, and getting a soft job back in Saigon somewhere. The high level commanders are more worried about political things than military considerations. District chiefs are the same way - they usually plan and go out on as few operations as possible, mostly worried about keeping the province chief happy from a political viewpoint. Nobody is really sure who to support - maybe tomorrow there will be another coup and the guy they supported will be thrown out. It's all highly confusing, but one thing is sure - it really hurts the military effort.

Captain James B Lincoln, American Advisor to ARVN

"William, what's the word from the Palace? These problems with the ARVN are not getting any better, have you been able to talk to the President?" Harkins looked across at Colby, the Chief of Station and someone who generally claimed to have influence with Diem through the President's brother, Ngo Dinh Nhu. Since 1960 the communist insurgency had been growing substantially, yet Diem and his cronies seemed to regard it as a uniquely American problem while they concentrated their efforts on controlling the country's very unhappy Buddhist majority.

"We've been doing a lot of work in that direction, General. The Strategic Hamlets Program is doing well and after that last disaster at Ap Bac the ARVN are working hard to regain their reputation."

"Christ, what reputation? They damned well need to do something, Bill. Jesus, what a mess that was."

"It wasn't all ARVN, General, there were some of our own guys there too," Colby retorted sharply. Harkins looked at him keenly. "What are you saying, that our boys can't fight?"

Colby sighed. "No, General, not at all. Our soldiers are amongst the finest in the world, well equipped and motivated. No, what I'm saying is politics, a question of where we're headed with this. Who is leading the army, what are their objectives, stopping the communists or the Buddhists?" Harkins interrupted.

"Christ, I hope you're not suggesting we take on the Buddhist population of South Vietnam too, Bill?"

Colby laughed. "No, I'm not. But why are we really here? I recall Eisenhower's famous quote, 'Finally, you have broader considerations that might follow what you would call the "falling domino" principle. You have a row of dominoes set up, you knock over the first one, and what will happen to the last one is the certainty that it will go over very quickly. So you could have a beginning of a disintegration that would have the most profound influences.' Is that what these people are to us, just a bunch of dominoes or are they valuable allies? We need to streamline the army leadership, to help them establish good government and infrastructure and protect them from the communists."

"Is that right?" Harkins sneered. "I thought MACV was here to fight and more importantly win a war. Am I correct, the M part of the title of my command does stand for military?"

"Well, yes, of course," Colby said hastily, "but…"

"So forget the dominoes, forget the cosy fireside chats with your friends in the Presidential Palace, I need more cooperation from the ARVN, you must make it your number one priority."

Harkins sat back. He rarely raised his voice, but the smooth Ivy League man seemed determined to make the simplest of matters more complicated than they needed to be.

"General, I think you overestimate my influence with the Palace," Colby continued warily.

"Even the influence of the Palace over the ARVN is not necessarily as, er, straightforward as we would hope." Harkins brought his mind to sharp focus.

"What have you heard? That sounds ominous, is there any chance of a coup?" he asked.

The CIA man hesitated. "I'd be lying to you if I said no

chance at all, there has been talk. But overall, I'm hopeful that things will stabilise along lines that are mutually beneficial to all of us."

What the fuck did that mean, Harkins thought?

"Have you debriefed your men, the two guys that were rescued from the North?"

Colby nodded. "Yes, we have General. Sadly, they were caught before they achieved anything useful to us, so it was something of a wasted effort."

Did he mean mounting the mission, or bringing back the two Americans? Again, Harkins wondered what went on in that Machiavellian mind. Almost certainly nothing that wasn't to the direct benefit of William E Colby.

"And the rescue party, the two Germans and the Special Forces guys?" Harkins continued.

"Well, we've had a report that they may have crossed the DMZ, but we're not certain."

Harkins finally lost his cool. "Colby, listen to me. You're not sure about anything, are you? About the politics and intentions of the government, the ARVN, even our own people. Could I ask you to come better prepared to our next meeting, or do I need to arrange for someone who can be better prepared?"

The two men looked at each other, both swallowing the anger that they each felt at the other's perceived inadequacies. Finally Colby looked away, intimidated by the iron resolve of the soldier.

"I'll do as you ask, General, I'll get my people on it right away."

Harkins nodded, stood up and stalked out of the room, startling his two aides who were waiting outside the door, and stomped towards the exit.

CHAPTER NINE

*Once upon a time our traditional goal in war and can anyone doubt
that we are at war? - was victory. Once upon a time we were proud
of our strength, our military power. Now we seem ashamed of it.
Once upon a time the rest of the world looked to us for leadership.
Now they look to us for a quick handout and a fence-straddling
international posture.*

Barry M. Goldwater, 1962

The most welcome sight of all greeted us several hours later
when we first heard the drone of the engines, then our C-47
came into view. Whoever was flying it was an expert, it could
only be Ritter. It banked neatly and flared in for a landing on
the tiny, rough airstrip. Johann would have needed at least one
pass to line up correctly and even then would have bounced
several times when he made contact with the ground. The
aircraft stopped and

the side door slid open, framing Ritter von Schacht in the

doorway. The piratical former Luftwaffe airman stood there, as ever his missing eye covered by the black patch that many of us had sometimes wondered whether it was assumed, but none would dare to ask him to remove it so that we could check. Johann appeared alongside him, pushed out a boarding ladder and the two men climbed down. I ran up and shook hands with Johann, and then Ritter literally hugged me, careful to keep his cigarette in its holder to one side.

"Jurgen, my friend, how are you?"

"How am I? You old bastard, we've been shot at and chased the length of Vietnam and you ask how am I?" Paul was embracing Johann, the relief we felt at getting back to our own people was beyond belief.

"Ritter, I've arranged for some fuel to be supplied to get us back, I'll get them loading it straight away and we can take off again."

"What? He looked dismayed. "Don't I get a chance to look at the nightlife, I've never been here before, to Khe Sahn. I need to find a bar."

"Time for that when we get back to Saigon, my friend, for the time being we just want to get out of here," I laughed. He sighed heavily. "As you wish, my friend."

A number of soldiers were rolling fuel drums across the flat ground towards us, Ritter went towards them and started bellowing at them to hurry up.

Within half an hour the aircraft had been refuelled and was ready to go. We climbed aboard, those of us left alive, the Special Forces, Abe Woltz, Joe Russo and Jack Bond. Then Paul Schuster and finally I shook hands with the base commander and closed the door. Ritter and Johann were already running up the engines and doing their final checks, less than a minute later and before I had a chance to strap in, the aircraft was rattling across the strip and took to the air. I went forward and checked that everything was good with Johann and Ritter, than I went aft and found a soft canvas tarpaulin that made a useful bed. I lay down and within seconds was fast asleep. The sound of the engine note altering woke me and I looked out of the cabin window to see the late afternoon landscape of Saigon appearing before me. I went forward to where Ritter was talking to the tower, in the background I could hear the sound of the radio playing 'The Lion Sleeps Tonight'. I put on a spare headset and listened to the familiar cheery voice of Nguyen Cam Le manning the tower as usual at Tan Son Nhat.

"Hey guys, where have you popped up from, you been on a mission to the North, dropping a bomb on Ho Chi Minh's bedroom?"

"Ritter laughed. "Ja, one day, my friend and we'll take you with us. Do we have clearance to land?"

"You sure do, winds are north easterly, speed ten knots, visibility is clear to two thousand metres, patchy cloud at five thousand metres, and it's a nice day here in Saigon. Come straight in, traffic is clear."

Ritter turned to me. "He's a good guy, that Nguyen Cam Le, hates the commies."

"Does he?" I nodded. He looked at me curiously. "Have you got some kind of a problem with Le?" he asked. I shook my head. "I don't know, maybe not. He seems friendly enough."

He focussed on flying the aircraft as the strip at Tan Son Nhat came into view. Expertly he trimmed the aircraft for landing, throttling back, gear down, flaps down and a smooth bank into final approach. Soon we touched down, a feather light landing. Ritter taxied us across to our company hangar and we disembarked, grateful to be back on friendly territory again. Or was it friendly, I had my suspicions? We shut the aircraft down, secured the ground anchors and went inside to the office where I found a bottle of Jack Daniels. We all toasted our safe return, the three Special Forces soldiers, Jack Bond, Joe Russo and Abe Woltz. Paul and I poured each other a hefty shot, Johann poured a modest glass and Ritter grabbed the bottle and literally poured it down his throat. It was a moment to savour, yet I stopped them for a moment and proposed a toast to those who had not made it back, Cady and Beckerman.

Almost immediately the telephone rang, it was MACV Saigon. Johann answered it, and then handed the phone to Jack Bond. We couldn't help but overhear his side of the conversation.

"Yes, Sir, we're fine, Russo, Woltz and myself. No, Sir, Captain Cady was killed, Beckerman too. You want us now? Right, we'll be ready. Mr Hoffman? Sure thing."

He handed the phone to me. "It's MACV, they want you." I picked up the phone.

"Hoffman here." I heard a crisp, military voice at the other end.

"This is General Harkin's office, Mr Hoffman, he wants you here right away. Could you come with the car we're sending for the other men?"

I had a deep, sinking sensation in my stomach. For every waking moment over the past few days I had wondered about Helene, would she survive, would the baby survive? "Is it about my wife, Helene, has she taken a turn for the worse?"

There was a hesitation and I died a thousand deaths in that short space of time, I felt myself growing dizzy again, the room going dark. "Your wife, Sir? No, I'm not aware of that situation. The General wants to discuss your recent mission to the North."

I let out the breath I was holding, it was to be a debriefing, for God's sake, I had to know about Helene. "Who am I speaking to, soldier?"

"Er, this is Captain Jane, Sir. I'm one of General Harkin's aides."

"Well, listen to me, Captain. I have to have some information on my wife's condition, I want you get that for me now. You do know she's in a military hospital stateside?"

"Er, yes, Sir. I do. I'll get onto that as soon as I can." I nearly lost it then. "Captain, if the General wants to debrief me you'd better make sure I have that up to date information when I get there, otherwise he can wait until you do. Is that clear?"

"Yes, Sir, I'll contact Washington right now."

"Thank you, Captain, I'll speak to you when I arrive. Give me a short time to grab a shower and change, when is the car due to collect us?"

"He just left, Sir, about fifteen minutes, I'd guess."

"Well he'll have to wait, see you later, Captain."

I hung up, they could wait. For a few moments I felt my

mind blank with the tension of the mission, the worry over Helene and the task I still had to achieve in front of me. I pulled myself together and finished my drink, thanked Ritter and Johann and asked the soldiers to wait while I changed. Ritter left to drive back to Saigon, I ran over to my damaged bungalow and found some clean clothes. I took them back to the hangar, showered in the basic facilities we had there and felt better with clean clothes on, chinos, a button down shirt and a pair of leather deck shoes.

The vehicle from MACV, a Willys jeep, was already waiting with the three Americans on board, I jumped in and found a cramped space on the back seat and we roared off to Saigon. The Willys pulled up inside the gates of 137 Pasteur Street and we climbed out and went in. I was ushered up the stairs and into the office of General Paul Harkins, the three Special Forces men were separated and led to another room, which surprised me. Inside the office were Harkins, a captain who I assumed to be his aide Jane and Miles Anderson. Harkins came forward, his arm outstretched.

"Mr Hoffman, my congratulations on your escape from the North."

"Thank you, General, but I explained to Captain Jane that I needed an update on my wife before I could be debriefed." He smiled. "Captain Jane has checked with Washington, she's doing well, the baby is safe and the surgeon expects her to make a complete recovery." He nodded to the Captain.

"Yes, as the General says, she's looking good. Their best guess is she will be okay to be flown back in about two more weeks."

"Thank you, Captain," I said to him. I felt a huge weight lifted off my shoulders. "Now, how can I help you, General?"

"Tell me about the mission, Mr Hoffman, especially anything that may be useful to us for future operations." I told them everything, except for the parts that I didn't want them to know just yet.

"So you think we have a traitor, here in Saigon?" Harkins asked. I nodded. "At least one, General. They knew we were coming, if they'd been better organised we wouldn't have got away with it."

"Any ideas, any names you have in mind?" he asked. I hesitated. "Miles, how's your leg?" I asked the CIA officer. They all looked startled at the sudden change of subject.

"My leg?" he asked in surprise.

"Yes, your leg, the one that was broken during your capture in the North, along with the cracked ribs. Hard interrogation, as I remember, that's what you said." He suddenly looked wary. "Yeah, well, it's starting to ease, still a bit painful, but yeah, it's not too bad."

"Show us, Miles."

"What?"

"Show us the leg, the broken leg. Maybe we should talk to the medic that fixed it for you, who did you see?" I asked him. "Right, it was one of our CIA guys," he finally said.

General Harkins was looking around suspiciously. "What's going on here, Hoffman? Why are you asking Mr Anderson about his leg?"

I didn't take my eyes from Miles Anderson. "General, give me a moment, will you? My reasons will become obvious once we can see the damage to his leg." Harkins hadn't got to where he was without being as sharp as a tack. He understood immediately.

"Miles, show us the leg, would you?" he asked him.

Anderson looked around the office, then shrugged and pulled the leg of his trousers up for us to see the dressing. "Satisfied?" He said with a smirk.

"Why isn't it in a cast, Miles? Broken legs need to be in a cast. Take off the bandage and let's have a look," I said. "Fuck you, Hoffman, I'm not taking off the dressing for anyone, you included," he said defiantly.

"Take off the dressing, Mr Anderson," Harkins said icily. Anderson looked around the room, I'd seen that look before, the look of a trapped animal, the most dangerous of the species. He bent to remove the dressing with one hand and I saw his other hand reaching under his jacket. He was much too slow, I'd been waiting for him to do exactly that. I took two quick steps across to him and reached under his coat and removed his pistol, a snub nosed Colt .38 revolver, before he had the chance to pull it. Harkins picked up the phone and called in the MPs, while Jane and I held the CIA man. Four burly soldiers with steel helmets and clubs drawn bustled into the office and at Harkins' orders, took over holding Anderson while I removed the dressing on his leg, then took off his shirt. No bruises, no broken leg, no cracked ribs. Harkins looked grim.

"So you're saying that Anderson is the traitor?" I nodded. "I am, General. He's been passing information to the communists about my mission, God knows how many other missions before this one."

"But why, why did he do it?" Anderson smirked at me. "That's bullshit, Hoffman. Just because I exaggerated a couple of injuries to look a little bit brave doesn't make me a traitor."

"That's true," Harkins said.

"Yes, it is General. But if you question his lover, you might find a different story."

"His lover, who the hell is she?" he asked. Anderson has gone white, the smirk fading rapidly from his face. "You mean he." I replied. "Nguyen Cam Le, the tower controller from Tan Son Nhat."

"But I've met Nguyen Cam Le and he hates the commies."

I smiled. "Really? If you check into his story I think you'll find it's the biggest load of bullshit you've ever been forced to swallow, General. He's a communist sleeper, prepared by Hanoi and fed into the system to do exactly what he's done, spy on your military. What better job could he have other than the man with access to every single take-off and departure from Tan Son Nhat? There've been so many leaks lately, everything points to him, especially with his relationship to this traitor. Think about it, the air traffic controller for Tan Son Nhat and a senior CIA officer."

"But that's crazy, Le's not even a woman, he's a man..." He tailed off as it all started to fit together, the awful treachery. "Jesus Christ. Are you a homosexual, Miles?"

The CIA man slumped. The way Harkins had said it almost made me laugh, as if that was by far the greater betrayal. Personally, I'd known a number of queers in the Foreign Legion during the 1950's, even in the SS during the Second

World War, despite the awful penalties that Hitler insisted on if they were caught. I couldn't give a damn about their sexuality, but I knew that not all men were quite as liberal and Harkins was probably less inclined than most to make allowances. A story had gone around when he first took over in Vietnam that when he was commandant of cadets and head of the tactical department at West Point, he was informed that there was a group of cadets, mainly among the football team, who were involved in a cheating ring. Harkins had made it plain that he felt that the behaviour was not in line with his vision of the academy. In a controversial decision he asked the cadets to gather information about the cheating. Eventually a formal inquiry was held and ninety cadets were dismissed from the academy, some of those had not participated in the cheating but knew of it and had not reported it, which was considered a breach of the Cadet Honor Code, 'a cadet will not lie, cheat, steal, or tolerate those who do'.

A true hardass, for whom homosexuality was a breach of every honour code known to man. I almost felt sorry for Anderson, but only almost, he had done his best to get us killed.

"Take this man to the cells," he ordered the MPs. "Then get an arrest warrant for Nguyen Cam Le, the tower controller from Tan Son Nhat. I want him brought in for interrogation, we'll check out their stories properly. Let me know when you've picked him up," he ordered. The MPs saluted and dragged out the hapless CIA officer.

"Jesus Christ, I can't believe it," Harkins said, "one of our own people, a CIA officer, this could be messy. Any idea how long it's been going on?" I shook my head. "None, but

I would assume the worst."

"Damn, you heard about Colonel Vann?"

"The advisor to Colonel Huynh Van Cao, the ARVN commander?" I remembered speaking to Colonel Vann over the radio when I had overflown Ap Bac with Anderson and Goldberg during the battle.

"Yeah, him. Vann started to criticise the progress of the war, MACV and myself especially. He even attempted involve the press with the supposed problems and went so far as to talk to New York Times reporter David Halberstam. I'm having Vann removed from his advisor position and sent home. Now we've got this, it's a fucking mess."

I made sympathetic noises. In truth, I thought the Americans were just as doomed as the French had been ten years earlier with corruption on a grand scale, theft, criminal gangs and nepotism. The communists seemed to have few of these problems, they simply shot anyone who didn't agree with them. Maybe they had a point.

Then the phone rang, Anderson had got away. Apparently he'd seized a gun from an unwary guard and shot his way out, leaving two dead and one wounded MP in his wake. Harkins erupted in rage, barking orders over the phone and I thought it time to leave. I said I'd call back the following day, and then left and went to a bar for a meal and something to drink. As I sat eating, I remembered the old French proverb, 'plus ça change, plus c'est la même chose'. The more it changes, the more it's the same thing. I finished up and got a taxi back to Tan Son Nhat, with Anderson on the loose I felt vaguely uneasy and wanted to check that everything was secure.

When I walked into our hangar I should have known that something was wrong, it was silent when normally Johann would have been pottering around fixing some piece of machinery. But as I reached for the light I felt a piece of metal pressed to my head.

"Turn on the light, Hoffman, then put your hands up." It was Anderson. I did as he said, when the hangar was flooded in light I saw the Johann's body lying in a pool of blood on the shabby office carpet. Paul Schuster was tied to a chair, his mouth gagged with a piece of rag. He was covered by Nguyen Cam Le, the air traffic controller, who was holding an American Colt .45 automatic pistol, the same as the one Anderson had pressed to my head.

"You've killed Johann," I said coldly. It wasn't a question. Anderson giggled, it sounded strange.

"He wouldn't cooperate so I had to put him down. Your friend Schuster will go the same way if you don't do as we say."

"So you want a flight out of here?"

"You'd better believe it, buddy. The sooner the better, so you'd better get your aircraft cranked up and ready to go."

"Where to?" I asked him. "I'll need to request clearance and file a flight plan."

Le nodded. "Yes, Miles, that is correct, it is the proper procedure."

"We're heading north, the CIA man said. "Tell them Hue."

"We won't make it before nightfall, they won't believe me," I said firmly, "you'll need to choose somewhere more local." They conversed between themselves in low tones. I imagined their actual destination would be Hanoi, where they would be treated as heroes. The trouble was, they weren't getting to Hanoi, not now, not ever, not in my aircraft.

"I need to check Paul and make sure he's ok," I said to Miles. He nodded.

I went and looked Paul over. He couldn't speak but his eyes spoke volumes. They raked to the right, over to a battered old couch we had in the office. Behind it there stood one of the AK47s we'd brought back from the North, taken off one of the Viets we'd killed in the last action. As far as I knew, it was fully loaded. Paul managed to convey to me that he would create a diversion, at least I hoped I'd read him correctly. Then I stood up to the side of the couch. Miles and Le carried on talking, and then Paul started to groan. At first, they ignored him, but I shouted at them that he was choking and couldn't breathe. They looked at him suspiciously, Miles went over to check him out while Le covered the office with his automatic. I walked over to stand next to Paul while Miles checked him out, then when Anderson gave me an impatient look I moved to one side, behind the couch.

I squinted at them, they were both still checking on Schuster, Miles had removed his gag. Paul was giving a command performance, moaning and groaning, it was now or never. I scooped up the Kalashnikov, flipped off the safety, aimed at Le and pulled the trigger. The blast literally tore him apart, he was thrown to the floor in bloody, bleeding shreds. Miles whirled around, bringing up his own Colt. Before he could pull the trigger I emptied the magazine into his body, sending him spiralling to the ground to join his lover and fellow traitor in death. Then the hangar was silent, just a wisp of smoke curling out of the barrel. Both bodies were totally still. I released Paul and he immediately went to look at Johann, and then shook his head.

"The bastards caught us unawares, poor Johann, he tried to fight back but he was an engineer, not a soldier. They shot him down like an animal. I knew what they wanted and hoped you'd see the AK47."

"I never thought I'd be so happy to see a Russian assault rifle again, Paul," I said. He nodded. "Me neither. But it was poetic justice, a communist gun to kill two communist traitors."

The telephone was still working and I used it to let MACV headquarters know what had happened and that the hunt for Anderson and Le was over. Half an hour later a convoy of vehicles drew up outside the hangar and a platoon of MPs stormed in and took charge of the bodies. Then General Harkins came through the door with a civilian.

"Mr Hoffman, are you ok?" he asked anxiously. "Yes, General. Sadly, my engineer was killed by Anderson and Le."

"I'm sorry to hear that. Gentlemen, this is Mr Colby, he takes care of certain interests here in Saigon for the United States government." I'd seen Colby once at a party when he was pointed out to me as the CIA Chief of Station. It was inevitable that he would be called in to clear up after Miles Anderson. We shook hands.

"Mr Hoffman, your engineer was killed by the Vietnamese traitor Le, no one else was involved," he said. "Let me assure you that the United States government will look unfavourably at anyone who suggests otherwise."

It was nothing new, I'd seen it happen countless times, the cover up to protect people's reputations. They called it politics, fighting soldiers called it bullshit. "And Miles Anderson?"

"He was killed while bravely trying to arrest the communist traitor, Nguyen Cam Le." We were silent for a moment while I tried to contain my rage. Johann was dead, yet all this bureaucrat could think about was covering his ass. Then I forced myself to calm down. Without doubt, Colby could cause trouble for my operations in Vietnam. Paul and I needed to run the airline and besides, I had a wife to worry about and a baby due, hopefully. I made myself a promise that if ever I got the opportunity I'd get some kind of payback for what happened to Johann, but how I would ever do it I had no idea. In the meantime, life had to go on. These people held the fate of my livelihood and my wife's health firmly in their greasy hands. It was not a time to make waves.

"Yeah, ok, I hear you." I turned away from him, Paul gave me a bemused look but I shrugged, what could we do? We couldn't fight the whole U.S. government.

"Hoffman, we need a word," General Harkins said form behind me. I turned around just as a team of medics came into the office and started to remove the bodies.

"Could you give us a few minutes, General," I replied. I didn't wait for a reply, Paul and I went to Johann and gently closed his eyelids. Then we covered him with the best blanket we could find, a thick woollen rug that Helene had bought one winter for when we had long flights up to the DMZ and one pilot slept while the other flew. It was little enough, but the least we could do. I turned back to speak to Harkins. "General?"

"Yes, I'm sorry for the loss of your engineer, Hoffman. I'll speak about some compensation, unofficially of course." I waved the offer away. "It won't bring back Johann, will it?"

"No, it won't, I'm sorry. Now, about the aircraft you lost in the North, as you were on government business, I'll make sure that you are supplied with a replacement aircraft. Was the choice of the Junkers 52 a business decision, or was it, you know, sentimental?" I grinned. "You mean did it remind me of the Eastern Front, General. No, none of us that were there wanted reminding of it. She was a sturdy, reliable aircraft that we picked up for a song."

"Yeah, I understand. I'll authorise the location and supply of a replacement Junkers, or a C-47, as you already fly a Douglas it might be sensible for you to standardise."

I thought for a moment. My wife was in hospital several thousand miles away, the corpse of my engineer was being transported to the mortuary, at that moment I hated everything about Vietnam, the country, the communists, the CIA and the army. But I had made it my home, it was Helene's home, Paul Schuster's home too. "We'll take the C-47, thank you General."

Paul nodded his relief, I knew he'd thought for a moment that I was going to tell the General to go to hell. "Good, I'll make the arrangements. Now look, Hoffman, I need to talk to you about a contract to take some of our people North."

Paul walked over and joined the conversation. "We've only just come back from the North, General. Exactly what do you mean by 'north'? In relation to the DMZ, that is." Harkins at least had the grace to look embarrassed. "Well, er, North North."

As we both started shaking our heads, he hurriedly went on. "Now look, gentlemen, I know you feel sore about what happened, but we've caught the traitors now, everything is different."

"We've caught the traitors? Who is 'we' General?" He nodded wearily. "Yeah, ok. You caught them. Well, him. In the end there was only one who was passing information to the enemy, wasn't there? But whatever, your experience and non-military status means that you can operate where our own people, military people, cannot."

"And the CIA?" Paul asked acidly. He swept his hand aside, dismissing them. "Forget the CIA. They have their own agenda which is not necessarily my agenda, the military agenda. Between you and me, there is going to be a massive military build up here over the next few months and there'll be a pressing need for air transport, especially to the more sensitive areas. You understand that when I say a contract, I'm talking about a long term proposition, you'll be paid a retainer as well as a substantial bonus for each operation. I'm talking big bucks here."

I could sense Paul's excitement, it would be our big chance to turn the airline around and make us major players in South East Asia. Or it could get us killed. But you could get killed crossing the road. "Paul, what do you think?"

"Yes, we should take it," he replied. "It'll be good for us."

"Very well. General, you've got yourself a deal, provided we can hammer out the details. I want to get my wife back before we start any operations. We'll also need to replace

Johann, that is urgent."

"I can get a list of available people if you wish, Hoffman." I smiled. "No thank you, General. I think we'd prefer to organise that ourselves, there are plenty of good people kicking around Saigon who would be interested."

"Ok, I have to get back. Come in to MACV tomorrow and I'll arrange for you to put a call through to Washington, to your wife. I'll get my people onto sourcing a replacement aircraft straight away, you'll have it within the month. Good day, gentlemen." He shook our hands and abruptly left. The office seemed strange, alien, just the two of us and all that was left of Johann was a dark brown stain on the floor.

"So, Paul. It seems we are to be mercenaries." He laughed. "At least the pay is better, if we're going to go into high risk theatres, we may as well earn the rate for the job." I got another bottle of Jack Daniels and broke the seal. I poured two glasses and gave one to Paul.

"To Johann, wherever he is now, you were a good comrade, we'll never forget you."

"To Johann." He raised his glass and we drank the fiery spirit down. Then we tossed the glasses against the wall in the old way. Time to get down to some work.

We still had an airline to run and after we'd cleared up we went into Saigon to try and find a good ground engineer. I knew just the person to ask, Ritter von Schacht. We found him in a disreputable bar, half drunk as usual.

"Jurgen, Paul, welcome, let me buy you a drink. You have more work for the best pilot in Vietnam?"

I laughed. "No, Ritter, not just now. Johann is dead.

Shot by a Vietnamese traitor." I told him about Nguyen Cam Le.

"Scheisse, I knew Le quite well, I thought he hated the commies."

"So did we all, but he was a traitor. Anyway, he's dead now, but he killed Johann in the process. Ritter, I do need an engineer urgently, who can you recommend?" He smiled and spread his hands. "Me, of course. Jurgen, I was tinkering with engines when you were pussying around Russia with your band of SS sissies. I did real work man, dangerous stuff, I learned to do much of the maintenance and ground crew procedures, it was the only way to stay alive. I can do a good job for you. Besides," he paused for a moment to take a swig of his drink. "I need the work, regular wages, Saigon is getting to be an expensive place to live."

I looked at Paul. "What do you think?"

"I've no doubt that Ritter can do the work, it's the sauce that worries me." He eyed Ritter's glass worriedly. "Hah! Is that all?" von Schacht snorted. "I don't see your American friends doing a very good job, even sober. But if it worries you it's no problem, I will guarantee to never drink on duty or shall we say eight hours before reporting for work."

"Twelve hours," I said firmly. He sighed. "Ten hours, and that's more than I need."

"Very well, it's agreed. Welcome aboard, Ritter. We haven't discussed pay yet." He gave an airy wave. "I've known you guys for how long? And in all that time have we ever double crossed each other? No, I'll settle for what you decide is fair. Now have a drink with me to seal our new relationship."

The barman served up three whiskeys and we toasted the future of our airline, which looked as if it was going to be very promising.

"I think we're going to be a lot busier," Paul said excitedly, "with all of the increased American military activity we'll be working night and day." I felt sombre. "You know what that means, Paul? It means that the Viet Cong will be working night and day too, you realise that?"

I noticed the barman give me a keen look, he was a male Vietnamese of about twenty five. I wondered what he did at nights.

* * *

'Any forces that would impose their will on other nations will certainly face defeat.'

Nguyen Giap

"So Comrade Nhat, your nephew failed us," Giap said sourly.

"My nephew gave his life in the pursuit of the American bandits," Quan Nhat, the Area Garrison Commander shot back. "What more could he do?"

"I do not recall that his orders indicated he should give up his life, do you, Comrade Duan?" The older man present at the meeting shook his head.

"My orders were straightforward, Nhat, I wanted them stopped and the German taken alive. What could be clearer than that?" Nguyen Giap looked at the Hanoi garrison commander. What a stupid, weak, useless man. Did he not realise that this war was more important than favouring one's relatives for petty promotions?

"Clearly my nephew was not sufficiently experienced for such a mission as this," Quan continued. "On reflection, an older, more experienced officer should have been sent."

"That is your opinion, is it?" Giap confirmed.

The garrison commander nodded, sweat starting to appear on his face. "Yes, yes, it is."

"In that case, Comrade Quan, why did you suggest sending your nephew when you knew how little he was experienced? You knew how important this mission was, how important to me personally, Comrade Quan. So why did you make such a flawed decision?" Quan looked down at the table unable to meet the gaze of the General.

"So, Comrade Le Duan, do you have anything to add?"

Le shook his head. Giap looked at Quan. "Comrade, you have been found guilty of acting improperly by criminally favouring your nephew and assisting the enemies of the revolution to escape justice. Guards!"

The door was flung open and four PAVN soldiers came promptly to attention. The first, a captain, saluted. "General."

"Take Comrade Quan to the cells, he has been found guilty of crimes against the state and will be detained pending our decision on his sentence."

"Yes, Sir. At once."

The captain barked orders and the hapless Quan was dragged from his chair and frogmarched out of the room. The door closed and silence returned to the room.

"You dealt with him severely," Le said to Giap. The commander of the People's Army of Vietnam, the PAVN, shrugged. "He was a weak fool, he was sure to fall sooner or later. We're better off without him and his idiot nephew."

"Yes. This business with the Americans, you seem to be taking it personally, Comrade."

"It's not the Americans, Le, it's the German who was with them. We go back a long way."

"I see," Le said uncertainly, although he didn't see at all. "Do you wish to mount an assassination mission against him in the South?"

Giap shook his head violently. "No, definitely not, he is not to be touched. Unless he comes North again, in which case this time he must be stopped and if necessary killed. But until then, he is an honourable man, a soldier, I want him left alone."

"We are all soldiers, Comrade Giap."

"True, but I want him left. Do not press me on this, Le."

Le Duan bowed his head in assent. General Giap was not a man to cross, not ever. It would be as he said. Briefly, he wondered how Quan would fare in the cells. Still, it wouldn't be for long, his sentence would be the usual one ordained by North Vietnam's leaders on those they regarded as criminals against the state. He would not live long enough to really suffer much at all.

CHAPTER TEN

'Our numbers have increased in Vietnam because the aggression of others has increased in Vietnam. There is not, and there will not be, a mindless escalation.'

Lyndon B. Johnson

We came into land in Hue, the most beautiful city in Vietnam, perhaps in all Asia, on the 8th May, 1963. On this occasion, Helene sat in the co-pilot seat. She was fully recovered from her injuries, the American military hospital had served her proud. In addition, she was heavily pregnant and her stomach was starting to bulge noticeably, before long a trip like this would be impossible. This was to be her last trip before she wouldn't be able to fly any more until after the baby was born. I was flying the newer of our C-47s, the one supplied by MACV to replace our Junkers 52 lost in North Vietnam. The army had done us proud, unlike our first C-47 this one had seen little use, probably it had been kept in reserve at an Army Air

Corps base. Everything worked as it should, the upholstery was still comfortable and showing no signs of wear and most importantly, the engines ran smoothly and reliably. We shut off the engines and gave instructions for the unloading of our cargo, and then we went into the city for a meal. Almost immediately, we ran into trouble.

It was the birthday of the Lord Gautama Buddha, a day very sacred to the majority Buddhist population. We asked the taxi driver taking us into the Citadel what was the reason for the obvious tension between large groups of sullen Buddhists and the many armed patrols who watched over them. He chatted away happily and explained what was obviously going to be another backward step in our adopted country.

"Under the 1958 law known as Decree Number 10, it is prohibited to display religious flags. This disallowed the flying of Buddhist flags on Phat Dan, the birthday of Gautama Buddha. The deputy chief in charge of security is a Catholic, Major Dang Sy. He is charged with maintaining public security and was commander of the Hue garrison. Major Dang has made it clear he will deal very harshly with any Buddhist demonstrations."

We looked at each other. "Will there be trouble, do you think?" I asked him. Trouble in Vietnam meant only one thing, shooting.

He laughed and shook his head. "No trouble, Sir. They will shout and rave at each other and threaten mass protests but in the end the Buddhists will back down, they are people of peace," he said, somewhat contemptuously.

"I take it you are a Catholic," Helene said to him.

"Yes, of course, like our President Diem."

We exchanged glances again, this was no way to unite a divided country threatened by a communist insurgency from the North.

We were dropped off at the Citadel, the old centre of Hue and found a good restaurant for lunch. We had been considering overnighting in Hue but, in view of the obvious tension in the city, decided against getting a hotel room for the night, it would be safest to make the run straight back to Saigon. The restaurant was almost deserted, as if the locals knew that today was not a good day to be away from home.

"Diem must be a total fool if he thinks that oppressing the Buddhists will do anything, other than play right into the hands of the communists," Helene said abruptly.

I smiled at her. "You are right, my darling, it's totally stupid. Sadly, being a total fool does not stop men from becoming heads of state. Look at your Napoleon in France, our own Hitler in Germany. Clever politicians, yes, but in many ways they were complete idiots. We just have to live with their idiocy."

"That's sad, Jurgen, to think that so many people have to suffer because of it. The Vietnamese, the American soldiers, even us, we nearly lost our baby because of it."

And you, I thought. Our meal was a sombre affair, there was little to be cheerful about. Something bad was brewing in this city and all we both wanted was to finish up and get out. We called a taxi and started back to the airport, it was then that the trouble began. We were stopped just before a bridge, a squad of steel helmeted troops had set up a roadblock and were turning everything back. A young lieutenant looked inside the cab and when he saw us white Europeans, told the driver to turn around.

"The road ahead is closed," he said angrily.

I leaned forward and spoke to him calmly, the situation looked tense and I didn't want to ignite any fuses.

"Lieutenant, I am a pilot under contract to the American military, I need to return to the airport to fly back to Saigon."

He sneered. "The Americans can take care of their own, we have our own problems here, the Buddhists are rioting all over the city. You must turn back."

As he spoke, he lifted his assault rifle in a way that stopped short of being threatening but was an unmistakable warning. I nodded and told the driver to turn around. As we started back, he said he knew an alternative way back to the airport if we didn't mind paying the extra fare. I told him to get us there by any means possible. I wanted Helene out of this tinderbox.

We drove through a series of back roads, tracks and lanes and seemed to be making progress back to the airport when we hit the second obstacle. This time it really was serious, a group of saffron robed Buddhist monks leading a procession of demonstrators. Their route had been blocked by a line of grim face, steel helmeted police. Their officer was shouting at the Buddhists through a loudhailer.

"What is he saying?" I asked our driver.

"He's telling them to disperse, that they do not have an official license for their demonstration. If they do not go back immediately he is threatening to shoot."

So far, the police had not levelled their rifles at the crowd and I had high hopes that people would see sense and both sides quietly back down. But neither side did back down. The officer stopped talking through the loudhailer and barked an order at his men. The sound of more than twenty rifles being cocked was like a roll of thunder. The barrels were levelled at the demonstrators, who as far as I could see were unarmed. For a few minutes there was total silence. The lieutenant shouted at them again, his face turning red with anger. There was no need to translate, he was clearly telling them to disperse or else. The crowd had gone silent, they just stood defiantly refusing to move. He shouted again, then again. Still nobody moved, then he turned to his men, shouted a single word and the gunfire started.

It was a slaughter, men and women screamed, the leading demonstrators crumpled to the road as dozens of them were wounded or killed outright. Astonishingly, the shooting didn't stop, they just kept firing and firing at the demonstrators, most of whom by now were running for their lives. Some stood too shocked to move, like rabbits caught in a vehicle's headlights, a few moved amongst the fallen, trying to help them until they too were hit and fell to the ground. Eventually, the shooting petered to a stop. We sat shocked into silence. The lieutenant started shouting more orders to his men who incredibly began to arrest some of the frozen survivors. The dead and wounded they left where they had fallen. I murmured to the driver to back up slowly and move away. This had all the hallmarks of a war crime and if the officer realised that we were witnesses he could turn his attentions to us. In the event, he took no notice and we managed to beat a hasty retreat. Helene, who was a trained doctor, was trying to persuade me to stop the cab so that she could give help to the wounded, but when I explained to her that her unborn baby would be at risk if the Vietnamese police decided that we were unwanted witnesses, she kept quiet. The driver continued to wend his way through the backstreets of Hue and eventually we got back to the airport unscathed. The air traffic controllers were unhappy about clearing me for takeoff, there was talk of a military clampdown until order was restored, but I played the trump card of U.S. military business and managed to get away. At last we were climbing into the air and I breathed a sigh of relief. Helene tuned the radio into the local AFN station, they were playing a frenetic rock song, 'The Twist', the singer was a new name to me, Chubby Checker. I wondered about the title of the song. It seemed very appropriate for Vietnam, the twist, that described everything here.

I had never heard Helene swear, so I was shocked when she spoke. "They are a bunch of total fucking lunatics," she said. "They have just recruited a large number of soldiers for the Viet Cong."

I laughed. "Welcome to Realpolitik, my darling." Realpolitik was politics or diplomacy based primarily on power and on practical and material factors and considerations, rather than ideological notions or moralistic or ethical premises. The politics of brute force. As practised in Vietnam, North and South.

"They're going to lose, aren't they, Jurgen?"

"You mean Diem, and his American allies?"

"Yes, they're playing right into the hands of the

245

communists, isn't that blindingly obvious."

"Yes," I replied. "Just as the French did before them, just as successive Vietnamese governments have done. I fear that within a few years the communists will be in power."

"So why are we here, Jurgen?" Why are we helping them?"

"Because it's our home, Helene. It's where we've chosen to make our lives, build our business and a home for our child."

She was silent for a full hour as we droned on over the endless Vietnamese jungle.

"Have we made a mistake, should we go elsewhere?" she said suddenly. I jerked in surprise and the aircraft leapt a couple of hundred feet higher.

"Possibly," I said after a moment. "But we are committed at the moment, once the baby is born and we have fulfilled our contracts with the U.S. military, we could consider moving somewhere else. The world needs aircraft to transport goods, we could consider setting up in a different country, we'll speak to Paul if you wish."

She nodded. "Yes, I think that would be a good idea, after the baby is born. Then we'll have a better idea of how things stand."

We landed back at Tan Son Nhat without incident, our intention was to go straight home to the bungalow we had rented while our own home was being repaired, but there was a surprise waiting for me. I taxied over to the hangar where there was a Willys jeep parked outside. Paul and Ritter came out, grim faced. I dropped down the ladder, helped Helene down and waited for them to speak.

"There's someone in the office to speak to you, Jurgen. Lieutenant Colonel Aaron Goldberg."

"What does he want?"

They both shrugged. "He refused to speak to us," Ritter said. "Said he wanted to talk to you and no one else."

It was nothing good, that was certain. If Goldberg would only talk to me that meant a secret mission of some kind and that could only lead to trouble. Well, I'd been in trouble before and had so far managed to get out of it. I went into the office, Helene came after me with Ritter and Paul. Goldberg was sat on our old couch, he immediately stood up and came to shake hands.

"Hoffman, good to see you again."

"Colonel, you too," I replied.

"How are things in Hue?" he asked.

"The usual, Colonel, a total fuck up. Did you expect anything else?"

He shook his head tiredly. "No, I guess not. I'm sorry about that problem you had with Miles, it could have been real bad."

I raised my eyebrows. "Bad, Colonel? As I recall it cost the lives of a Special Forces captain, two sergeants and countless other lives including many Vietnamese civilians and our own engineer. That was 'real bad' enough for us."

He looked suitably abashed. "Yeah, sorry about that, it wasn't one of our finest moments. Now look, I want to talk to you in confidence," he looked significantly at Helene, Paul and Ritter.

I smiled at him. "You are talking to me in confidence,

Colonel. These people are totally trustworthy, proved time and again. As I recall, it is your own people who you have problems with. As a matter of interest, you're sitting two feet from where one of them killed Johann, if you look hard the bloodstain is still visible."

I felt Helene flinch, but I felt I had to make a point. Goldberg relaxed and smiled.

"Ok, I'm not getting very far am I? Maybe I'd better come right out with it. I need your aircraft, Jurgen."

"So what's the problem, you want a standard charter of one of our C-47s, just put in the paperwork and we'll deal with it?"

I was being deliberately naive and we all knew it. A senior officer coming out here personally and waiting for me to return was no standard charter.

"I want both of your C-47s to ferry troops and equipment to Da Nang, can you handle it?"

I looked at Paul and Ritter. This proposal stank worse than a manure heap. "You know we can handle it, Colonel. What's the catch?"

He thought for a moment. "Well, there are one or two aspects of the operation that I can't discuss with you, but essentially it's a straightforward ferry job, out and back. Take the men up there, refuel and wait for forty-eight hours and bring them back."

"Can I discuss it for a moment with my people, two aircraft is a major charter for us?"

He nodded, and I indicated to Helene and the others that we needed to speak privately outside the hangar. We went into the late afternoon sunshine and I asked them what they thought.

"They want us to go to the North," Paul said immediately.

Ritter nodded. "My thoughts too, Jurgen. They could use any number of their own aircraft for a simple ferry job to Da Nang."

Helene had paled. "Oh God no, not again. Not the North."

I spread my arms. "That's almost certainly what they want, so let's proceed on that assumption. What do we do?"

"Say no, of course," my wife said. "You mustn't do it."

I smiled at her. "It's not that easy, my love. We have certain obligations to the U.S. military and we can't refuse them out of hand. Let's face it, we knew this was coming."

I could see a tear forming in her eye. I felt angry that the Colonel had come to put this one on us so abruptly, but I guess he had his orders.

"We'll have to do it," Paul said. "We owe them a lot, but let's just make sure they pay heavily for the privilege."

Ritter nodded. "I'm up for it, you'll need me for a two aircraft job. We'll need a second co-pilot too."

"I'll do it," Helene said. I stared at her. "You cannot be serious, you're five months pregnant."

"If you're going, Jurgen, I go too. I'm not sitting at home waiting to hear you've been killed. If it happens, I want to be with you."

"You're not cleared for twin engine aircraft," I said lamely. Her license was single engine only. But it was a stupid argument and she just laughed.

"You cannot be serious? What are they going to do, arrest me for not having the correct paperwork?"

We argued back and forth for almost half an hour. In the end we compromised, she would come with us to Da Nang but not cross the DMZ, and to get that agreement I had to repeatedly remind her of our unborn child. We went back into the office.

"You've got your aircraft, Colonel, provided you agree to our terms. What is the destination?"

"That's excellent, Hoffman. I told you, Da Nang."

I heard a laugh from Ritter von Schacht. "We are not children, Colonel," he said, "you have more than enough aircraft of your own to take your men to Da Nang. Tell us, exactly where is the destination?"

Goldberg sighed. "Ok, you're right. Initial destination is Da Nang, but yes, we want you to take our group over the DMZ and return for the pick up approximately forty-eight hours later. It's a straightforward in and out, you've done it before."

"So have you, Colonel, as I recall it was anything but straightforward last time."

He winced. "Yeah, point taken, but this time it's much simpler."

"When do you want to depart?" Paul asked him.

"Tonight."

The four of us stared at him as if he was crazy.

"You can't mean that, Colonel," I said to him, "that's ridiculous and you know it."

He nodded. "I do, you're quite right. We had a contract

sorted with another airline, Air America, but this morning there was something of a disagreement on policy between their managers and MACV and they've pulled out."

"Why didn't the CIA want to fly this one?"

"CIA?" he asked. "What do you mean?"

None of us replied, we just waited for him. Air America's slogan was 'Anything, Anywhere, Anytime, Professionally'. This was not an exaggeration, as Air America aircraft, including De Havilland Canada DHC-4 Caribous and Fairchild C-123 Providers, flew many types of cargo to countries such as the Republic of Vietnam, the Kingdom of Laos, and Cambodia. It operated from bases in those countries and also from bases in Thailand and as far afield as Taiwan and Japan. It also on occasion flew top-secret missions into Burma and the People's Republic of China. The airline was directly owned and operated by the CIA, through a maze of front companies and they provided direct and indirect support to CIA operations.

Goldberg shrugged. "Yeah, you're right. Politics, I guess. There's been a falling out between CIA and MACV, each has their own view on how the war in South Vietnam should be run. Meanwhile, people like us have to keep the real war going."

"Ok, it's nothing new. Here are our terms. Triple the normal fee and the military fully insures our aircraft against loss or damage."

"Triple?" He was shocked. "That sounds a bit steep."

"I'm willing to bet it's a lot cheaper than Air America," I replied, but I was holding my breath. A triple fee would make a big difference to us.

He relented, he was obviously desperate and under orders to get results. "Yep, ok, we can do that. How do you want payment?"

"Half the fee up front in cash, and a certified cheque for the value of each of the aircraft. If everything goes well we tear up the cheques. Other than that, we'll ignore the paperwork. The balance to be paid when we return."

"Yeah, we can't put anything on paper. Very well, I'll be back here in four hours, we fly to Da Nang, take on some extra supplies and refuel and then push on across the DMZ tomorrow evening."

"We'll be ready, Colonel. Don't forget the money."

He smiled as he walked away.

"Paul, would you and Ritter get both aircraft refuelled and pre-flighted. I'll take Helene home for a quick nap, a shower and change of clothes, it's been a long flight in from Hue and we've got another long one ahead of us."

"We'll be ready," Ritter said. His eyes were shining, obviously he enjoyed the chance of seeing some action. I hoped to God he would be disappointed and it would be a milk run. We went to our bungalow and slept for a couple of hours, then showered and ate a hasty meal. Helene was unusually quiet.

"I don't know," she said when I asked her what the problem was. "I'm just sick and tired of all this nonsense, that business in Hue upset me, it was so stupid and unnecessary. Now this, it's like little boys constantly playing Cowboys and Indians. When will it ever end so that people can live a normal life, people like us? I want out, Jurgen, as soon as possible."

I agreed that when we got back we'd start looking into getting out of Vietnam. Shortly afterwards we were back at the hangar, Paul and Ritter were just finishing their pre-flight checks when two military transport vehicles arrived and disgorged our passengers, thirty tough looking soldiers, they carried no unit insignia but were almost certainly Special Forces. There were several wooden crates containing their equipment and these were quickly loaded. Thirty minutes later we were in the air, Helene flew with me and Paul and Ritter flew the other aircraft. Von Schacht was in the left hand seat, a gracious nod from Paul to the old Luftwaffe pilot's undoubted superior skill.

We droned on through the night towards Da Nang. I went aft to check the passengers twice but they were very uncommunicative, Helene and I were just the taxi drivers. That would do for me, I was quite happy to earn my pay by avoiding any contact with either them or the enemy, I was getting too old for that, it was best left to the youngsters. Da Nang airfield had lit up the runway and we were able to land without difficulty. We were directed to a far corner of the field where the soldiers hurriedly disembarked and were collected by two lorries. Shortly after the dawn arrived and we were left to our own devices throughout the day. We chatted, caught up on sleep, ate the sandwiches that Helene had provided and checked the aircraft twice over. During the day a fuel bowser came and we refilled the tanks until they were right to the top. I saw Helene to the officers' quarters at the airfield where they had allowed her the use of a room, and then returned to the aircraft as darkness fell. The lorries re-appeared with an additional four men, they were all wearing army camouflage but they were no soldiers, their slumped civilian bearing gave them away. Colonel Goldberg joined me in the right hand seat to help navigate to the landing field. I called over Paul and Ritter and as they crowded into the cockpit we went over his maps.

"This is our destination, Vinh. Specifically a level field on the outside of the town, we'll be far enough away to get in without the locals noticing we've arrived. We've got some people of our own who'll be putting out markers for the landing, so it shouldn't be any problem getting the aircraft in. Only room for one at a time, though. Can you handle that?"

"I suggest the second aircraft leaves slightly later, Colonel. I don't think we want it circling over Vinh while the first aircraft unloads."

"Oh, right, yeah, I never thought of that. Ok, we'll do it your way."

We smiled at each other, it was pretty basic not to have an unarmed defenceless aircraft circling over enemy territory for any period of time.

"Who are the civilians, Colonel?"

"We haven't got any civilians."

He saw our sceptical look. "Yeah, ok, you're right. They're intelligence guys, translators and code breakers. The mission is quite straightforward, we got wind of a cache of enemy documents related to the insurgency, local leaders, intelligence people in the South, they're at an address in Vinh. We're going in to check out the documents and take photos of anything interesting, then leave them apparently undisturbed. It could be quite an intelligence coup, especially if they don't know we've seen them."

I didn't say anything, it sounded ridiculous. But if that was what they wanted to pay us for, so be it. At least there was a good chance of avoiding enemy contact. It was time for departure, the troops were already aboard. I went into the cockpit with Goldberg, we were the leading aircraft and we started up, got clearance and took off. Navigation was something of a challenge, we were looking for a small field in a darkened area west of Vinh but I managed to take bearings from the stars to assist my compass heading and within three hours we started to descend. There were lights below marking out the landing strip, arranged in an arrow to mark the wind direction. As I came in to land, Goldberg snapped out an order for the men to be ready and the cabin echoed to the sound of weapons being cocked.

He needn't have worried, I brought the C-47 to a halt and the soldiers leapt out, weapons raised, but there were only friendly voices raised in greeting. Immediately I took off again to clear the field for the second C-47 and as I gained height I saw it reflected in the moonlight as it approached the field for a landing. I flew back to Da Nang and when I landed Helene was there to greet me. Shortly after Paul and Ritter landed and the first part of our mission was over. We went into the military bar and bought drinks and then sat in silence. It was an odd feeling that for once the Special Forces were in enemy territory and we were safe at Da Nang, almost a feeling of guilt, as if we should have been with them. We felt powerless, unable to influence events as we had so often in the past. All we could do was wait. Eventually we gave up and went to bed, avoiding each other's eyes. The following day we spent servicing the aircraft to be ready at any moment, but the call didn't come. Neither did it the next day and by the following night we were beginning to get worried, they were very overdue. We waited half the night and still the radio was silent, the following morning we sat around waiting again. Then an army communications sergeant came over to us from the tower. They were in trouble.

"Message from Colonel Goldberg, Mr Hoffman. They've stirred up a hornet's nest over there, they want you ready to go in as soon as they can clear a safe landing strip."

He gave us the full text of the message. They'd been jumped by a large force of North Vietnamese regulars and had been forced to make a fighting retreat to the outskirts of Vinh. MACV were liaising with the United States Navy and the Air Force to arrange for an air strike on the enemy, as soon as they were due to go in they wanted us airborne.

"We'll be ready, you can acknowledge, let us know as soon as we can take off."

"Yes, Sir." He went back to the tower and we sat on edge, waiting for the word to go. An hour and a half later, we were told to take off immediately and pick them up from a point five miles due south of Vinh. We climbed aboard our aircraft and minutes later I was flying north. I was wondering about navigation if things got difficult when Helene appeared in the cockpit. I nearly leapt out of my skin.

"What the hell are you doing, you're supposed to be waiting at Da Nang?" I shouted at her.

"You needed a co-pilot, Jurgen, you've got me so shut

up and let's get on with it," she said matter of factly as she sat down in the right hand seat. She'd timed it beautifully, it was too late for me to head back to Da Nang and remove her from the aircraft. I swallowed the angry retort I was about to make and did as she said, I shut up.

After two hours we had crossed the DMZ and were well on our way to the pickup point outside Vinh. I saw movement out of my starboard window and glimpsed two squadrons of Douglas A-4 Skyhawks, heading for Vinh. They were travelling at high speed, inside of a minute they had disappeared from view.

"They obviously mean business, sending that many aircraft over," I said to Helene. She just pulled a face. I kept scanning the sky, then saw even more aircraft, a squadron of Grumman A-6 Intruders, ground attack bombers, they were new in Vietnam and carried a very heavy bomb load. I assumed they'd been launched from an aircraft carrier offshore, but it was too far away to see their markings. I looked again, a further squadron of aircraft were flying escort above the A6 intruders. One dipped down and came to check us out, they were F-100 Super Sabre fighter bombers.

"I think they've sent every fighter aircraft in Vietnam to join us," Helene said drily.

I nodded, I was staggered at the awesome display of airpower, there must have been at least sixty aircraft in the air, maybe more. As we approached the vicinity of Vinh, we saw the results of their intervention. Half a dozen A4 Skyhawks were circling around a point several miles south of the town, occasionally one or two would swoop down and blaze away at a ground target. The wing leader came onto our frequency.

"Civilian C-47s this is blue wing leader flying escort patrol over your party, acknowledge you have the LZ in sight."

I peered down and could see a large group of men in a defensive position either side of a sports field, it was Goldberg's party without doubt. They were besieged by a number of North Vietnamese regulars who were themselves pinned down by the relentless firepower of the Skyhawks.

"Civilian C-47s, acknowledged," I replied.

"Very good C-47s, let us make one more pass and then you can go in for the pick up."

"Acknowledged."

All six Skyhawks banked hard and swooped down on the North Vietnamese. The air came alive with rockets and cannon fire, the twenty millimetre cannon shells hammering the enemy ground troops to shreds. One by one they delivered their deadly ordnance and swept back up into the sky. I throttled down, dropped flaps and went straight in for a landing, Ritter followed suit and landed exactly parallel to me, showing off his superb flying skill as usual. As I taxied over to the men, Helene ran back to open the door, then they were pouring into the aircraft. Inside of a minute, Goldberg came into the cockpit and started when he saw Helene.

"I didn't expect to see you aboard, Ma'am," he said. "Jurgen, we're all aboard, you can take off right away?"

I didn't need any further encouragement, I opened the throttles wide and got us into the air. Ritter was right behind us and I felt comfortable to see several Skyhawks fall in around us as escort. Back in the cabin there was uproar, somehow they'd manage to locate some booze and were celebrating. Goldberg came into the cockpit. "Hoffman, I don't suppose you take a drink when you're driving?" He grinned.

I shook my head. "No, thank you, Colonel. What are you celebrating, it sounds like a party back there?"

"Jesus Christ, man, we got out, we really hit those commies hard. Did you see those fighter bombers go in?"

"I saw them, yes. I assume your mission was a success, Colonel?"

"Hell no," he laughed, "it was a total mess up from start to finish. But we got out with only a couple of minor casualties and the air force gave them a damn good pasting. Christ, it's something to celebrate," he laughed again and went back into the cabin.

We flew on in silence for almost an hour, then Helene spoke to me. "What are you thinking?"

"I was wondering whether it would be worth us considering buying a Douglas DC-4, it's a much bigger aircraft, four engines and over eighty seats."

She stared at me. "You cannot be serious? These people are lunatics. Those soldiers back there are celebrating a failed mission and the total devastation of a North Vietnamese town. Crazy."

I laughed at that. "Did you not realise that before, Helene? Of course they're all crazy, war itself is lunacy. But it's the way things are, I can't change it or them."

"They'll never win a war if they fight it like this, you know. The people on the ground must hate them," she snapped back.

I shrugged. "I expect they do hate them. But it's not my

problem, I'm not dropping the bombs."

"So that's all it is to you, Jurgen, just a way of making money?"

"That's all this business has ever been, Helene, a business like any other. When I fought here in the Legion I fought hard and honourably. Now I run my business just as honourably. What would you have me do, retire and become a missionary?"

She laughed then. "No, perhaps not. I can't see you preaching the word of God."

"Good. And what about the baby, won't you want him to have a decent home, nice clothes, a good education? Maybe the Sorbonne? We could get an apartment for when we visit."

She laughed. "You're so sure it's going to be a boy?"

I shrugged. "Maybe, I don't know, I'll be happy either way."

"That's ok then. Paris, the Sorbonne, yes, that would be wonderful. But I don't know, it's a terrible way to earn a living."

"So is being a soldier, at least this pays better. It's our business, Helene, it's what we do."

She went quiet for a while as we droned on. Just before we came into land at Da Nang, she suddenly turned to me. "If we were to stay here for a while longer, Jurgen, what does a Douglas DC-4 cost these days? I hate it all, but we do have to think about the future of our child."

I grinned. "A lot of money, my darling, but at this rate we'll be able to afford it. Providing the war goes on for a few years."

I smiled, French women were both beautiful and very practical and my brave, lovely wife possessed both of these qualities in full. How could any man be as lucky as me, to have a wife like her? We were both survivors, both battered by the forces of war and both able to keep looking forward.

"Oh, the war will go on for some time," she said. "But you know that sooner or later we'll have to leave South Vietnam?"

"You mean when the communists take over."

She nodded. "Exactly."

* * *

Once upon a time our traditional goal in war and can anyone doubt that we are at war? - was victory. Once upon a time we were proud of our strength, our military power. Now we seem ashamed of it. Once upon a time the rest of the world looked to us for leadership. Now they look to us for a quick handout and a fence-straddling international posture.

Barry M. Goldwater

General Harkins looked out of his office window. Jurgen Hoffman and his pretty wife Helene were walking out of the building having just signed a new one year contract with the U.S. military. Jurgen was carrying their new baby, a girl named Celine, apparently after Helene's grandmother. They were a happy, prosperous looking couple, he reflected, more prosperous now that they had the new contract to make payment on a Douglas DC-4. He looked around as an aide, a major, walked into his office and saluted.

"Sir, the news has come through, Diem is dead, the information minister Tran Tu Oai has declared it was a suicide."

"And?" Harkins pressed him.

"It was General Duong Van Minh, Sir. Together with the Army Chief of Staff, Tran Van Don. Just as we expected."

Harkins nodded. That would leave the way clear for someone who would be more acceptable to the Buddhist majority.

His thoughts turned to the other problem, the New York Times correspondent David Halberstam. Four months ago they were having a Fourth of July celebration at the American embassy when David Halberstam became so angry that he refused to shake hands with Harkins. When the host called for a toast to the General, Halberstam shouted 'Paul D. Harkins should be court martialled and shot!' It was all bullshit, of course, but that kind of bullshit tended to stick.

It was lucky that he had the ear of President John F Kennedy, at least Kennedy would be there for the long haul, he wasn't likely to go the way of Diem in this fly-blown country, assassinated by his own people.

Even the Times correspondent, Lee Griggs had the impertinence to compose a sarcastic rhyme about him.

We are winning, this I know, General Harkins tells me so.
In the mountains, things are rough,
In the Delta, mighty tough,
But the V.C. will soon go, General Harkins tells me so.'

These damn traitors ought to be shot, he thought to himself. Thank God for the United States.

THE END

ALSO BY ERIC MEYER

DEVIL'S GUARD: THE REAL STORY

Following the myths and legends about Nazis recruited by the French Foreign Legion to fight in Indochina, Eric Meyer's new book is based on the real story of one such former Waffen-Ss man who lived to tell the tale. These were ruthless, trained killers, brutalised by the war on the Eastern Front, their killing skills honed to a razor's edge. They found their true home in Indochina, where they fought and became a byword for brutal military efficiency.

SS ENGLANDER:

The Amazing True Story of Hitler's British Nazis. The incredible story of an Englishmen imprisoned in Germany at the outbreak of World War II, then forced to join the SS Liebstandarte Adolf Hitler. In 1944 he was given the task of assisting in the formation of the British Free Corps, a volunteer Waffen-SS Unit consisting mainly of British POW's and deserters.

CPSIA information can be obtained at www.ICGtesting.com
Printed in the USA
LVOW072149131111

254810LV00001B/120/P